ADAMANT

THE ALLIANCE SERIES:
BOOK ONE

Emma L. Adams

Disclaimer: This book was written, produced and edited in the UK, where some spelling, grammar and word usage will vary from US English.

Copyright © 2015 Emma L. Adams

Cover design by Amalia Chitulescu

Stock photographs purchased from Shutterstock.com

ISBN: 978-0-9931319-3-6 (Paperback)

I dedicate this book to the online writing community and to my readers for making this the best job I could possibly have, in any universe.

CHAPTER ONE

ADA

Pulling up my hood to hide my face, I slipped from the fog-shrouded London street into a narrow alleyway between two abandoned buildings, a smile forming at the prospect of breaking the Alliance's rules. Rule number one: no trespassing in the Passages. Rule number two: no leaving Earth without a permit.

Lucky they didn't know about this particular door.

I rubbed my arms, the chill from the alley wall penetrating the thin fabric of my coat. Several feet in, the brick gave way to a fake section of wall which wasn't obvious at first glance. This area was so off-radar, no one would ever come looking for trouble here, not of the magic variety. But my fingers found the familiar cracks between brick and metal, and a gentle push made the fake part of the wall slide away, revealing cold metal.

I didn't know who'd first discovered the Passage here, nor who'd concealed it. The Alliance had logged every single one, not that there were many on Earth, but this was hidden even from them. A nice irony that the biggest illegal offworld operation was in the same city as Earth's main Alliance branch.

Nothing was quite like that first thrill when magic made itself known, buzzing under my skin as my fingers brushed the metal wall. It was icy to the touch and functioned like a sliding panel, moving back to reveal a dark corridor. Heart beating fast, I stepped over the threshold.

The Passages were always freezing, no matter the time of day. There was no sun here, and on the lowest level, where I was, it felt like the inside of a gigantic refrigerator. The lowest level, or "level zero", was the most dangerous, which was most likely why the Alliance hadn't found the door. Even Alliance guards could get eaten alive by the monsters down here.

Luckily, this time it was quiet, though the lingering stench of Cethrax's swamp followed me through the corridors. That world was not on my list of tourist destinations. But once I'd escaped the warren of the lower level via a concealed staircase, I was in the Passages for real. The first-level corridor opened before me, branching out into countless others. All identical—high-ceilinged, ten metres wide, and lined with metal doors like the one that led to Earth. All were labelled with numbers in an order only the Alliance knew, to ensure nobody but them could tell which door led to which universe. There were thousands in total, spread throughout these corridors. Maybe even millions—I hadn't seen them all.

For me, imagining was part of the thrill. Every hum of the wind in the dark whispered promises of worlds beyond imagining, every door held something new behind its cold metal exterior. I'd come here too many times to count, yet I'd never set foot beyond one of those doors. But God, the temptation was so intense I could taste it.

And then there was magic. You couldn't really *see* magic on Earth the way I could here, like the shift of a tinted lens, enough to make the world look one degree different. And I could feel it under my skin, like I was plugged into a live wire. Something in the Earth's atmosphere stifled magic, which was why the Alliance relied so much on their offworld technology. No denying they needed it, seeing as they were the one force standing between Earth and the mercy of a thousand offworld threats. And yet, I'd be at *their* mercy if they found me here. Using an unregistered Passage to help illegal magic-wielders from another world that the Alliance deemed 'dangerous' would mean instant imprisonment, if I was lucky.

I walked swiftly, with the occasional glance behind to make sure I wasn't being tailed. I had long since figured out the pattern of the Alliance's patrols and could avoid them, but despite having come here frequently since I was eight years old, I couldn't pretend I knew all the Passages' secrets. They'd been set up by the original Alliance. That was about as much as anyone on Earth knew. Not how they'd put the doors in place, not how they found each world. Classified, Nell had said. The Alliance guarded its secrets well.

My phone buzzed in my pocket. I fished it out and glanced at the screen. "Level 2, Door 65. You're late."

Rolling my eyes, I slid my phone back into my pocket. Delta

had been the one to hook up my phone to Inter-World Communications so I'd have a means of contacting him from Earth. A pretty handy extension. Not quite as fancy as the flashy communicators members of the Alliance carried, but it worked for me. I could call anyone within the five neighbouring worlds and the Passages between.

Second level. I suppressed a shiver of unease, and the smile faded from my face. I knew which world I'd be dealing with this time.

The staircase to the upper level was invisible to most people, but I found it, coat whipping behind me in the chill wind of upper level. Shivering, I climbed the twisting staircase and hurried through the corridors, not daring to glance at the doors hidden in the gloom. I couldn't imagine the horrors on the other side. On the top floor, a place restricted even to Alliance employees, these were worlds torn apart by war, worlds barred from ever joining the Alliance.

One of them was my homeworld.

Reaching the corridor I needed, I paused, looking out for the familiar figure. Delta waved at me from a shadowy corner near door 65.

"You took your time." Delta faced me with a smile full of elongated teeth.

"Can't be too careful," I said, mimicking Nell's lecturing voice, and he grinned. His hair stood up like the bristles on a toothbrush.

"Right. There's a family coming through. They should be here any minute now. They've been checked over. No magic, and no weapons training."

I nodded. No magic usually meant it was easier to get away. Not that the Alliance didn't think we'd all start a magical war anyway, given the chance.

"How's it going?" he asked. "Is Nell still being paranoid? I thought she'd locked you up."

"Not going to happen," I said. "She knows I'd break out and come here anyway. What's she think will happen? I can hardly go swanning off to Valeria without a permit—though I wouldn't turn down an invite," I added, not so subtly.

"Nice try, Red," he said.

"Ugh. Enough with that stupid nickname already." Though my dyed dark-red hair had an even more vivid glow in the Passages. Blue light shone from the walls and ceiling, like an alien nightclub. "Seriously, though. Hover boots? Valeria has actual hover boots now?"

"New patent," said Delta, with another grin. "Not on the market yet, but I'm going to get my hands on some as soon as they are."

"If you don't let me have a go in them, I'll never forgive you," I said, crossing my arms. Delta and I were like weird cousins... who happened to live in different universes. I'd never met most of his family, and all I really knew about them was that the Campbells worked in magi-technology in Valeria's capital, trading with other universes. When they weren't smuggling offworlders through the Passages.

"Sure thing, Red." He ducked as I pretended to aim a punch at him. "How's Gary?"

"Long gone, thank God," I said. "He took issue with my–" I made quotation marks with my fingers–"'wild lifestyle'. I made the mistake of going over to his place after that fight with the selver and he thought I'd been in some neon orgy or something."

Delta snickered. "That's priceless. You went over there with selver drool all over you?"

"I couldn't help it! That stuff doesn't clean off easily. I glowed in the dark for a week! I had to throw away my clothes, Delta. The sacrifices I make for you."

"I'm sure you'll get over him."

"Already have."

Such was the price I paid for a double life. Part-time cashier and part-time assistant at Nell's home business by day. Owner in chief of an illegal shelter for offworlders by night. Any time between, I spent in the Passages. And none of it could I share with another person. I was surprised my now ex stuck around that long. For some reason, most guys weren't particularly enthused when you refused to tell them where you lived or how you spent most of your time. "I know a dozen ways to kill a man with my bare hands" didn't go down well as a conversation-starter. Even if you followed it with "Wait. I've not actually done that."

There was a slight possibility I needed to work on my conversational skills.

"Good. How's Nell doing, anyway?"

"Same as ever," I said. "She's thinking about expanding our business into offworld markets."

"Might as well, seeing as you have the connections," he said. "The Alliance upped their cross-world trade restrictions not too long ago. A lot of people are angry about it. You'd have support."

"Yeah, not exactly legal, though, is it?" I gave him a meaningful look. We were breaking a dozen laws between the two of us just by standing here talking.

"You could always join the Alliance," he said with another toothy smile.

My own smile froze. "That was a joke, right?"

"Right." He gave a rather forced laugh. "Sure. Just, you know, it'd give you an alibi. You could come here more frequently, help more people…"

I bit my lip. I couldn't pretend it had never crossed my mind, and I knew *his* family had connections with Valeria's Alliance. As an Alliance member, I'd have legal access to the Passages without worrying about being intercepted by guards. But I'd also be expected to work for *them*. And that I couldn't do. I couldn't pretend to be one of them. Not even for money to pay the shelter's bills. Their council, as Nell reminded me on a weekly basis, had left my homeworld to ruin.

"Nell isn't the ruler of the Multiverse, you know," said Delta.

I smiled at that. "No, but I reckon she could give the Alliance a run for their money."

A faint noise sounded behind Door 65.

"Let's get this sorry business over with," said Delta. He nodded at me, and then tapped the door once, twice, three times. Safety signal.

The door opened in a silent sliding motion, and I caught a glimpse of a gleaming tunnel beyond, which led to the transition point. Not Enzar itself, of course—all the Passages directly into the war zone were closed off. Instead, the lucky few who managed to escape via hidden tunnels were taken to a between-world transition point before being smuggled out. Earth was an obvious choice because it was so low-magic and innocuous—not to mention right at the Alliance's centre—that no one would possibly suspect it might be at the heart of an operation like this.

It was a family this time, a mother and two kids. The woman turned in my direction, frightened eyes peering from under layers of sand-coloured scarves. I fixed a reassuring smile on my face. She was a couple of years older than me, by the look of things, early twenties at most. Her face was oval-shaped and delicate with eyes like glittering amethysts—a dead giveaway, if the expression of utter desperation wasn't enough. Nell always said you could recognise a person from Enzar a mile away. Everything about the Enzarian Empire used to be beautiful.

The little boy broke free of his mother's grip and ran to me. I smiled at him, too. "You're going to be safe now," I said.

"Yeah, Ada will take care of you," said Delta, stepping back. "You okay from here?"

I nodded. "Sure thing. Take care."

We parted ways, and I led the family towards the staircase. "Just down here," I said, with another encouraging smile, as the boy peered warily down into the dark. I held his hand and led the way.

The woman let out a sob, adjusted a grip on the little girl curled into her. "Thank you," she whispered, in English. I didn't speak Enzarian, though I'd asked Nell to teach me a dozen times. She'd have learned English at the transition point, like Nell had. There was no going back to Enzar.

It broke my heart every time, but I couldn't afford to lose my concentration. I tensed at every noise, gaze sweeping into the darkest corners as we made our way downstairs and then back through the Passages. Only the sound of our own footsteps on the metal floor followed us. What they were made of, I didn't know—certainly nothing found on Earth. The bluish glow was ever-present, as was the shiver of magic, making the hairs stand up on my arms, like it lived in my very skin. Perhaps it did.

All too soon, we climbed the stairs down to the lowest level. The stench of Cethrax was stronger than ever, like a corpse left to rot—and that about summed up Cethrax, which even the Alliance called the cesspool of the Multiverse.

A too-long shadow that appeared to belong to nothing crept along the corridor. Something followed us. I picked up the pace, my heart thudding. I had to get the family out of here, and stop whatever it was before it noticed the door.

There: the way back to London, Earth. The door that had saved my life, and Nell's, and too many more to count.

"You'd better get through that door, now," I said to the woman. The little boy clutched her hand, and she nodded. "Wait for me outside."

Only when I was sure they were safely out of the Passage, on Earth, did I turn around, bracing myself. The shadow crept over the floor like spilled ink.

"You can't have them anymore," I told it. "They're gone."

A growl answered me. My hand slipped to the dagger concealed in my boot. I'd had a feeling another of these nasties would show up. They never had the guts to interrupt a patrol, but stragglers in the Passages were easy prey. Or so they thought.

Magic crackled beneath my fingers, ever-eager to strike, but I couldn't use it now. It'd draw too much attention, and I could fight well enough without it. Trouble was, it was always there, as irresistible as a drug, and about as safe as juggling lit matches. So instead, I let my opponent reveal itself to me, layer after layer of shadows peeling away, and three rows of jagged teeth in a wicked smile. Oh, brilliant. A chalder vox.

They liked pain. *Really* liked it. It was like tripping on acid for them. I had to kill it.

I held up my left hand and tapped into the magic in the air, the red glow warning it I wasn't to be messed with. The chalder vox didn't even blink. It shuffled forwards, and I saw that it had three arms, one sprouting from the middle of its chest and ending in curved claws. Its ears were the same length as its rocklike face. Lovely. Creatures like this one were slow and clumsy, but also six feet of rock-hard skin.

One stonelike fist hit the wall, inches from my face. I dodged, kicking high at the hand that grabbed for me, and my foot connected with something solid. The creature hissed at me, its face stretched in a hideous grin. It was enjoying this.

I backed up and prepared to spring.

The monster's hand swiped as I jumped, magic flowing through my hand to propel me higher—I'd used it without thinking. Again. *Oh, all right, then.* Using magic in a closed space was generally a stupid idea, like firing a rocket in a cubicle. It was like any physical force, and if you weren't careful, the backblast would knock you out.

As it was, I aimed well. My feet connected with the creature's face, and when I let go of the magic, the backlash bounced off the ceiling and knocked into the back of the chalder vox's head, driving its teeth into the heel of my padded combat boot. Ouch.

With one hand, I gripped the side of the chalder vox's elephant-sized ear for balance and pulled myself upright, dagger aimed directly at a dip in the back of the creature's neck.

It flailed, almost throwing me off, but I held on and stabbed. The blade sank into the monster's weakest point. There was no blood, but a horrible screech echoed off the walls and the chalder vox fell to its knees. I leaped back quickly. Shadows flowed from the hole in the back of its neck, thick as blood. It went still. Dead.

Talk about an obvious weakness. Replacing the dagger in its sheath, I turned my back and went through the door, back into the foggy London alleyway. The static buzz of magic faded as I stepped back onto Earth. With the low-hanging clouds and tall buildings, it felt more enclosed than the Passages, and the smell of exhaust fumes never really went away. The woman and kids waited for me, looking uncertainly around.

"Sorry," I said. "We were followed. The Passages are dangerous, as I'm sure my friend Delta told you."

The woman bowed her head. She understood she'd never be able to go home. The kids wouldn't even remember it in a few years. I hoped so, anyway. My heart twisted all the same.

"Okay," I said, slipping a hand into my coat pocket. "You need to wear these all the time," I said, handing the woman a small packet. "They're contact lenses," I explained. "Your eyes will attract attention here. People on Earth don't have eyes that colour. Take your pick—blue, green, brown, grey. But stick with one colour." I glanced down at the little boy. His irises were pale grey, almost white, like mine. "They aren't mageblood?" I asked.

"I'm half mageblood," the woman whispered, face clouded with sadness. My heart twisted again. *Oh, boy.* Half magebloods had a death sentence on them from birth in Enzar. She was lucky. Really lucky.

I nodded. "If the kids start developing the pigment, get them more of these lenses. Ask Nell. She runs the shelter. It's this way," I added, pointing towards the street at the alleyway's end. Nell had rented the empty three-floor apartment building for convenience, as it was a short walk away from the alley. No one saw us, but I kept an eye out while I unlocked the door and led the family inside. I didn't need to tell them to keep quiet.

Nell was still up, waiting in the dark hallway. She looked much younger than her real age, even with her dark brown hair pulled into a bun. Her oval-shaped face hadn't a single wrinkle, though a jagged scar marked her right cheek. A souvenir from Enzar, she'd told me. More scars marked her strong, tanned arms. Her light blue eyes met mine as she nodded. Her natural eye colour was pale purple and could pass as blue, but she wore the lenses anyway. Even her hair was dyed; most Enzarians were fair. Another reason I'd dyed mine dark red.

"Welcome," she said to the woman, extending a hand. "I am Nell Fletcher."

In her typically quiet-but-authoritative manner, she led the family upstairs, leaving me in the dark hallway. I pushed open the door to the kitchen and helped myself to a glass of water.

We lived on the ground floor. Officially, the upper floors were out of use, and no one ever came to check, since we owned the building. No nosy landlords asking questions. Nell had set up this place herself, after she'd come to Earth with me. When I was less than a year old. Our odd family had later added Jeth and Alber, my brothers. None of us were related by blood, but we were as close as real siblings.

Nell came back into the kitchen, having helped the family settle upstairs. We had only a limited number of rooms, but this place was more of a transition point. We'd get the refugees new identities, help them adjust to living on Earth as best we could. We had contacts with other shelters throughout London. All illegal, like ours. Nell would never forgive the Alliance for adopting a noninterference policy twenty years ago that meant there *was* no legal way to help anyone from the worlds on the second level of the Passages.

Now, she narrowed her eyes at me. "Your coat's singed," she said.

I glanced down. She was right, of course, the edge of my black trench coat was smoking slightly. "A chalder vox," I said. "I got it, though."

Nell had nailed the disciplinary stare. "Ada. You need to stop challenging those things."

"I couldn't let it run around in there. It might have attacked someone. Or got through one of the doors."

"Then it's a problem for the Alliance. Not for us."

The old argument. "Thought you said the Alliance were blind to what's in front of them," I said.

"Tell me the three principles of magic."

I rolled my eyes. "Do we really have to go through this again? Can't I just go to bed?" I was bone-tired after the fight, though using magic often left me restless and irritable. Like it called to the part of me that belonged to Enzar, my homeworld, even here on Earth.

"Just tell me."

"Magic is a force which either acts on a person or an object. Every use of magic has an equal backlash effect, and there are three levels of increasing severity. All is tied into the Balance."

"Good."

"You know I'm not going to forget," I said, with a sigh. "Look, I didn't have a choice. I only used a little."

"Someone might have seen," said Nell, pressing her mouth into a thin line. "Magic creates a ripple effect. You know that."

She was right, of course. But I'd only used level one. It barely registered. It wouldn't affect the Balance. Only a major magical disturbance would cause the levels of magic across the universes to tip. A *major* disturbance. It had never happened, not as far as the Alliance knew, and from what Nell had told me, their records went back over a thousand years. Hell, the Alliance guards themselves used magic-based weapons in the Passages. I was careful.

"Yes, I know," I said. "Can I go and get some sleep now? I've got an early morning shift."

"Make sure you don't sleep in, then."

Nell didn't even *like* my job—well, there wasn't much to like about a part-time stint in a supermarket, but it was more than most graduates could get these days, and it had stopped her giving me grief for not going to university. It hadn't seemed worth adding to our debts with a mile-high stack of student loans I'd never be able to pay back.

I wanted to keep doing what I did: helping people. But I couldn't live at home forever. Nor did I want to. There was more to the world than this. More to the Multiverse.

Delta had said I should join the Alliance. But I knew better than to mention that aloud to Nell. It'd only set her off again. Yes, I knew that the Alliance's council had ruled against interference in the war, but sometimes it felt like Nell held them single-handedly responsible for every problem in our lives.

"Night, Nell," I said instead, and headed to my room.

CHAPTER TWO

KAY

"Watch out for wyverns." The text message came through on my brand-new, Alliance-issued communicator as I waited, not-so-patiently, at a red light. Rolling my eyes, I took one hand off the wheel and typed a response to Simon's version of a *Good luck at the new job* message: "Watch out for giant rats."

I could already see the Central Headquarters of the Alliance towering over the surrounding buildings, three sides of obsidian-coloured glass gleaming under the barely-risen sun, as I manoeuvred my car through the narrow streets of south-east London. No wyverns here. At least, I hoped not. It wouldn't be out of line with my usual luck. Though getting mired in early-morning traffic was torture enough. With all the technology of the Multiverse at their fingertips, you'd think the Alliance would have come up with a way around that.

Simon's profanity-ridden reply came a minute later. He didn't appreciate the reminder of our memorable encounter with giant swamp rats in the Passages during the Academy's final-year test two weeks ago. I grinned, recalling Simon's exasperation when I'd said, "You haven't lived if you've never taken a wrong turn into Cethrax's swamp." I'd decided not to mention that it wasn't a wrong turn—it was just the better alternative to being eaten by the monster that had chased us all over the first level. Good times.

Even he had to admit it had been worth it. Now we were both Alliance employees. Simon had transferred over to the branch in New York City, while I'd stayed in London. And we both had a lifetime ticket to the Multiverse. Monsters included.

I squinted against the glare, changing gears and making a turn towards the open gates leading into the car park. Words had been engraved into the gate: INTER-WORLD ALLIANCE, EST. 1988. Technically, the Alliance had been around much longer than that, but that was the year they'd gone public. The year my late grandfather had decided to unleash the truth about magic upon an unsuspecting planet Earth.

Back then, of course, there was a real risk of a war between the universes. Now, the black skyscraper looked out of place amongst the grey tower blocks, more like a tourist attraction than the centre of Earth's defence against offworld threats. The exterior wasn't made of regular glass, but adamantine, a rare offworld substance impervious to magic and virtually indestructible, which gleamed black even at night. To most people, it was an eyesore that drew attention to itself rather than hiding in the shadows like Alliance guards were supposed to. But Central was just a front—it was offworld where all the action happened.

As I pulled into a parking space, the beep of a horn and an

angry shout drew my attention.

"That was my space, you asshole!"

Killing the engine, I climbed out of my car to face the person who'd yelled. A surly face curtained by long black hair poked out the window of a black van behind me.

"I said, that was my space!"

"I don't see a name on it," I said. "Tough shit." For God's sake, half the car park was empty. He was just being a dick.

"You must be from the Academy," said the guy in the van, parking alongside me. "Nice manners. Humans." He gave a derisive snort.

I blinked at the way he said *humans*. "But you're…"

The words stopped as a *centaur* climbed out of the van. He wore a jacket, shirt and tie, but his back half was that of a tan-coloured horse. Easily six and a half feet tall—well, he towered over me, and I was five eleven. It was reason enough that I'd assumed—and I imagined most people would, for that matter—that the few centaurs on Earth didn't drive. They could kick up speeds of eighty miles an hour on their own four feet. I mean, hooves. Seriously.

"What're you staring at?"

The centaur's back foot kicked up, like he intended to knock me down. I met his eyes, indicating he didn't scare me. Not *entirely* true, but he didn't have to know. Come on. Was I really going to get tackled by a centaur before I even stepped into

Central? This was ridiculous, even for me.

The centaur moved back onto all four hooves, and laughed—well, more like a *neigh*, really.

"You didn't seriously think I was going to hit you, did you?" he said, snorting with laughter. "Priceless. I don't give a crap where you park your fancy vehicle."

"Who the hell are you, the welcoming committee?" I said, all thought of good first impressions going clean out the window. "Which department do you work in?" I turned my back to lock my car. I'd never met a centaur in person before, because—no shit—they hated humans and most never left their homeworld of Aglaia.

"First floor. Same place you're heading, if I'm not mistaken, Academy kid."

Kid? If he wanted to piss me off, he was going the right way about it. I made for Central's front entrance instead of replying, but the centaur tailed me across the car park.

"What?" he said, over the sound of clip-clopping hooves. "You're trying to picture me in an elevator. Am I right? Humans. Making assumptions because I have two more feet than you do."

I'd been thinking nothing of the sort. But of course, now he'd mentioned it... how in hell did a centaur get into a lift? I hid a smirk at the mental image.

"Speaking of making assumptions," I said, pulling my key card from my pocket, "don't call me *Academy kid.*"

The centaur laughed. "What would you prefer me to call you?"

"My name's Kay," I said, over my shoulder, as I swiped the key card and the glass front doors of Central slid open. "And this conversation is over."

The centaur laughed. "Direct and to the point. You can call me Markos. And seeing as we're going to be working on the same floor, Kay, we might as well get acquainted with one another."

I'd already made a mental note of the layout of the entrance hall. Reception desk on the right staffed by a sleepy-looking blond woman, open booths on the left, three gigantic glass elevators at the far end, stairs leading to the guard offices and cells—and everything sparkled like someone had upended a bucket of glitter all over the place. It felt alien, to say the least. But this was where I'd be spending the majority of my time now. The Alliance was more than a job.

"See?" said Markos, cantering ahead of me into the lift. "These things can carry a full centaur patrol."

"Is that likely?" I asked, resigned to him following me to the first floor. I hit the button, and the doors slid closed. Slowly, with a screeching sound not unlike a wyvern with its tail caught in a door, the lift began to climb. I turned back to the centaur.

"You never know. Wait." He frowned at my name badge, pinned to the front of my shirt—yeah, enough people worked at

Central to make those badges an unfortunate necessity. "Walker? You're his son—well, that explains it."

Damn. Should have known even an offworlder would make the connection sooner or later, though no Walker had set foot in Central for over twelve years.

I looked at him will well-practiced blankness. "Is there a problem?"

The centaur gave a self-satisfied nod. "Ha. Now I get it, Academy kid. Nepotism wins every time, even at the Alliance…"

"About not making assumptions," I said. "Don't finish that sentence."

Nepotism? Seriously? At twenty-one, I might have been the youngest in my year, but like the Academy, the Alliance didn't play favourites. I'd—naively, it seemed—assumed everyone knew that. I was more annoyed with myself than with the centaur.

Markos gave me an appraising look. "Tell me what to assume, then, Academy kid."

Either he had some issue with the Walker family, or he just wanted to start an argument. "How about we assume that I had my own reasons to join the Alliance?"

"Well, your diplomatic skills leave much to be desired."

"I don't pretend to be diplomatic before coffee," I said. There was a pause, and then he laughed.

The lift stopped without a sound, the glass doors sliding

open. In contrast to the glittering entrance hall, the first floor had the appearance of a modern office divided into booths with separate rooms for senior staff. "Office Fifteen" covered one section of the floor, and a sign pointed the way to Mr Sebastian Clark's office. My new boss had seemed amiable but absent-minded when he'd interviewed me, but at least he hadn't called me *Mr Walker* or even commented on the name. Nepotism indeed. Like I wanted everyone to look at me like they'd looked at *him*, before he'd relocated to another world to help with peace negotiations. They must have had a hell of a long negotiation, because that was five years ago.

"Kay Walker," said Mr Clark, as I knocked on the half-open office door. He spoke loud enough that everyone in the vicinity turned in my direction. They all knew who I was, all right. Stupid of me to think even for an instant that I could walk in here and *not* be recognised, name badge or none. Still. It was unlikely that any of them would have spoken to the old council, and the exact same thing had happened at the Academy when I'd first joined. I could handle it.

Mr Clark peered at me from behind a wall of paper, glasses sliding down his nose. "It's lucky you're here early. I have something I need to get from the archives, but I can't really leave the office. I'm expecting a phone call.

"Sure," I said. "That's the fifth floor, right?"

"It is." He disappeared entirely behind the stack of papers. "I need a document on the properties of bloodrock. It should be somewhere in the seventh section, I think. Markos knows the archives backwards. He'll be able to take you to the right place. There he is." And sure enough, the centaur appeared behind me, waving at Mr Clark. Guess things were casual in Office Fifteen.

"This should be fun," said Markos. "I have coffee, by the way." He handed me a paper cup.

What game was he playing now? I settled for saying, "Thanks". I wasn't complaining.

"What's he got you looking for in the archives?" Markos asked as we rode the elevator to the fifth floor.

"Something on bloodrock. What even is that?"

"I have no idea. Odd. Clark is an odd one, though."

"You're one to talk," I said, downing the rest of the coffee and crumpling the cup in my hand. Through the glass doors, I glimpsed more offices, all identical-looking—the Alliance liked everything to be uniform, apparently. Deceptive in its ordinariness. In those offices, the Law Division resolved offworld issues, the technology department worked on top-secret Alliance-only technologies from simulator tech to weaponry, and the council made statements that swept the Multiverse. But I sure as hell didn't intend to stay in an office forever.

"It's fun to wind up you Academy kids," he said, earning a glare from me. "You *are* kids," he said. "I suppose being a

Walker would help, but… that reminds me. I'm intrigued to know your thoughts on the Alliance's current noninterference stance on the war in the Enzarian Empire?"

I blinked. Was this some kind of test? "Enzar's been off radar for twenty years," I said. "The council think the war's none of Earth's business—we don't have the resources to interfere in magical warfare." That was the official statement, signed by one Lawrence Walker. Maybe that was the centaur's issue? Though Aglaians in general didn't take an interest in offworld affairs.

"Yes, but I want to know what *your* opinion is."

"I'm not intending to be a voice on the council, if that's what you're implying," I said. No way in hell. "But I'd have put out a call for offworld aid, at the very least. With all the magic they're throwing around, there's bound to be backlash on the Balance, too. I'd send people—magic-wielders, of course—to try for a peace treaty. That's what the Alliance is for, right?"

Markos nodded, brow furrowed, like he was trying to figure out why I'd said the stark opposite of my father's statement. Let him think on that one.

"Okay. Well, that's an unusual position."

"Idealistic, maybe," I admitted. "Any particular reason you wanted to know?" The high-magic worlds were usually kept under close scrutiny, but Enzar was a mystery. Even in the Alliance's information files logged into my new communicator, that area was glossed over, save for the statement that the

Alliance had withdrawn all involvement with that particular world. Seeing as magic was involved, it wasn't surprising.

"Just curiosity. It's the one world no one knows anything about, even here, and I've worked at Central for ten years." Well, that explained his fluency in English and familiarity with all things Earth. Centaurs weren't generally known to adapt to human customs. They stayed well away from humans on their homeworld.

The lift finally dinged to a stop at the archives, and the sound of Markos's clip-clopping hooves followed me through the aisles. It turned out there was one file on bloodrock, and it was two pages thick.

"What does he want this for?" I said, on the way back down. "Bloodrock. I'm not familiar with the term." It had to be classified, then.

"When it comes to Clark, I'd assume it's a whim. Things are pretty quiet at the moment. He's probably bored and needs something to amuse himself with. Most of the admin supervisors in the past have complained that the novices get to have all the fun, but he doesn't seem to mind that he doesn't have to run dangers in the Passages."

"Hmm." Not an Academy graduate, though I'd guessed as much. Most tended to want something a little more exciting than admin. Like Alliance Ambassadors, who had free run of the Multiverse when they weren't on missions. Give it a few months and I'd be there. For now, chasing monsters seemed a decent alternative.

"You, on the other hand… I'm taking a wild guess that's what you're thinking of right now."

He'd got me. "The Passages are where it all happens," I said.

"So they say. They always put the Academy kids on the late-night shift in the lower level. Savage creatures down there, or so I'm told. Chalder voxes… the odd wyvern or two… ever been face-to-face with a wyvern?"

"I have, actually," I said, and then wondered why I'd risen to his bait. It wasn't something I went around shouting about, though everyone at the Academy had known about the infamous wyvern incident.

Markos raised an eyebrow. "You're lying."

"Nope."

"Prove it."

Typical. Once centaurs fixated on something, they never let it drop—the phrase "stubborn as a mule" came to mind, not that I'd be saying *that* aloud unless I had the sudden desire to become part of the interior decorating. Centaurs weren't easily freaked out, but maybe this would deter him from asking any more questions. I pushed up my shirtsleeve to show the tip of the claw mark scar across the back of my forearm then flipped it over to show the identical mark on the other side.

"Damn," he said. "Well, that could have come from a

wyvern… or a really vicious stinging nettle."

We reached the first floor, sparing me from having to reply. File in hand, I approached the open door to Mr Clark's office. Behind all the papers, I saw he was on the phone, so I laid the file down and backed out of the room just as someone else passed by.

"Hey—you're new here? I'm Ellen." She read my name badge. "Kay…Walker?"

"Just Kay," I said.

"Nice to meet you, then, Kay," said Ellen, brushing dark blond hair from her eyes and smiling at me. "Wait—someone was just talking about you. Aric Conner."

I stared. "Aric Conner… from the Academy?"

"Yeah, he started this week, too." She gave me a puzzled look. "You know him?"

Well enough that I'd like to string him up and use him for target practice. "We were in the same class. That's all."

Oh, I wished that was all. I'd thought he'd gone to join his sister at London's West Office, and good riddance, but it seemed the universe wasn't done screwing with me yet. If ever anyone deserved to be trampled by a wyvern on the first night shift, it was the bastard responsible for the incident which had almost got me and two other students killed. And he'd got away with it.

My communicator buzzed in my pocket.

"That'll be the patrol rota," said Ellen. "I'll see you around, okay?"

"Sure thing," I said, skimming down the touch-screen. The rota said I was up tonight. Now that was more like it.

And then I saw Markos's name next to mine—and Aric's.

Yeah. The universe definitely wasn't done screwing with me.

CHAPTER THREE

ADA

Morning brought the smell of hot chocolate and a certainty that I'd slept through my shift. A glance at my alarm clock confirmed it. Ten thirty. My shift had started two hours ago.

Groaning, I rolled out of bed and gave my clock a shake. Oops, I'd forgotten to set it before I left for the Passages last night. Way to go, Ada.

I unplugged my phone from its charger, trying to think of an excuse I hadn't already used to text my supervisor. I settled for, "Sorry, I thought I had an afternoon shift", which would probably have got me fired from any other job. My boss was known for being lenient, even if reliability was *not* listed on my CV.

I dressed in jeans and a long-sleeved top, leaving my combat boots by the door. I pulled out my dagger from the sheath and put it back with the other knives I'd acquired, stacked on the bedside table. My room was little bigger than a cupboard, a problem when you hoarded the way I did. Books were stacked creatively on every surface, often with trophies from various martial arts classes balanced on top, and "souvenirs" Delta had given me from offworld. When I was twelve, I'd fetched a ladder and painted the ceiling with stars. Not representing the actual stars outside, but the worlds in the Multiverse. Like the doors in the Passages. Close, but distant. Untouchable.

The aroma of hot chocolate beckoned. My legs were stiff from yesterday, but I could still feel the electric tingle of magic in my blood. My bad mood cleared. The lingering aftereffect of using magic meant I'd be able to use it on Earth, at least for a short time. Today was going to be good.

Nell was in the kitchen, washing up. She looked like an innocuous housewife from the back—and people had been known to regret making that assumption. "You must be Ada's clone, seeing as she's at work," she said.

"Ha ha," I said. "Guess I was more tired than I thought."

Nell turned around. "Have they fired you yet?"

"They won't fire me. They like me." I gave her my most innocent smile.

Nell made a disparaging sound. "Can't imagine why."

"Nice to know you care. Is that hot chocolate I smell?"

"On the table. Don't say I don't spoil you."

So it was, and also a stack of toast. I shoved half a slice in my mouth. "You're amazing," I said, my voice muffled.

"Don't talk with your mouth full. You're lucky Jeth and Alber aren't around."

I swallowed the mouthful of toast. "Alber's not up yet?"

"Hangover. His own fault."

I grinned. "Hey, you let him go out." Unlike me, my seventeen-year-old brother Alber fitted in fine with people his own age. He'd got a handle on the double life better than I did.

"And Jeth's at work."

Here we go. I could sense a work-related lecture coming a mile off. Jeth was two years older than me, twenty-three, had a 'real' job in IT, and was saving to move into his own place. In other words, exactly what Nell wanted me to do. Well, it wasn't like there was an abundance of affordable flats in London, much less for someone young, single, broke, and who kept a collection of knives in their room. A conventional landlord would kick me out.

"Ada," said Nell. "The real world won't go away if you ignore it."

I glanced up at the flickering light. "I'm not ignoring it. I'm helping people. Same as you." Okay, I'd left my adult card behind today. But I was tired, and kind of ashamed at myself for sleeping through my shift. As well as being the first time I'd done that in a while, it was a reminder that a double life came with a price.

"Well, I don't want you to waste your life away. You can't save everyone."

Her face clouded. She never really talked much about her life before she'd moved to Earth. All I knew was that she'd

37

taken me to the transition point to be assigned to a new world and was coached on language and customs. I could never wrap my head around the idea that Nell had known nothing about Earth until she'd been there, and had learned English from scratch. Within a couple of years, she'd been able to pass as an Earth native, and nobody had ever doubted the same of me. When I'd asked why she'd never taught me Enzarian, she'd said, *We're never going back. We have to let the past go.* She never spoke about how hard it must have been to accept that.

"Duly noted," I said. "Look, I'll... find a better job. Honestly, I didn't plan on spending my whole life stacking shelves." Pity even a degree wouldn't qualify me for more. The exception, of course, being the Alliance. They'd interview anyone for an entry-level position, provided they passed their entrance exams. I probably had more practical experience in the Passages than most of their novices, at least, the ones who hadn't been to the Academy, and could speak three offworld languages to boot.

The one job I might be qualified for was the one Nell despised more than anything in the Multiverse. That figured.

"What's happening with that family?" I asked. "Do you have their papers sorted out? Need me to get anything?"

"Actually... you're changing the subject," Nell said, sternly. "But yes, we're out of powdered bloodrock."

I frowned. "I thought you had a ton of the stuff?"

"We burned through most of it three weeks ago."

Ah. That had been the biggest job of the summer, when a huge group of people from the collapsing world of Zanthar had come through the Passages at once. There was absolutely no way a Zanthan could pass as someone from Earth—they had gills, for one thing—so Nell's friends, the Knight family, must have used all the bloodrock to make the concealment concoction using Nell's recipe, a delightful combination of pure bloodrock and human skin tissue. It worked like magic—ha—to completely change a person's appearance. Permanently, if you kept applying it every year or so. I'd never used it, but it seemed to be some kind of hi-tech illusion – you only needed to dip your hand in it, and the effect would transfer to your entire body. Pretty ingenious. Except there was only one place bloodrock, a highly classified illegal offworld substance, was available.

"I get to break into Central's stores?" I said, cracking a grin.

Nell turned, hands on her hips. "I never said *you* had to do it. You've been reckless enough this week already."

"Might as well keep it up," I said. "Come on, I'm not working. There's less risk in it for me than the others."

At that moment, Alber came into the kitchen, yawning. "I'm dead," he announced.

"You're walking," I pointed out.

"This is my reanimated corpse," he said, opening a cupboard. The door fell off. "This house is literally falling apart," he announced, propping the door back in place.

"It is a bit," I admitted, glancing up at the cracked ceiling. The house had been "lived-in", as Nell put it, when we'd moved here fifteen years ago. Now, it seemed like something broke every day. The kitchen light flickered constantly, shelves fell down with little warning, and the dripping tap was a permanent fixture.

"Well, when you've found the universe where money grows on trees, let me know," said Nell. "I'm going to check on the others upstairs."

"Sure," I said. "Enjoy last night, Alber?"

"Never speak of it again," he muttered, running a hand through his blond, spiky hair and downing a glass of water. "Why is there no food in this house?"

"Because you and Jeth ate it all," I said. "I have good news, though. I'm breaking into Central tonight."

Alber's eyebrows shot up. "You serious?"

"Yeah, Nell's out of powdered bloodrock. You want in?" Hey, I never said I was a good influence on impressionable teenagers.

"Hell, yeah." He set the glass down, grinning.

"Great. Today's Monday, so patrols are every hour until

eight, then every two. I think we should set out at ten, to be on the safe side. They'll be in the Passages when we get there, so there'll be fewer guards at Central."

"You know all their patrols by heart?" said Alber. "Wow. That's dedication to law-breaking, right there. And shouldn't you be at work?"

"Shouldn't you be at school?"

"School finished a week ago," said Alber, rolling his eyes. "Which universe have you been in?"

"Ha ha." I pushed back from the table. If I had a few hours to kill, might as well do something productive. Like practicing throwing knives in the garden.

Alber followed me out the back door, having swiped the remains of the stack of toast from the table. "Nell's being a neglectful parent again," he said, perching on the garden wall. Weeds grew between the cracked paving stones and from the back, the house looked run-down and abandoned. Nell had let the ivy grow out of hand to block the windows, not that anyone ever came back here anyway. A chain-link fence and an alley separated us from the neighbouring house.

"She's just busy."

Running both the shelter and a home business was no joke, even if the business was basically all online, selling disguises to offworlders who wanted to build new lives on Earth. Nell might have wanted a normal life for me, but she could never escape her own roots.

The magic still zinged through my veins as I lifted a knife in my right hand, focusing on the target. Usually, I wouldn't be able to do this, but today magic was on my side.

I gripped the knife and sent a jolt of power into it, letting go as I did so. It struck the target dead centre, and then rebounded. I jumped into the air and caught it by the hilt, exhilaration mingling with the power still surging through me. Nell had lectured me half to death about throwing away my weapon during a fight, seeing as one time I'd done that, I'd ended up missing and almost getting speared through the eye with my own weapon. But with magic, I could get my dagger back to my hand without the enemy grabbing it.

"Show-off," said Alber, his violet eyes flashing. He wasn't wearing his contacts. He jumped back as the knife whizzed past and stuck point first in the target. "And you wonder why Gary was scared of you."

"Did you have to bring that up?" I said, shuddering at the reference to my ex. "It's not like I brought knives to our dates. Wait. Okay, there was that one time."

"I rest my case," said Alber.

"Oh, don't you start," I said. "Thank God Nell's not the type to want me to settle down and get married. Ugh."

"No." He smirked. "Can you imagine *her* dating anyone? I'm pretty sure she sleeps with three knives under her pillow."

"See? Makes me look almost normal."

I handed the knife over to Alber. He was right-handed, but landed a perfect hit with his left hand. Again, the knife soared back at him and he caught it in his right hand, grinning.

"I know all your tricks, Ada," he said. "You're not the only mageblood here."

I smiled, but it felt suddenly like a sharp object caught in my chest. I had no idea why Nell hadn't told Jeth and Alber what I really was, especially considering I knew everything about them. I knew Jeth's world, Karthos, was the only world to have ever been kicked out of the Alliance for human rights breaches after a bloodbath. He'd been five when someone had smuggled him to the transition point, and Nell had taken to him immediately. Alber was from Enzar, like me, and Nell had adopted him at three from another shelter. But he was mageblood. He didn't know I was related to the Royals, the ruling nonmages who'd wrested power from the magebloods on Enzar, forced them into servitude, or killed them outright. He didn't know Nell had been the Royals' servant, that she'd risked her own life smuggling me away as the magebloods and Royals alike were swept into a massacre.

That was all she'd told me. I'd only been a year old when

I'd left, after all, so I had no memories of Enzar. My blood family might still be alive for all I knew. From the little I'd heard from the survivors brave enough to share their stories, I didn't want to know their fate.

But I wouldn't have minded knowing why I had the same magic level as a mageblood when I was supposed to have none at all.

I whiled away the hours until sundown practicing throwing knives and going through self-defence exercises, while Alber lounged on the side-lines, skimming one of my paperbacks. Reading about other worlds might seem a poor substitute for the real thing, but it was all we had and they were good stories besides. Personally, I thought Earth people did a great job compensating for the lack of magic in their own world. Tolkien had the right idea.

Early evening, I decked myself out in standard breaking-and-entering gear, black from head to toe, long black trench coat and combat boots. This summer had been unusually damp and gloomy, and it was cold outside. Mist pressed against the window and a chill seeped through the thin walls. We didn't have the most reliable heating system and with no money to fix it, winters weren't fun. Still, it was the best we could get and we were lucky to have it. As I knew all too well. Sure, we might joke around, but it was that or live in a permanent state of despair. Nell always said she'd spent so many years living in fear, she was damned if she let the horrors of what was happening on our homeworld take away our happiness, too. We were the epitome of hope for everyone we helped.

I checked my reflection, slipping my phone into the inner pocket of my coat. My dark red hair was a little conspicuous, but at least it ensured that I'd never in a million years be taken for a refugee from Enzar. None of us went as far as to use bloodrock to hide our appearances—there were others who needed it more than we did—but you could never be too careful.

"Snazzy," said Alber, appearing from the gloomy hallway. "You're going for the Alliance guard look? What is it with those guys and tight leather?"

"Technically, it's not leather," I said, following him out into the hall. "The guards' uniform's made of some kind of magicproof material, isn't it?"

"Don't ask me. You're the one who spends all your time spying on them."

"I do *not.*" Okay, I'd followed a patrol… once. A couple of times, then. How else was I supposed to know their patrol routes?

"Uh-huh."

"Have you got Jeth's Chameleons?"

"Got it," he said, tossing one of the small, metal objects

to me. I caught it in one hand, checking it was switched on. Jeth, technological genius, had created a set of devices coated in powdered bloodrock, which had once belonged to the Alliance. I had no idea which world it was from, but it was like pure, powdered magical energy—or "fairy dust", as Jeth sometimes called it—and if you developed it in the right formula, it could change the appearance of anything. Object, person, whatever. In its purest form, it could also be used to create a chameleon effect. Hence the name. Hit a button and they went invisible, and so did anything that came into contact with them, including us. Plus, he'd also developed a set of three-way-communication earpieces, also coated in bloodrock. Alber passed me one of those, too.

I clipped the Bluetooth-style earpiece on, slid the device into my pocket and grinned at my foster brother. "Ready for a little law-breaking?"

"You," said Nell, appearing at the top of the stairs, "are a terrible influence."

"Wonder where I get it from? Come on. You said we need the bloodrock. ASAP."

"Yeah, it's gathering dust at Central," said Alber. "What do they even use it for?"

"Nothing. It's an illegal offworld substance," said Nell, her eyes narrowing as they always did when someone mentioned the Alliance. So, about twenty times a day.

"See? We have to go there," I said. There were people who needed our help *right now*. This was more important than the Alliance's petty laws.

"Just be careful," said Nell.

"Always am," I said.

This time, Alber and I didn't take the alley to the Passages, but the regular normal-person route to the tube station. Lights from the pubs and twenty-four-hour convenience stores spilled onto the roads, making me feel even more like we were spies or criminals, sneaking through the shadows. A world apart, almost literally.

Thankfully, the public transport system wasn't too crowded at this time of night. I wished the Passages could transport us right there, but the doors only led to certain points. There were five registered in the UK, two of which were in the London area. Central had, in fact, been constructed near Earth's main Passage, which had been around longer than London—longer even than humans had walked the Earth. It meant that they'd had to put in a back gate, right by the entrance to their stores, I assumed for a quicker route to the Passages. Prime target for breaking and entering.

The Alliance's Central Headquarters was visible the instant we exited the tube station at London Bridge. It towered over the Thames, a colossal three-sided skyscraper of gleaming black glass piercing the cloudy sky like a knife. Sleek, but ultimately for show. For all the money they'd invested in their fancy headquarters, I was willing to bet they hadn't spared a penny to help Enzar. Hypocrites.

Alber and I parted at the gates. He'd keep a lookout and tell me if anything changed, and I was the best at stealth. I crept around the outskirts of the fence.

Magic waited for me, thrumming under my skin. I could feel it pulsing from the fence, too, and I knew that if I as much as put my hand on it, I'd get zapped. The Alliance had ways of harnessing magic like electricity using offworld technology, less damaging than an actual electric fence, but just as much of a deterrent.

Except for me. I reached the back of Central, where the fence gave way to the back gate, and waited in the shadows, checking my watch. Sure enough, a group of four shadowy figures came out of the gate and headed down the back road to where I knew the Alliance's official entrance to the Passages was located. Few people lived on this road, but the handful of parked cars told me that it wasn't totally deserted. Some people would risk anything for cheap rent. Not that monsters tended to escape onto Earth. Most of the time. Claw marks on the side of one of the more run-down apartment buildings told me it had happened at least once.

I'd come here before to watch patrols leaving, and to

figure out how things operated. Including how to unlock the gate. Turned out it wasn't magic at all—they never expected anyone to sneak around this way. Complacence at its finest. As for the padlock, I had a small lock pick ready. Nothing fancy, but it worked. I'd had enough practise that it took only a few seconds to open the gate.

Not that I was relaxing. Now I had to get *inside* the building. The front door was key card operated, not to mention guarded, but at the back, there was always a changeover between patrols. I'd timed it to the minute—and I had to, because the Chameleons had limited battery life. The guards would notice an open door, but a window, I could get away with. Especially one I'd used before, and had wedged a folded piece of paper into it in such a way that it looked closed from the outside. It wasn't like anyone checked close up; the guards were more focused on potential intruders than a small ground-floor window nobody ever opened. It wouldn't have surprised me if most guards didn't even know it was there.

I reached beneath the visible world for the buzz of magic and pushed at the air, hard but carefully. The tiniest crack spiderwebbed across the pavement, but the momentum had already knocked open the window. I shook my hands to stop the buzzing as the adamantine walls of the building objected to the level-one hit and then climbed onto the windowsill and pulled myself inside. I pushed the window enough that it looked like it was closed, from a distance, again. No one on patrols had ever come close enough to check. But my heart thudded in my ears all the same. If I failed, I'd cost us everything.

I trod lightly down the corridor, pressing myself flat to the wall when I came in range of the security camera. I reached for the Chameleon and hit the button for cloaking, clipping it to the inside of my sleeve. Its effect depended on skin contact.

It was a bizarre experience to watch my hand fade away, then my arm, then the rest of my body. A shiver ran through me as I looked right through my own body, even though I knew it was still there. Invisibility cloaks, eat your heart out.

Time to go. I moved faster now I couldn't be seen, racing through the dark corridors until I found the door I was searching for. It was harder to manipulate an invisible lock pick and I fumbled it a couple of times, but within less than a minute, I was inside the store room.

The Alliance kept everything in crates. As usual, it was hard to resist opening some of the others and seeing what mysterious offworld substances they didn't want the public to know about, but I had ten minutes, tops, before the invisibility wore off. Here on Earth, you could only put a small amount of a magic-based energy source into a device like the Chameleon without risking it backfiring on you. Sadly, no exploring time for me. I opened the crate labelled 'bloodrock' and pulled out a handful of small bags, then rearranged the rest so it didn't look like anything was missing. I backed out of the room, and retraced my steps back to the window I'd come in by.

A group of guards stood a few feet away, engaged in urgent conversation. I went completely still, my heart thudding. Sweat beaded on my forehead. I had to get out silently. Why were so many of them close to the back entrance?

Relax. You're invisible. And yet, for once, that didn't reassure me. I quickly pushed the window wider, pulled myself out, and tiptoed around the group, ready to run.

"Hey! YOU!"

Voices. Shouts, echoing in the night. Shock surged through me, and this time I ran for real, coat flaring behind me. I pelted for the gate, which was open, but there were people outside. Too late to slow down. I shot right past the group—was that a *centaur?*—No time to stop. I didn't even pause to draw in a breath until I'd reached the street's end, and then I kicked up speed again. I paid no attention to where I ran, to the ground hitting my feet, the cold nipping through my coat, the sharp pain of my own breath—

I ran smack into someone, who stumbled back. "Jesus, Ada!"

I gasped out, "Alber—thank God—need to go."

"What happened?" He stared at me, the whites of his eyes bright in the lamplight.

"I'll tell you on the way back." Panting, I glanced over my shoulder. I'd lost my pursuers, but the sense of danger persisted. I'd never been spotted before, never messed up.

Only when we stood on the train, alone, did I let the tension seep out of my limbs. I collapsed into a seat, shaking all over. "Crap. Crap."

"Okay, Ada, you're really starting to worry me now. Did someone see you?"

I swallowed. "Yeah. There were people outside Central…lots of people. I don't know what they were doing. The Chameleon just stopped working." I removed the earpiece and unclipped the Chameleon from my sleeve. Dead battery.

"I swear I charged both of them," said Alber, frowning. "Did you get the bloodrock, at least?"

"Yeah," I said, slumping farther back. I didn't want to mention that they probably knew I'd taken something. I'd done enough damage already.

"I'm going to kill Jeth," said Alber. "Him and his bloody contraptions."

"Never mind that," I said. "I don't want to end up on the Alliance's hit list." For more than one reason. Who else would help the refugees?

"Yeah…I think you should lie low for a bit."

I gave him an eye roll. I felt a little better. But that didn't mean I looked forward to Nell's reaction when we got back.

CHAPTER FOUR

KAY

"Isn't this fun?" said Markos, smiling around at the group. "I can tell we're going to make a superb team."

Yeah, right. The four of us—me, Markos, Aric and a guy named Lenny—stood in the entrance hall of Central, dressed in standard patrol gear made of a material that looked like leather but was magicproof fabric manufactured offworld, designed to protect from both magic and nonmagic damage. Right now, it looked like the damage would most likely come from a fistfight between me and Aric, if he didn't quit being a smug bastard and sucking up to the supervisors, then making snide comments to the youngest of our patrol. Lenny, a skinny redheaded kid barely out of his teens, stood as far away from the rest of us as possible as though afraid he'd get speared by the intense glaring contest between Aric and me. I figured he was here on an apprenticeship and hadn't been to the Passages before. If Aric mentioned wyverns one more time...

"Right," said the night supervisor, Carl, striding over to us. He was late twenties, I guessed, with a ropy scar on the left side of his face. Definitely a claw mark, from an offworld monster, I'd wager. "Three of you are new, right? Damn that idiot Clark. The patrols are supposed to be an even split of novices and experienced assistants. No offence to you, Markos, I know *you* know what you're doing."

"Actually, we ran drills at the Academy," said Aric, with an air of superiority. "Same format as the patrols. Except keeping quiet and alert with a *centaur* on the team might be a bit difficult."

And here comes the bigotry. I was content to let Markos take care of this one, and when he turned on Aric, the blood drained from the idiot's face. Lenny let out a terrified whimper and backed away so rapidly he tripped over his own feet.

"It might be difficult to move stealthily with both your legs broken," said Markos. "Want to find out?"

"Enough!" said Carl. "Aric, you're forgetting the first principle of the Alliance. You *never* insult a fellow team member if you want to keep your job. Nor do you speak in that manner to a colleague regardless of homeworld, race, whatever. Don't let it happen again."

Ha. I gave Aric a scathing look, but he was too busy defending himself to Carl.

"He threatened me!" he protested.

"You deserved it," said Carl, and I decided I liked him. "Right. You have one hour. You'll know where the entrance to the Passages is, am I right?"

Carl went through the standard safety lecture, specifically on the use of the knives all guards carried as part of our uniform. The term 'knife' was misleading, because they were far from the flimsy, stainless-steel implements carried by morons attempting to look tough. These were the Alliance's specially developed automatic blades made of adamantine, with hilts of reinforced wyvern hide—an irony that wasn't lost on me—and could cut through virtually anything, magic reinforced or otherwise.

Of course, they were never, under any circumstances, to be used on another human, if it could be avoided. We were only to incapacitate, not kill. But monsters were fair game. No one could bring down a chalder vox using hand-to-hand combat alone. I'd already learned *that* lesson at the Academy. I watched Aric out of the corner of my eye, not trusting him in the slightest. True, we had an implicit understanding that neither of us would mention anything of our history at the Academy to anyone at Central, and some things were best left buried, but there was still the chance he'd try to start trouble anyway. Because he couldn't leave the hell alone.

"That's all," Carl finished. "Any questions?"

"There aren't any monsters, are there?" asked Lenny.

Aric snorted. "Kid, if you can't handle it, get out."

"That's enough," said Carl. "Markos will lead the way, as he knows the route. Return in an hour and report to me. If you see anything out of place, tell me via communicator. Obviously, there shouldn't be anyone coming in from offworld at this time, but you'd be amazed how often someone decides to wander this way from Valeria."

"Absolutely, sir," said Aric, back into sycophant mode. Carl, however, did not look impressed.

"Whatever the hell you guys have a problem with, I'm not interested. Do your jobs. Keep an eye out for trouble. And no *whining*. That clear?"

"Sure thing, boss," said Markos. "As long as that asshole keeps in line."

Aric started to retaliate, but Carl interrupted. "Enough! Talk to Clark about your patrol preferences, but I have no interest in why you all hate each other so much. Keep your personal opinions out of your work life. Got it?"

"I wouldn't worry," I said. "Aric hates everyone with more brain cells than he has. So, everyone."

Carl actually looked amused. Aric glared at me, but didn't retaliate. Carl tapped a button on his communicator. "The last patrol has checked in. You're up."

"Excellent," said Markos.

Much as I hated to admit it, Aric had a point about stealth being difficult for a centaur. Aside from his size, the clip-clopping sound of hooves was difficult to mute. Still, it wasn't like Academy drills, where they sometimes set monsters loose in the Passage to give us a taste of an emergency situation, always obtaining permission from the Alliance first. Except for the wyvern incident, of course.

Even Aric wouldn't be idiot enough to try any tricks in a real patrol, but I sure as hell didn't trust him, especially knowing he carried a fully charged stunner. Then again, so did I. It was shaped like a remote control but had only one switch, and I could feel the static charge as I tucked it into my pocket. Three shots were all it could handle, but a level two would still temporarily paralyse anyone or anything that got hit.

"Well, this is a rather frosty atmosphere we have going on here," said Markos. "Lenny, I don't believe we've met. You're Mr Clark's assistant, am I right?"

Lenny made a nervous sound. "Aren't we supposed to keep quiet?" he asked, tripping over the kerb. His communicator fell out of his pocket with a *clang*, and he fumbled to pick it up.

"Did you know," said Markos as we turned away from the gate and headed down the back road behind Central, "there's supposed to be a ghost in the Passages around here."

Aric gave a derisive snort.

"It's true," said Markos, with a straight face. "There was this guy who thought it'd be funny to shoot a gun in the

Passages. The magic didn't like that. He blew his own head off."

"That's bullshit," said Aric.

"It's true," said Lenny. "I mean, I don't know if the story's true, but you can't fire a gun in the Passages, right? The magic interferes with it."

"Everyone knows *that*," said Aric, shooting me a glare. *Oh, get over yourself.* If he wasn't careful, he'd be getting a well-placed zap with the stunner.

Markos pressed his hands against the wall of the building facing us. I hadn't used the Alliance's official entrance to the Passages before, but I knew that there'd be a sliding panel somewhere, where metal hid beneath the brick facade. The building behind looked like a disused factory, but like other Passage entrances, it was just a cover. Markos stepped back and part of the wall slid aside, revealing a wide metal door-like shape. That, too, slid back, and the cold tunnel of the Passages beckoned us.

Despite the late hour, I was wide awake and ready to face whatever waited ahead. In fact, bring it the hell on. It had been two weeks since the final Academy tests in the Passages, and now, it was almost a disappointment to find a monster-free corridor waiting ahead, lined with doors on either side.

My skin buzzed, like a mild shock from the stunner, as

we followed a path through the winding corridors of the first floor, lit by the faint bluish glow from the walls and floor. I didn't acknowledge the presence of magic even though it pulled at me like a seductive whisper. I had no intention of tempting fate, not again. I'd dreamed of the Multiverse my whole life, since long before I'd known I was a magic-wielder, and I was damned if I let anything wreck my chances of making Ambassador and seeing the worlds on the other side of these doors. Top of my list was Valeria, one of the few worlds which was similar enough to Earth to be easy access for Ambassadors. And okay, maybe I wanted to test-drive one of their premium hover cars.

As a faint shuffling noise came from up ahead, Lenny made a terrified sound and moved closer to Markos.

"Honestly," Aric muttered, who'd got out a torch regardless of the ever-present blue light, and was aggressively shining it into corners. "I don't know why the Alliance hired you. You're useless."

"Well, they'd filled their dickhead quota," I said.

"Shut it," said Aric.

Markos stomped a hoof, so close to Aric he almost fell over.

I smirked. "A little jumpy, Aric?"

"Quit laughing at me, Walker," he snarled.

"Only when you stop being so entertainingly stupid."

Aric swiped at me with his stunner, but I'd already moved out of range, my own stunner in hand. It wasn't like I was planning to use it, but it didn't hurt to be armed, too.

Markos let out a loud, sudden *neigh* sound. My heart damn near jumped out of my chest, even though I knew it was only the centaur. Lenny whimpered and backed away, and even Aric didn't laugh.

"Right!" he bellowed. "As much as I'd dearly love to watch the pair of you kick the crap out of each other, we're in a restricted area and… insert serious lecture here. I'm done."

I shot Aric a glare and followed, Lenny stumbling behind us.

No one murdered each other on the way around the corridors, which was some achievement. The buzz of magic was starting to get on my nerves by now. It was always there in the Passages, and no doubt it'd be the same offworld. Especially on high-magic worlds. Some, like the Enzarian Empire, had been torn to pieces by magical warfare. Hell, it had nearly happened on our neighbouring worlds, which was part of the reason the Alliance had revealed itself to the public on Earth. But even the Alliance couldn't control magic. It was a force all on its own, and on no one's side.

"Pretty quiet tonight," Markos commented, as we made our way back. "'Course, this is only the first level. They'll have you down in the lower-level corridors soon enough." He threw a glare at Aric, who'd tapped Lenny on the shoulder in the dark and scared him half to death.

"I'm shaking," said Aric. "Bet you've never been down there, seeing as centaurs can't climb-"

"I wouldn't finish that thought," I said. "Did you know when centaurs reach peak speed, they can turn anything they trample on into paste?"

"You're a liar, Walker," said Aric, but he took a step or two away from Markos. The centaur grinned at me. Of course he knew I'd made that up.

"You'd be a mess of blood and splintered bones," said Markos, and Lenny moaned behind me. Really, he'd picked the wrong career.

"Yeah. He almost trampled me earlier," I said.

"I did. It would have been a shame. He's pretty, for a human. Pity I can't say the same for you."

"Oh, go fuck yourselves, both of you," said Aric.

The centaur chuckled softly. "Humans. So easy to wind up."

Lenny gave a weak laugh. Markos tilted his head to face him.

"Please don't hurt me," said Lenny.

Markos sighed. "It's a pain, looking so intimidating. In my world, I would be called majestic. It's wasted on you people."

"My heart bleeds for you," I said, rolling my eyes.
Centaurs.

As we came out of the Passage and headed back down
the road to Central, I almost dared to think things would
pass without a hitch. Then the clamour of urgent voices
broke the quiet. Even in the dark, between the fence bars, I
could see a crowd had gathered outside the back door.

"There's never that many people at Central this late," said
Markos, frowning. "Something's up."

"No shit," said Aric. "Get out the way. We have to find
out what's going on."

Just before we reached the gate, a small figure ran
through, turned left and pelted into the night, so fast it
appeared a shadowy blur.

"Oi! You!"

Two guards followed, vanishing into the shadows too.
Markos cursed under his breath.

"What the hell?" I said. "Was that—?"

"Trespasser, probably," said the centaur. "Come on. Let's
see what's up."

Trespasser? Who the hell would have the nerve to break
into Central?

We went through the gate, towards the crowd. The entire
night guard had congregated out back, by the look of things.

Carl beckoned us over, and he, along with everyone else wore a dead-serious expression… like someone had died.

Oh, shit.

"What happened?" Markos got there first.

"Mr Clark," said Carl. "He's been murdered."

No way. I looked from Markos to Carl and back at the guards. Like someone would reveal this to be an elaborate prank.

"What… how?" I asked.

"Strangled from behind, we think. In his office. You knew he was working late?"

"Yeah. He spoke to us. Before our shift." Damn—we were the last people to speak to him. "When did this happen?"

"We're still trying to determine that," said Carl. "No one has *ever* been murdered on the premises before. Not in thirty years."

A shiver went down my spine. "Damn," I said.

"Who would do that?" Lenny blurted. "He—he was…"

"A supervisor," Aric cut in. "He wasn't a higher-up, right?"

A blond woman stepped forwards to glare at him. I recognised her as Ellen, whom I'd met earlier that day. She'd been part of the next shift.

"Might you show a little respect?" she said to Aric. "A

man has died. *Your* supervisor, to be precise."

It seemed unreal. I'd spoken to Mr Clark that *day*. Barely an hour before he died. He'd been reading those papers I'd fetched from the archives.

"How could a killer have got in the building?" I asked Carl. "It's magicproof and there's no way to climb up the walls, right?"

"Unless it was someone who worked here," said Aric.

Lenny moved away from him in panic. "No way! None of us are killers."

"The police are here, but it's looking like we'll need the Law Division in on this one," said Carl. "They've never had to investigate a crime within our own headquarters before."

"It's messed-up," said one of the guards. "Who'd strangle Clark? He's harmless. Never hurt anyone, never really spoke to anyone outside his department."

"Yeah, that's why it's suspicious," said another guard.

"We saw someone run," Markos said. "They were being chased down by guards."

"How the hell did *they* get in?" I said. "Did anyone see anything odd when we were on patrol? Because the Passages were quiet. Nothing out back, either."

"That's the point," said Carl. "There's literally no trace. None of the cameras picked anything up until this girl appeared...over there." He pointed at a spot near the building's corner. "I did find an open window when I went in the back way, but I figured that was a mistake. Now, though… perhaps that's how they got in. Glass isn't magicproof. There should have been a guard there."

"When was this?" asked Ellen.

"Not long ago. I went right to the back door after these guys left. I saw the window open a bit later, and figured someone had just forgotten to close it. Damn stupid of me, but it's happened before."

"So the killer got in through the window?"

"The gate was unlocked when we came back," Markos said. "It shouldn't have been, right?"

"I normally check every ten minutes," said Carl, "but the alarm went off and people started gathering out here. The killer must have run fast, if that's when they got in."

"Something's not right," Markos said. "That girl we saw. She's the killer? Did anyone see her face?"

I didn't even see it was a girl. She'd moved wicked fast.

"Hopefully, the other guards will bring her in," said Ellen. "We were supposed to be headed for the Passages now."

A burly guy beside her nodded. "Yeah, we've the next shift. Reckon we'd better get a move on."

"Hold it," said another guard. "We all have to stay here, wait for the police to come down. They want to speak to everyone who was here."

A collective groan from everyone. "Seriously," Aric muttered. "They expect us to stay here all night?"

I glared at him from out of the corner of my eye. If anyone here were capable of committing murder... but of course, he had an alibi. And no motive that I knew of. My mind was already racing through the possibilities, even though I knew there was nothing we could have done.

It was going to be a long night.

CHAPTER FIVE

ADA

"You were foolish," said Nell for about the fiftieth time, from the other side of the kitchen table. She'd waited up for us, and I'd predicted her reaction dead-on. "Never assume that you're invulnerable no matter what tricks you have up your sleeve."

"It's Jeth's fault," said Alber, and our foster brother glared at him. He *hated* it when one of his treasured technological contraptions failed to do its job. He was fiddling with the Chameleon device and had scattered dismantled bits of metal and wire and God-knew-what all over the table.

"Look, everything glitches sometimes," he said. "These Chameleons are ninety-nine point nine percent reliable. By that, I mean they've never just stopped working before. It should have had at least another hour's charge in there. I checked them all. Honest."

"Yes, well, that's not the important thing," said Nell. "Ada, you shouldn't assume that because something has always worked, it will continue to work in the same way."

"What was I supposed to think?" I said. "Besides, there were a ton of people gathered out back at Central. They have two guards, and they never come near the back entrance. Something must have happened."

"Let's hope no one saw your face," said Nell. "Their cameras, too."

"I had my hood up," I said, with more confidence than I felt. I hated feeling vulnerable. "Still, I got the powdered bloodrock, and plenty of it. We won't need to make another trip there for a while."

Nell sighed. "Well, that's good news, at least. I'll send one of the others to hang about the Alliance for a bit tomorrow, to find out what happened."

And that was that. Unsurprisingly, I didn't get much sleep that night, and when I did, it was only to wake sweating and shaking from nightmares of being chased down the Passages. Just as I was finally dozing off, someone banged on my door.

"What?" I groaned. "I'm asleep."

"It's midday," said Alber. "Nell wants to talk to you."

"I thought she was done lecturing us already."

"Nope. She's just getting warmed up. Also, someone died at Central last night."

I sat bolt upright. "You what?" Sliding my feet into slippers, I went to the door. "You're joking."

"Nice pyjamas." I was wearing the blue rabbit-patterned ones Jeth had bought me as a joke. Idiot older brother.

"Seriously, though. Some supervisor or something. He was

killed at Central last night. That's why there were so many people outside."

"Oh. Shit. We were there."

"I know. Damn. Hope no one saw you."

"You and me both."

I wished I was working. Not that I'd spoken to my boss since missing my shift yesterday. Oh, crap.

On cue, Nell's voice rang through the hallway: "Ada! Stop hiding in your room. I need to talk to you."

The dreaded words. I came out into the hallway, still in my rabbit-patterned pyjamas. Nell was in the kitchen, and on the table in front of her was the bag of powdered bloodrock I'd taken from Central. The bag was half-open, revealing the transparent glittering dust.

"Someone was killed last night?" I asked. "For real?"

"Skyla called me this morning," said Nell. "She heard two Alliance guards talking about it."

"How did they die?" I asked. "Was it when we were there?" When I was in the building? They wouldn't have seen my face—I'd moved too quickly—and yet I'd run right past a group of them by the gate. And at least one of those guards could have seen me. I looked at the powdered bloodrock and wondered if it was worth formulating a disguise for myself. But there were others who needed it more than I did.

"I don't know," said Nell. "No one knows. This person was working late, alone in the office, and someone went in there and killed them. No clue about motives. Not to mention how they got in there in the first place."

I thought of the Chameleon and shivered. Jeth was the only person who had those devices, I knew that much, and we'd never shown them to anyone else. It was a fairly major thing to be able to use magic-based technology on Earth and have it actually work how it was meant to. Most people didn't know much more than the three basic principles, which were broadcast on the news daily because the media thought the public needed a constant reminder. In case they started, I don't know, waving wands and trying to conjure things. The most even a magic-wielder could do was fire a first level power jolt, no more damaging than a static shock. I'd used it to open the window…

What if the killer got in by the gate I left open?

No. I wasn't going to feel guilty for the death of a stranger. It had nothing to do with us. The last thing I wanted was to get wrapped up in the Alliance's business. As horrible as the idea of a murder was, it didn't affect us. We could just go on as normal. We had to.

"That's bad and everything," said Alber, "but we don't need to go back there again anytime soon. As long as we keep our heads down, we should be fine, right?"

"In theory," said Nell. "But this gives me a bad feeling. Also, I need someone to take this bloodrock to the other shelters."

"Thought you didn't want me running any more risks," I said, but I brightened at the idea of getting to talk to some of the others. People like us, and the few Nell trusted.

"Jeth's at work," said Nell. "Take it to the usual places. Save a third of it to give to the Campbell family. They need a bunch of it, ASAP."

"Wait, what?" I frowned. "You mean, Delta or one of his brothers? But that would mean going back into the Passages." Valeria's citizens were allowed to leave their world as they pleased, which was how Delta and I had met, incidentally. He'd sneaked up on me and I'd almost choked him to death. The start of a beautiful friendship.

"Yes..." said Nell, slowly.

"Taking an illegal substance into the Passages right after what happened? Seems a bit..."

"Don't you pretend to be concerned about safety, Ada Fletcher. You're just trying to get in my good books." She knew me too well. "It's not ideal, I know, but there's a big group of Karthos rebels coming through next week and it's going to be a challenge to get them all in without causing suspicion."

The doorbell rang, making us all jump.

"I'll get it," said Alber, while I hurried back to my room to dress in something a little more dignified than rabbit-patterned pyjamas.

It turned out to be Skyla, who'd come to check up on us. She was about a year younger than me. Her thick dark hair was swept in a high ponytail and she wore a smart shirt and trousers which looked odd on her. In the five years she'd helped at the shelter, I'd never pictured her as the type to work in an office as a secretary. She looked like she should be running gym classes instead.

"I was trying to call you earlier," said Nell. "Ada's going to need your help to make a couple of deliveries."

"Ah, I'm on my lunch break at work, so I can't stay here long. I wanted to make sure Ada was okay after last night."

So she'd heard about the whole debacle. I said, "I'm fine. Honestly."

"Well, if you say so. I'll give you a hand with those packages of…" Her eyes widened as they landed on the bloodrock. "Is that what I think it is?"

"Yeah, that's what I almost got caught stealing," I said. "But I only just found out someone was killed. Do you know what happened?"

"No more than anyone else does," said Skyla. "I listened in on a conversation on the way to work. Guy strangled in an empty office. Total chaos in Central, seeing as it's the first time someone's been murdered on the premises. Of course, it's nothing to do with us, but it might make using the Passages tricky. There's a chance they could alter their patrols."

"Dammit," I said.

"Yeah," said Skyla. "I've never seen them like this. They're interrogating all their staff. Well, that's what I heard them talking about, anyway. Wouldn't wish it on anyone else."

"I'm more concerned with whether they recognised Ada," said Nell. "If anyone saw her face…"

Shivers ran down my back. For once in my life, I didn't want to go outside and deliver the packages, but only Alber and I knew the addresses of all the others who helped the refugees. Nell wouldn't trust anyone else with that information.

"I can help," Skyla offered. "Not that I really want to be caught running around with that stuff—also, I have half an hour before I have to be back at the office."

"I'll go with Ada," said Alber.

"Tell you what," said Skyla, with a glance at her watch. "I'll meet you after work and come to the Passages. I can be your lookout. Okay?"

Nell's eyes narrowed. She implicitly trusted Skyla, because she was sensible and didn't take unnecessary risks, and we'd gone to meet Delta in the Passages together a few times before. But after everything that had gone wrong in the past twenty-four hours, Nell's barriers had gone up again. She turned back to the bloodrock, contemplating the six heavy bags, and sighed heavily.

"Alber, Ada, you two go make the usual rounds. Save the Passages till last. Skyla, would you have the chance to check if the Alliance are running their usual patrols?"

"Sure, I'll take a look," she said. For all her pretence of posh office girl, part of the reason Skyla had interviewed for a job at that particular office was because it'd give her the perfect view of Central, patrols and all. I'd never seen her workplace, but it was on the road facing the Alliance building. "Come on, Ada, Alber. We'd better go deliver this contraband." She grinned. Like me, she couldn't resist a challenge.

"Sure, I'll get my stuff," I said, heading back to my room.

"It would help if you put socks on," Skyla called after me. "No shift today?"

"Haven't talked to my boss yet. Crap." And sure enough, there were several unread messages on my phone, which I'd not heard when I'd been asleep.

"Ada, I need to talk to you. Two p.m. tomorrow."

"Crap." This had 'bad news' written all over it. Plus, I could hardly show up for a meeting with my boss carrying a ton of bloodrock, even if most people on Earth wouldn't have a clue what it was. He'd probably think I was trading illegal drugs or something. "Alber, could you hang onto that stuff while I go meet my boss?"

"You couldn't have picked a better time?"

"I don't have a choice," I said. "I'll be quick as I can."

"I'll head back to work, then," said Skyla. "I'll message you, okay?"

"Sure." I'd have to run if I wanted to make the meeting.

"I'll come for moral support if you buy me a Coke," said Alber.

I needed more than moral support. I needed a miracle.

***

KAY

"This is a disaster," Markos said.

"No shit," I said. Markos, Ellen, Lenny and I hovered around the main office the following afternoon, all in varying degrees of tiredness. Markos stood by a filing cabinet and occasionally shuffled papers. Ellen had given up on work entirely and was texting someone. And Lenny hadn't stopped shaking. He'd been called out for questioning three times already—the rest of us had got off lightly with once each, but Lenny had made the mistake of admitting he'd been the last person to speak to Mr Clark before he'd died. It was obvious he was the least likely candidate to commit murder, but then again, there was no evidence to speak of.

With no one to leave instructions, we were at a complete loose end, turfed out of our old office, and most of the area was under investigation. Nothing was out of place; all the offices had been in the same state we'd left them at the end of the day. That was the last time we'd seen Mr Clark alive.

How could any of us have known that? Death wasn't uncommon in the Alliance, by any means—the average guard ran into more than their fair share of near-fatal situations, and Ambassadors risked their lives every time they went into hostile offworld territory. The death list was a mile long. But there was a world of difference between that and a brutal murder right here at headquarters.

I'd been too rattled by the murder to sleep in the few hours at my apartment last night and now that I was wired on caffeine, hanging about the office all day was slowly driving me insane. I paced back and forth, counting the seconds to my next patrol shift so I could get the hell out of here and do something useful.

"Oh, for heaven's sake," said Markos. "Quit your bloody pacing. You're making my head spin."

"Well, what am I supposed to do?" I said. "It's a waste of time us even being here."

"Tell me about it," said Ellen, yawning. "It's all right for you guys. You have an alibi. I arrived ten minutes before Clark died and they've given me a right grilling."

"It's awful," Lenny mumbled. "And that's just the regular police. The Law Division's going to be involved later, and then we'll all be screwed."

"Your optimism is infectious," said Markos. "Where's that idiot Aric?"

Good question. He had zero moral scruples, if the wyvern incident proved anything. But killing our supervisor? Even I thought he'd have to have a damn good reason. Besides, he'd been with us.

"No idea," said Ellen. "That guy's the most disrespectful ass I've ever met."

Markos looked at me. "What's your guys' problem with each other?" I groaned inwardly. I was not in the mood to discuss Aric. Typically, we were both on the same patrol later. Someone up there was having a really good laugh at my expense.

"We both went to the Academy. He didn't quite grasp that he needed to actually study and not try to bribe people to do it for him. He scored an 'A' in 'Being a Twat', of course." I stopped pacing to open the window. It was too damn stuffy in here.

"Hmm," said Markos, plainly not satisfied with that explanation. "He needs a reality check. Most offworlders wouldn't stand for his bullshit."

"Well, he must have got in on connections," I said. "His family are offworld technology tycoons with links across three universes."

"That explains it," said Markos. "I tried to quiz him on the new restrictions in offworld trade. He didn't seem to appreciate it."

"Considering it probably lost his family a crap-ton of money, I'm not surprised," I said absently. The Alliance were right to push up barriers on offworld trade, considering the absolute chaos that inevitably resulted when magic-based technology went wrong on worlds like Earth, where knowledge of magic was next to none. It was like time-travelling back to the Stone Age and handing out grenades.

"Most Academy graduates who come in here haven't a clue how to deal with the reality of non-Earth negotiations," said Markos.

"The Academy did cover offworld law, believe it or not," I said, pacing again.

"Thought it was more about chasing monsters," said the centaur.

"That too," I said, and Ellen laughed.

"Sounds exciting."

"Sounds *mental,*" said Lenny, shuddering.

"Not the first time I've heard that," I said.

"Wow," said Ellen. "I think I'm glad I went through an

apprenticeship instead, but I always wondered." She was still looking at me. "Did you get to go offworld?"

"Aside from the Passages? No. Guess they didn't want a bunch of teenagers running amok with hover cars in Valeria."

Ellen grinned. "Fair point."

"Never been offworld?" Markos inquired, giving me an assessing look.

"Not yet." I *could* have, since I'd turned twenty-one, but the permit application process was so long-winded and tedious that ultimately I'd decided to hold off until I'd graduated and had full access to the Passages and the main allied worlds as an Alliance employee. Now I was regretting that decision.

I paused by the filing cabinets at the office's end, checking my communicator again. "Law Division's coming down here this afternoon, by the look of it."

"Crap," said Lenny, paling. "They're not going to arrest me, are they? I didn't murder anyone. None of us did."

Ellen sighed. "I think we should do something." She indicated the walled-off section of the corridor outside, which led to Mr Clark's office.

"Leave it to the Law Division," said Lenny. "Can they use magic to track who killed him? Or weren't there DNA traces or anything?"

"Apparently, the killer hid their tracks," said Ellen. "Didn't you hear them?"

"He was being questioned," Markos reminded her. We'd all eavesdropped on one of the discussions that had taken place among the guards and law enforcement, in which it seemed apparent that the killer had somehow removed their own DNA traces from the victim.

Magic, was my immediate thought. Surely they'd have taken it into consideration. Though I had no idea how many magic-wielders there were at Central. I'd never met another. You couldn't tell by glancing at someone. That was what made magic so damned unpredictable. I'd expected the question to come up when I'd been interviewed for the job here, but it hadn't, so I'd played it safe. For all I knew, being a magic-wielder might work to my advantage later on, but I'd also discovered it while breaking the law. Not exactly something I wanted to mention on the job application.

"The Law Division. Christ." Lenny shuddered.

"I wouldn't have thought they'd get involved just yet," said Ellen. "I know it's murder, but there's nothing offworld about it, is there?"

"Don't be so sure," said Markos. "Clark was strangled, but it could have been done with magic. If they'd had a source. A stunner wouldn't do it. They should have magic experts on the case soon, I'd assume. In a place like this, sad to say, it's always a possibility."

Of course. It had slipped my mind that on Aglaia, Markos's

homeworld, magic was second nature, at least to humans. Centaurs, not so much. But there were bound to be more offworlders here.

"Interesting," said Ellen, switching off her communicator. "I've always been intrigued how it works. Magic, I mean."

Don't be, I thought. If I never had anything to do with magic again, it'd be too soon.

"Useful interest for a secretary," said Markos.

"Everyone needs a hobby."

"Looks like Clark's cost him his life," Lenny said, and I glanced in his direction. "He was poking into weird things when he died. So the officers said."

Weird things. Bloodrock.

"He's always had odd interests," said Ellen.

"How long have you worked here?" I asked, out of curiosity.

"Two years," she said. "It's going to be weird without Clark here."

"It is," said Markos. "He was a good guy. Not that I'd normally say that about a human, but he was."

It felt like I trespassed on a stranger's funeral. I'd been here only a day. I hadn't known Mr Clark, at all. And yet the image of the strange file on bloodrock was never far from the back of my mind. No—I was being paranoid. His death had nothing to do with that. Right?

But it didn't take a genius to see the wrongness screaming out from the whole situation. Even the police's interrogations were directed solely at people in the building. No one seemed to take into account the girl who'd broken into Central last night. I hadn't seen her face, but like the bloodrock file, it kept coming back to me. I guessed the file was back in Clark's office, and it took all my willpower not to pace in that direction to have a look.

Paranoia. Just paranoia.

Someone rapped on the door, making Lenny jump.

"Are you admin?" A fair-haired man opened the door. His name badge identified him as Alan Gregory.

"Yeah," said Markos. "You know that, Alan. I'm the only centaur in the building."

"All right, just checking. Your new supervisor's been assigned. One Ms Danica Weston."

Markos's face pinched inwards. "Ouch."

"I wouldn't say that in front of her," said Alan, withdrawing. "Best of luck."

"Well, that sounds encouraging," said Ellen. "Weston... crap. She's not from this department."

"She's transferring over from the Law Division," said Markos, forehead creased in a frown. "I've never heard of that happening before."

"Well, what's she like?" I asked, seeing as Lenny didn't seem inclined to ask the obvious question.

Before anyone could answer, Alan opened the door again. "By the way," he said, "the Law Division has sent out an official announcement. As of today, all patrols have new privileges, approved by the police… to arrest and apprehend anyone they find acting suspiciously in or around the Passages."

"Wait, what?" said Markos.

"What I said. Who has a patrol today?"

"I do," I said. "They're giving us permission to arrest people?"

"So it would seem," said Alan. "Good luck."

"Well, damn," I said. Okay, I'd been through the drill a hundred times at the Academy, but this had got serious fast. I'd never thought I'd have the authority to make arrests on my second day at Central.

Alan left, and I turned and saw Markos smirking at me. "What?" I said.

"Nothing," he said. "I just find this amusing. You look so thrilled to be playing at law enforcement."

"Ecstatic," I said. I was fully aware of the irony, though there was no reason for the centaur to know I'd been arrested twice before. My record was clean, thanks to the Academy, who'd decided it was in the Alliance's interests if the rest of the world didn't find out it had been the youngest Walker who'd burned down the family estate. Besides, murder was a tad more serious than that brief spell of delinquency when I was sixteen. Markos's questioning had lasted three times longer than mine had. He'd spent the past hour muttering about 'bloody suspicious humans'.

"I wouldn't think you're off the hook," said a voice from behind a filing cabinet. I recognised it as Aric's.

"What're you doing back there?" Markos said. "Eavesdropping?"

"It's a creepy habit of his," I said.

"Doing my job." Aric's face appeared around the corner, levelled in a glare. "Getting the office ready for our new boss."

"I thought we weren't allowed back in the office," said Ellen, putting her phone away.

"We are now," said Aric, with an air of superiority. "Which you'd know if you weren't slacking off over there."

"Oh, pull your head out your ass, Aric," I said, earning a *neigh* of laughter from Markos. "We're coming."

"You watch it," said Aric. "I hear the Law Division thinks it was a rogue magic-wielder who killed Clark. You'd better watch your back on patrol later, Walker."

"I'll keep that in mind," I said, scanning the message on my communicator screen to distract from the urge to punch him in the face. *Crap*. The Law Division really did suspect illicit magical activity. It was more than a theory.

And I knew already that in the Passages, it could be fatal.

CHAPTER SIX

ADA

"Nell's going to kill me," I said to Alber later. We hung out at a coffee shop waiting for Skyla to come and meet us.

"Yes," he said, ever the supportive sibling. "She is. You really landed yourself in it now."

Nell would *not* be happy that I was now officially unemployed. No job, and potentially on the Alliance's "wanted" list. I'd really screwed up.

"That job was crappy, but at least it was paid." I stared dismally into my hot chocolate like it could give me answers.

"Yeah. Should have heard Nell ranting the other night, when you were out. We're in debt."

"We've always been in debt." I chewed on my lower lip. Stress habit. "I know. I should have… I don't know. It's done now. I'll figure something out when we get home. If Nell doesn't bury me in the garden."

"Come on, Nell's kind enough to give you the dignity of a quick death," said Alber. "It'll be painless."

"What on Earth are you two talking about?" said a voice from behind us, causing me to jump and spill hot chocolate everywhere. Skyla had arrived, clad in leather—actual leather, not guard uniform. Probably meant she was hoping for a fight. For once, I was *not*.

"Ouch," I said, dabbing at myself.

"You're as twitchy as Nell," said Alber. "Remember when she threw a knife out the window at me when I came home late?"

"Hey. No talking about my murderer. I want to enjoy my last hour on Earth in peace."

"Do I really want to know where this conversation's going?" asked Skyla.

"Lost my job," I said. "As of tonight, I'll be the first in the Fletcher family's emporium of stuffed human corpses."

Alber laughed so hard he knocked his glass of Coke over, too.

"You two," said Skyla, shaking her head. "We should head out. Who are you meeting again?"

"Delta," I said, waving my phone. Lucky bugger could leave Valeria whenever he wanted. Delta was always running around other worlds having adventures, or so it seemed to me. Hell, there wasn't even an age restriction on travelling offworld. Earth's Alliance was ridiculous in that respect. You had to be twenty-one to even apply for a permit, and all applications were Alliance-scanned, so I'd never have been able to leave Earth legally even if I'd wanted to. Right now, it felt like I'd got the shitty end of the deal. That could easily have been me, if Nell and I had been assigned to Valeria, not Earth. The offworlder population there was high enough that although using a magic-shot was illegal, it was easier to get away with it. And there were hover cars. But then again, I'd brought Delta for a tour of London and he'd been enraptured by the public transport system. Each to his own, I guess.

Still, talking to Skyla raised my spirits a touch. As it was light outside, we took our time getting to the alleyway which housed the entrance to the Passages, waiting to make sure no one was watching. Bruise-coloured clouds crowded over the brick buildings, promising a storm later. The biting air was far too cold for a summer evening.

"Are you sure it's safe taking that stuff in there?" asked Skyla, with a glance at the bag. "Magic and the Passages don't mix, do they?"

"This is dormant," I said, shaking the bag. "Harmless, at least until you use it in a formula. Are *you* sure the Alliance patrols are running as usual? We can't really afford anything else to go wrong."

"I'll go into the Passages, if you're worried," said Skyla. "I don't mind, honest."

I hesitated. It wasn't that I didn't trust her—she was one of maybe five people who'd won my trust over the years— but the idea of handing over the bloodrock made the image of Nell's stern face rise in my mind.

"I'll take it," said Alber. "You can be our lookout, right?"

No, I thought. Yeah, I'd had a close call, but it shouldn't be this big a deal.

"Come on, we have to go," said Skyla, and she found the sliding door behind the brick wall.

"See you in a bit, okay?" said Alber, and before I could protest, the two of them had disappeared into the Passages.

And I was left outside, on Earth, alone.

The minutes crawled by. I grew bored contemplating the cracks in the opposite wall and began surfing the Internet on my phone. I sent Delta a quick text warning him he'd not be meeting me, but didn't get a reply. The magic from behind the door sparked against my skin, and it took supreme effort not to pull on it. It was like an addiction I'd been born with, a craving for something more than the life I had on Earth. It wasn't fair to Nell at all, or to anyone else, but now, with all the Multiverse a mere foot away, the pull to explore ached within me, even more insistent than usual. It would take only three steps.

Two.

One.

A scream rang out from the Passage. I jerked back, heart thumping, hand going for the dagger in my boot. Caution warred with instinct for a brief struggle, and then I ran through the door.

An icy breeze swept over me, and the magic exploded all around me like fireworks. Something had caused a major disturbance, and it definitely hadn't come from Earth.

I ran, feet striking the stone floor and echoing off the walls. I was sure the scream had been Skyla's. Skidding around a corner, I collided with Alber, and the two of us fell to the ground. He shook all over, and it was pretty obvious why.

A gigantic reptilian creature towered over us, at least eight feet tall, stooped under the ceiling and perched on two legs like a dinosaur with two short, skeletal wings. It opened its beak and screamed, and frantic scrambling sounds told me Skyla was trapped on its other side.

I recognised it from pictures, though I'd never seen one before. A wyvern. Where in hell had it come from? *Stupid question*, I thought, as its barbed tail flicked through the air, its deadly stinger aimed for the spot where I'd stood half a second ago. Those stings held enough poison to kill you in less than a minute. Icy fear flowed down my spine.

"Skyla!" I shouted. "Get out of there!" She lay flat on the ground, blood spattered around her, and my heart plummeted—*please don't let her be dead!*

She pushed to her feet, breathing heavily. Wait, that wasn't human blood. The wyvern was hurt, its wings covered in numerous deep cuts. But the monster was heading right for her, its back to me. I couldn't get to her. Cursing, I let the magic flow to my fingertips and the response vibrated in my bones. I fired a bolt of energy at the ground and then jumped, the energy rebounding and striking the wyvern in its scaly hide. The beast roared, its barbed tail knocking into a nearby door. The resounding sparks of magic burned holes in its skin through gaps where someone had knocked scales off, and it flailed, tail thrashing with enough force to break concrete. The floor shook, and I took a couple of steps back. No amount of magic within my blood could save me from that poison. And its half-metre-long claws were equally deadly. They could tear you to shreds.

Skyla leaped out of the way of its swiping claws, slashing with a dagger. A hideous screech told me she'd hit her mark. Alber slumped against the wall, eyes wide in terror. He'd never been good at dealing with monsters. I made sure he was well out of range, and then ran forwards.

My own dagger ready, I leaped and struck the wyvern from behind. I'd never fought a creature with so much external protection, and most of my strikes simply bounced off its armour. I had to keep withdrawing out of range of its thrashing tail.

Worse, I didn't dare use magic above level one, otherwise it'd blow the place up. Second level magic might pierce the armour, but I was losing power with every strike I aimed. Burnout? Or was its armour partly magic-proof?

This wasn't good. Gathering energy in the form of a crackling red orb, I put everything I had behind the dagger in my right hand, and hurled it as the beast bowed its head. If I hit just the right point, it'd pierce through the brain.

I missed, and the dagger clattered away down the Passage, sending sparks of red magic rebounding after it. Cursing, I dodged the tail again and grabbed for my second dagger. The beast swung around, Skyla still clinging to its side and striking it with her weapon. Crap. Now it was between us and the door. A claw swiped and Skyla yelled, letting go. She rolled out of the way of its rampaging feet and came to stand at my side, but we were hopelessly outmatched. And if it moved a few metres to the left, it'd be loose on Earth. Where no one would arrive in time to keep it from attacking other people, because the Alliance didn't know about that Passage.

Shit.

Skyla grabbed my arm and dragged me out of the way of a claw. The monster reared up to its full height, letting out a roar loud enough to make my eardrums hurt. Claws slashed madly, and the beast drove us farther and farther back, out into another, narrower corridor.

"We've got to lure it away," I gasped, my dagger suddenly

a flimsy knife in comparison to those claws.

"This way!" Skyla pulled me down a side tunnel, panting, hair plastered to her face with blood from a cut on her cheek. The wyvern screeched, angry its prey was escaping, and struck out. We backed up down the tunnel. The ceiling was narrow, so I'd hoped the wyvern wouldn't be able to fit, but it dropped to the ground and began to slither in a rapid, snakelike movement. I knew we'd driven ourselves into a bigger trap. Skyla's nails dug into my arm. We backed away, and as its teeth snapped, pure panic took over.

We ran, the beast's cries echoing behind us, faster, faster—claws swiped at our backs and I felt my coat tear, shredded to ribbons. Another swipe, and the dagger clattered from my hand. *No!*

No time to stop. My heart pounded in tandem with our frantic steps. We ran through corridors even I didn't know, until I skidded to a halt at a dead end.

Dead. We were dead.

Skyla leaned against the wall, gasping. "Shit. Shit."

I looked around wildly. Nothing but blank, blue-lit wall… wait. One section of wall didn't look right. A hidden staircase. I grabbed Skyla's arm and pulled her towards it just as the wyvern came slithering into the corridor. Cursing, we scrambled up the stairs, higher up into the Passages—the first level.

And the wyvern was still following us. Crap. *Crap.* The corridor we stood in ended at another dead end. Only one way to turn, and we ran. I'd never been here before, not this part of the first level, I didn't have a freaking clue where we were going, how we'd ever get back. But the only thing between us and death was running like hell, until we lost the monster. The roaring breath at our heels told me that wasn't happening anytime soon. I couldn't run forever. My muscles screamed, my legs ached, Skyla was chalk white and the cut on her face was streaming blood, and we couldn't stop. I wouldn't die in this place.

Corridor after corridor. A maze with no way out. And a monster raging behind us, getting closer–

It was too late to stop, to avoid running into the people suddenly up ahead…

Alliance guards.

***

KAY

Go time, I thought as we left Central that evening. The Law Division had sent out yet more alerts. London's West Office had closed their Passage entrance, forbidding even people with permits to travel offworld. The UK Alliance had put Earth's main corridor, used by people from hundreds of worlds, on lockdown. They really did think there were illegal magic-wielders out there. Carl had given us each a pair of metal handcuffs along with the standard stunners.

"They're laced with obsidiate and adamantine," he'd said. "Not that you're likely to have to use them, but if you do catch a magic-wielder, it'll incapacitate them. They're rigged to go up to second level with no more backlash than a gun's recoil, but just be aware there's a kick to it."

I hadn't missed the significant look Aric gave me. Maybe I should just lock him up in the handcuffs and leave him in a corner somewhere.

"Scared?" he whispered behind me at the door into the Passages. "There might be something dangerous waiting in the dark…"

I stepped back onto his foot. Hard.

"Bastard," he said, between clenched teeth.

I turned to give him a humourless smile. "Shouldn't startle me like that," I said, softly. "It might well be your face next time."

And then I followed the others, stunner at the ready in case he decided to ambush me from behind.

A clamour echoed from the corridor ahead. "There's trouble," said the leading guard.

I was already prepared, but a new tension seared my veins. I recognised that cry.

Wyvern.

I couldn't help it—I glanced at Aric. If he had anything to do with this... but no. His eyes were stretched wide with terror, his face stark white.

We rounded a corner and met total chaos. Sparks of magic danced off the walls, creating a haze of blinding light, and I swore, flicking the stunner to life in my hand. I couldn't see more than a few inches in front of me, and running headlong towards a wyvern blinded was the height of stupidity. But the others on our team were already on the case.

"I'm calling backup!" yelled the leader. "We'll take care of the lizard—stop those magic-wielders!"

Hell. Those sparks were pure, raw magic energy—level two. These were the real deal, all right. Blurred figures moved in the dark, and when one of them pelted towards the exit, I took off after them.

I might have been blinded, but I was faster than they were—faster than she was. My arms locked around her waist and sent us both sprawling to the ground. She kicked and squirmed but I held her pinned down. Screaming curses, she twisted around to glare at me from behind wild dark red hair. She was little more than a kid, I realised—but I couldn't afford to let her get away.

I went for the handcuffs. And the floor beneath us began to shake.

Damn. She'd hit the ground with magic, and with us both down, the backlash could hit either of us. I had the advantage of magicproof uniform, but she didn't. An untrained magic-wielder? Dangerous, whoever she was. I dragged her away from the backlash, a ripple that pulsed through the air from the spot where she'd hit. The magic was so thick here, I could see the backlash ripple outwards, strike the wall, and rebound. Swearing, I ducked, and the girl took the opportunity to squirm out of my grip. *Oh no, you don't.*

I lunged forward and grabbed for her leg, cursing the lights that blurred my vision. Another cry came from up ahead.

"Get away from me!" she screamed, as my hand locked around her ankle. "Let me go, you bastard—"

The air exploded with magic again. I lay flat and it bounced over my head, and the girl threw herself to the ground, too. She clearly didn't have a clue what she was doing, and if she didn't stop, this place could blow sky-high.

"You're going to hurt yourself if you keep doing that." I pulled on her ankle, dragging her over the metal floor.

"I'm not doing that, idiot!" she yelled, twisting. I went for her shoulders instead and yanked her upright. We needed to get the hell out of this corridor. I couldn't see the magic rebounding anymore, as it had disappeared into the general chaos. But it was still out there. I could feel it, the static buzz beneath my skin more pronounced than ever. Pushing magic's temptation away, I tightened my grip on the girl's shoulders. She swore at me over and over, kicking and hitting with elbows and knees, but I managed to manoeuvre the stunner to brush against the back of her neck, and flicked the switch.

The bolt had more recoil than I expected, vibrating through my hand and stopping as it hit the magicproof sleeve of my jacket. But it had a worse effect on the girl. She gasped, eyes widening, limbs shaking, and her knees gave out. I caught her before she fell, fighting the bizarre impulse to apologise. I gripped the back of her coat. It had been shredded, by the wyvern's claws. She'd had a narrow escape.

"What have you done to me?" Her eyes glazed over, her teeth clenched in pain.

I didn't answer. Where the hell were the other two guards? And Aric, come to that. Maybe that reckless magic shot had been his stunner, or one of the other guards'. No way to tell.

Get on with it, Kay. I took advantage of her weakness to get out the cuffs and clamp them around her wrists. The shock brought her back to life, and she fought every step. I steered her back towards the door outside. Hers were the frantic movements of an animal caught in barbed wire, and although it might have been easy to knock her out, it seemed wrong, somehow. Who was she? Outside the Alliance, the number of people who could use magic here on Earth was hardly worth counting. For all her flailing, I could tell she'd had some kind of combat training—but she'd been trying to get away, not do serious damage.

"Let me go!"

A bolt of magic shot over both our heads. I pulled us both to the ground. Someone else was throwing magic around in here. And judging by the vibrant red colour of the energy stream, it was someone with a stunner. Aric.

Moron. He should know that firing the stunner into empty air in the Passages was a stupid idea if you wanted to get out with all your limbs intact. Not that Aric specialised in common sense, but still. The girl was wriggling away from me again, kicking out with her thick combat boots.

"Dammit, Aric," I muttered, pulling her to her feet again. "You're going to draw every magic-eating monster from downstairs."

"You deserve it," the girl said through clenched teeth. Her eyes were still glazed. The cuffs were only supposed to have one jolt of magic, so… she had an internal source. Had to be.

Goddammit. I dragged her down the corridor by the hands. She fought me every step of the way, and yet she was weakening.

You wouldn't find someone with inbuilt magic wandering the streets on Earth. Was she even *from* Earth? She didn't look British, but I couldn't put my finger on what was different about her, what might point to her being offworld. Her skin was tan, and her blue eyes were a shade too bright to be natural. Contacts? Her hair was obviously dyed, but that didn't tell me much.

"Get these freaking cuffs off me," she snarled, trying to grab at the edges of the door. One more step and we'd be outside.

And then the Passage behind us exploded. Once again, the two of us were sent flying. After the Passages, the shock of hitting the rock-hard tarmac was jarring as I rolled over to avoid the impact, but it was worse for the girl, who'd been flung sideways into the brick wall.

I twisted around in time to see Aric fall out of the Passage, swearing.

"The hell happened to you?" I said, getting to my feet and walking over to the girl. She lay in a crumpled heap, a bruise swelling on her forehead. I tried not to hurt her any more when I pulled her to her feet again by her cuffed hands.

"Wyvern," said Aric, not sounding nearly as cocky as usual. "They got it, though—wait, who's that?"

"Trespasser," I said. *Wow—that was almost a civilised conversation.*

The two other guards came out of the Passage, dishevelled and covered in dust.

"There you are," said the lead guard. "You caught one of them?"

The girl spat blood at them, and the two guards moved out of the way.

Aric said, "I think we need to teach this one respect."

"We'll take her into custody," said the guard. "Good job.

Want me to cuff her ankles?"

"Knock her out," said Aric, looming over her.

"None of that," I said, stepping between them. "We'll take her back to Central. Right?" I looked to the others for confirmation.

"Yeah. But at least one other trespasser ran away."

And the other glared intensely at me. "They'll kill you," she said. "You'll be sorry."

CHAPTER SEVEN

ADA

Captured.

Alliance Guy had a firm grip on my upper arms, just tight enough to tell me there was no chance I was getting away. *Bastard.* I'd never, ever been overpowered so easily. In the times I'd watched the guards patrolling, I'd never considered how downright terrifying it would be to encounter them up close. From a distance, they'd been a source of fascination to me. I'd wondered what their lives were like, if they lived one step apart from the world like I did, unable to connect with normality. Now, I wished I'd never seen them. In particular, the guy who'd appeared from the shadows like a freaking ninja and presumed to *lecture* me.

Two other guards walked a few feet in front, a man and a woman, and a second man was behind, the blond, muscular guy who'd threatened me. He kept glaring at me, and though I did my best to glare back, I couldn't stop shivering. The shock from the handcuffs had left me weak and shaky, and my feet dragged on the ground as Alliance Guy steered me down a road—not the alleyway, but somewhere else. Now the haze of magic from the Passages had faded, I could see the tall dark shape of the

Alliance's Central Headquarters over the rooftops.

Oh, God. No.

No escape. Nowhere to run. I hadn't seen where Skyla went. Skyla had set off a magic-based firework-type device to distract the guards after the wyvern had fled—whatever the guards had done to it sent it packing. Alber had presumably got away. That was something, at least, but I was still a prisoner.

Hopelessness burrowed in my chest. I had no magic, and they had those freaking Taser-like things. Alliance Guy could have killed me when he'd zapped me. It had been like an electric shock right through my bones. Level two magic, at least. I didn't think that was even allowed in the Passages. But these guys were the Alliance's police force, effectively. They could do whatever the hell they wanted.

Nell was right. I should never have assumed I could get away.

I recognised the street now. It was the same one I'd fled down from Central. The gate was locked, but one of the Alliance guys was already unlocking it. I tilted my head to look up at the guy holding me in case his attention had slipped, but it hadn't. His eyes were such a dark shade of brown they appeared almost as black as his hair, and narrowed when he saw me watching.

The blond guy closed in behind me. "I'll take her from here."

"Leave it," said Alliance Guy, the slightest tension in his voice. Okay, I could tell these two didn't like each other. Maybe I could use that to my advantage.

I pretended to lose all strength in my legs, going limp.

Alliance Guy tightened his grip in response and held me upright. Well, it was worth a try. Now I paid attention, I realised that my coat was shredded, and there wasn't a whole lot holding it together. The beginnings of another scheme began to materialise.

I let myself go limper. The other guard finally looked away to follow the others through the gate. My sleeves—or what was left of them—rubbed against the handcuffs. Only Alliance Guy's eyes were on me now… I slumped my shoulders, and his grip on me slipped. Just for an instant, but it was enough. I moved fast, tearing free of my coat, and sprinted for my life.

"Shit!" Alliance Guy came after me—damn, he was fast—and caught me before I'd moved more than a few metres. I came down on my knees, hard, and clenched my teeth to stop myself making a sound.

Before I knew it, Alliance Guy lifted me off the ground and slung me over his shoulder. If there was one thing I hated, it was being carried. I abandoned all pretence and tried to kick him, but the other guy had already grabbed my legs.

"I've got it, Aric!" snapped the first guy. But Aric had already yanked me free of Alliance Guy. I choked as Aric's hands closed around my throat.

"Stop that," snapped Alliance Guy. "That's *not* necessary."

"She's a dangerous criminal," snarled Aric. "She tried to run."

"Wouldn't you?"

Aric's grip tightened. Spots danced before my eyes. My throat burned.

"Get *off* her." The pressure loosened. Alliance Guy's hand gripped Aric's, forcing him to loosen his hold. I gasped.

Aric hissed between his teeth. "Get your fucking hands off me, Walker."

"Stop choking her," said Alliance Guy and squeezed harder on Aric's wrist. Aric let go, cursing. There was a scuffle and a yelp of pain, and suddenly, it was Aric pinned to the wall. Instinct took over and I stumbled away—*damn these handcuffs!*

"She's getting away!" yelled a voice from ahead. Crap—the other two guards had turned back.

Alliance Guy—Walker?—cursed and spun around, and then both he and Aric were bearing down on me. I tripped over the kerb and fell, knees striking the hard ground again. Hands grabbed me, and I kicked out. My foot connected with someone. I twisted to see who. Oh, crap. I'd hit Walker instead of Aric, my combat boot catching him in the face. Oh, well. They both deserved it. Yeah, he might have stopped Aric strangling me, but he'd put the cuffs on me in the first place.

"Jesus Christ," said Walker, hauling me to my feet. He ran his free hand over his rapidly bruising face. I couldn't have responded even if I'd had a clue what to say, as my throat was still raw from Aric's half strangling me.

"Is there a problem back there?" another guard demanded.

"We've got it," said Walker, apparently oblivious to the blood dripping from his nose. And he didn't let go of me again.

Aric glared daggers at both of us. *If looks could kill...* But then, Walker was pretty scary-looking, too, with his face covered in blood. There was absolutely no mercy in his expression now. His pitch-dark eyes were trained on me.

Holy crap. I'd really landed myself in it this time, managing to piss off an entire Alliance guard patrol.

Still. I could glare back. And did so. It was the one defence I had left.

Walker didn't let go of me until we'd reached Central. Another group of guards had gathered by this point, surrounding us and asking questions. I tuned them all out, concentrating on finding a way I could escape. Opportunity was key, and I had no intention of squandering my chance. Perhaps they'd take the cuffs off when we got in the building.

"Right, we'll take her from here," said one of the guards, and Walker handed me over to them. Like a freaking game of pass-the-parcel.

"Sure." He glanced at me, like he wanted to say something else, then shook his head.

And then I was left alone with the other guards. A sinking feeling descended. Had Alber made it home? Did he know I'd been captured? What about Skyla? Was our house safe—were the refugees safe? Too much to worry about.

And the guards were taking forever. The one who held me had a hand on my back, but relaxed, and he wasn't looking at me.

I moved, quick as I could, ducking out from under his hand and sprinting through the guards. But I didn't even make it a metre. A heavy body slammed down on top of me, knocking the wind from my lungs. I gasped for air, blood filling my mouth. I'd bitten my tongue again. Spitting out blood, I kicked blindly at the guard. Without magic, I was useless. I'd never pushed it to its limits before like that, and now I was on Earth, I'd lost my edge. But I had the feeling the cuffs were doing something to me, as well. The burning sensation wasn't because they were too tight, but it was like a pressure lay on whichever part of me could use magic, making me weak and shaky. I hated it. God, I hated it. It was the stark opposite of the static buzzing of magic in the Passages.

The guards dragged me in through the glass doors at the front of the building, into the biggest entrance hall I'd ever seen in my life. Tall glass elevators waited at the end, while countless doors led off to the sides. Everything gleamed. Adamantine. The cuffs must be made of the same stuff, I realised—antimagic. They were quite literally magicproof.

Damn. I'm screwed.

The guards steered me towards the elevators, but then veered off to a staircase nearby. As they lifted me clean off the ground, blind panic took over. I kicked out at the guards, but there were many of them and only one of me. Two guards carried me downstairs, ignoring my feeble attempts to break free.

Into a corridor lined with rooms. First door on the left—I made sure to memorise the way out. The door led into another corridor with yet more doors. One door was pushed open, and I was carried inside. The guards sat me down on...a bed? The room was bigger than my bedroom at home but with no windows, and bars over the small one in the door. It had only two pieces of furniture—a sink in the corner and the bed I sat on.

"You'll spend the night here. Your questioning will take place tomorrow." They said more words, but everything blurred together. Unbearable tiredness descended on me. It was so wrong. I shouldn't be here. I shouldn't be a prisoner. But I was, and they were removing my boots. They did another weapon search, and when I elbowed the guard—who I was positive was feeling me up—he actually hit me. The sharp pain across my face threw me back onto the bed.

"Don't hit her!" said another guard. "We're not supposed to harm her. She's hurt already."

The first guard glared at me, and left the room. When one

guard remained—I could tell he was senior because of the badge on his jacket, and the long scar on his face told me he'd had a close call with a monster before—he said, "I'm going to remove your handcuffs. If you attempt to fight, I'll put them back on."

Yeah, that's pretty clear. At least this guy—Carl, his badge said—wasn't as much of an asshole as the other dude. I didn't fight when he removed the cuffs. The sight of the number of guards crowded outside the door had squashed that notion entirely.

He withdrew from the room, and the door closed.

I was a prisoner of the Alliance now.

I bit my lip. I wasn't going to break down. Okay, so nothing like this had ever happened to me in my life. And yes, I'd probably deserved to get knocked down a peg for being so convinced I could get away with breaking the Alliance's rules. But this…

I was powerless to help anyone. Not my family. No one from Enzar, either. And now the Alliance was on full alert. And they might suspect me of murder, too.

I just wished I knew more about the Alliance's Law Division. I'd broken no overly serious laws, not that they'd seen. I'd trespassed in the Passages, used magic, and brought others into it. That was all. I'd pretend I'd been curious for a glimpse of another world. People had got away with that with a slap on the wrist. Or a night in here. Nell said even some of the Academy kids sneaked into the Passages for a laugh when they weren't yet at that level. Okay, so the timing wasn't perfect. But they had no grounds on which to convict me. If Alber and Skyla had got away, they wouldn't even know about the bloodrock.

But there was a tight feeling in my chest. I flexed my wrists, half expecting to find burn marks from the handcuffs. I wondered how many people they arrested for using magic. It wasn't technically a crime—but in the Passages, it was illegal, of course.

You're going to hurt yourself. I clenched my fists as Walker's words replayed in my head. Condescending dickhead. Did I know magic was dangerous? Of course I did. The idiot who'd been firing his Taser in the Passages had done more damage than I had. When I recovered the magic that lived under my skin, I'd be out of here.

I hoped.

***

I must have fallen asleep, because I jerked awake when someone turned the key in the lock. I sat up, wincing as the bruises all over my body made themselves known. I'd struck the wall pretty hard in the street. Plus, my knees had taken a beating when I'd fallen onto the pavement. I was pretty sure nothing was broken. My eyes stung a little, but I didn't dare remove the lenses.

I tensed up as the door inched open. A woman came into the room. Japanese, probably about ten years older than me, a badge saying, "Medical Division" pinned to her shirt. She carried a clipboard, and when she met my eyes, her expression wasn't unkind.

"I just need to check you over," she said. "I'm Saki."

I gritted my teeth together, but she was surprisingly gentle when she gave me a once-over. I kept my eye on the unguarded door. When she moved to my left arm, I prepared to run. And then she pulled out a syringe.

"I'm going to take a blood sample…"

No. I stuck out an elbow. Saki let out a squeak of surprise as it connected with her chin, but I was already at the door, opening it–

Crash. Stars winked before my eyes as a sharp object caught me on the skull. *Ouch!* She'd hit me with the clipboard. My hands scrabbled at the door, but Saki twisted my arm behind my back so hard, and so unexpectedly, I yelped aloud. Running footsteps sounded, and guards came into the room, surrounding me. Hands held mine behind my back, while several others restrained me.

"Get the cuffs!" one of them shouted.

And just like that, I was cuffed again. My hands locked behind my back—and my ankles too to add insult to injury.

The energy drain was so intense, I slumped onto the bed, feeling like the life was being sucked from my body. I couldn't sit up, even when they surrounded me. Someone stuck a syringe in my arm. I managed one last kick, but missed. My legs felt like lead.

"Get...the hell away...from me," I whispered, as the world faded away.

CHAPTER EIGHT

KAY

I paced by the window, which looked out over the car park, the Thames and the glittering skyscrapers beyond, waiting for Ms Weston to call me into her office. Each of us had a mandatory meeting with the new boss. And I felt like the universe had literally kicked me in the face.

"What the hell happened to you?" asked Markos, cantering past with a cup of coffee in each hand.

"Lost a fight with a door," I said absently, then cursed myself for the stupid lie.

"Looks like it kicked you," Markos commented.

Crap. Was it really that obvious? On the drive back from Central, the blood on my face had freaked out a few people, who'd probably assumed I was a murderer coming back from burying his latest victims. But I'd been too out of it last night to look at the damage. Not like it was the first time I'd been in a fight.

Now, I glanced at my reflection in the window. Dark circles under my eyes—nothing new there—and the unmistakable, bruise-coloured imprint of a boot across the bridge of my nose. Damn. No getting around this one.

"By the way, you're up next. Good luck."

Okay. Time to face the new boss. *Hope this one lasts longer than a day,* I couldn't help thinking morbidly, as I headed to her office. They'd already removed the sign with Mr Clark's name from the door. I knocked, wondering if it wasn't the tiniest bit unnerving to occupy the room where someone had been murdered not long before.

One glance at Ms Weston told me she wasn't the type of person to get unnerved at such things. She had the manner of a severe schoolteacher, and her appearance was as impeccable as her desk, some achievement in itself, given what a state it had been in when Mr Clark had been here. I guessed the police, or the Law Division, had taken everything away.

"You're Kay Walker." She studied me, indicating I take a seat. "And you started working here recently?"

"Just two days ago."

She said nothing for a few long moments. I was pretty sure her intense stare was focused on the boot-shaped mark on my face. But she hadn't commented on my name, which was a surprise.

"I can imagine it's been quite eventful for you," she said. "Your supervisor murdered, and you've already made your first arrest."

"Is the girl still here?"

Ms Weston's eyes narrowed at the question. "She is in the holding cells. I am planning to question her myself, and then we will decide the next step. Can I have your exact account of what happened?"

She didn't look away once as I recounted the patrol last night, including the wyvern, and the other trespasser.

"The girl has accomplices," Ms Weston said. "She talked to you?"

"Not really. She was mostly trying to break free."

"Yes, I gathered she put up quite the fight." Oh, she was staring at the footprint, all right. I only hoped Aric had kept his mouth shut about our tiny disagreement.

I didn't say any of this to Ms Weston, who continued to watch me. I could tell she was the type who stared until you backed down. When I still didn't look away, Ms Weston finally spoke again. "You showed initiative, I'll give you that. But the situation...it should not have happened. The wyvern's attack made what should have been a straightforward arrest into a more complicated scenario. I'm going to need you to fill out these forms." She slammed a stack of papers on the desk. "We need a full account from the person who made the arrest. I'm going to talk to your comrades who were patrolling that night, and to the girl, too. But first, I want *you* to talk to her."

What? "I thought you planned to interrogate her."

"I plan to try different questioning tactics. It may be that she responds better to you, seeing as you showed her…mercy."

Aric said something to her. Interrogation hadn't been on the job application, either. Okay, so one of the primary tasks of an Ambassador was effective communication with people from offworld. But interrogating *her?*

"Sure, I'll talk to her," I said. "I don't think she'll be inclined to give up information, though."

"You say you think she has instinctual magic?"

"I can't think of any other way she could have done what she did. Not without, I don't know, a talisman or something. A source."

"You think she's from offworld."

"Perhaps." It bothered me how difficult it had been to tell, considering I could usually discern someone's homeworld at a glance, or at least if they were from one of the allied worlds. She was a mystery.

"Haven't you seen her yet?" I couldn't help asking.

"She has been sedated for most of the morning. She attacked the nurse who went in to check on her injuries."

I couldn't say I was surprised. "And you think she'd be willing to have a civilised conversation?"

Her eyes narrowed, registering the touch of sarcasm. "I want to see what you can do, Kay. These are hardly ideal circumstances, but I was intrigued to meet the youngest Walker."

That was the first time she'd acknowledged my name. And I had the odd sense that she'd done it on purpose. To get a reaction, maybe.

"Then I hope I'm not a disappointment," I said.

"I hope not, Kay. Take those." She tapped the pile of papers. "Bring them back to me as soon as you can. Also, this." She stacked another file on top. "Return it to the archives."

"Okay," I said, taking the stack of papers. The Law Division was single-handedly responsible for the destruction of the rainforest, apparently. "When should I speak to the girl?"

"I will send for you when I receive word that she's woken up," said Ms Weston, with a dismissive wave.

That went well, I thought, leaving the room. And if there was one thing I hated, it was tedious paperwork.

"What's all that?" Markos asked, raising his eyebrows at the stack of papers as I set them down on the desk.

"Our new boss decided I have to file a report on last night," I said. "Or about a hundred of them."

"She did? Good luck with that. I'm up to my neck in old files." Papers were scattered all over the standing desk he worked at, too. Central preferred reports to be handwritten, firstly because handwriting was hard to fake, and secondly due to the frequency of technological meltdowns inevitable in a place which had so much contact with magic.

"Have you spoken to her?"

"I have. Surprisingly, she didn't comment on my being a centaur. At first, I thought she couldn't see me."

"Yeah, a centaur's difficult to recognise," I said. "Can't say I know what to think of her. Except I don't think she accepts any bullshit."

"Yeah, I got that impression," said Markos, tapping a pen on the desk. "She scared the hell out of Lenny."

"Do the police still think he killed Mr Clark?"

"They've handed the case over to the Law Division," said Markos. "I don't think any of us are under suspicion anymore. Not now that girl's been caught."

"You think she's a killer?" I put down the papers, frowning. However hard she'd fought, she hadn't drawn her weapons. She'd been desperate, but not enough to use magic above first level, though if she really did have an internal magic source, she'd certainly been capable of it. Even more so with all the level two shots flying around the Passages then. Third level killed in a heartbeat. She could have done it at any point before the cuffs touched her. But she hadn't.

"I don't know. I never met the girl. Looks like she gave you a rough time, though."

I rolled my eyes. "I'll live. I think she was aiming for Aric." Judging by the guilty look on her face, I'd say so, anyway.

"Bad luck."

"Ms Weston said I have to go and talk to her. She didn't say that to you too, did she?"

"No. Is it because you arrested her?"

"I've no idea. I doubt she'll tell me a thing. Most prisoners aren't inclined to disclose information."

"Perhaps she thinks you can charm the girl," the centaur said. "Or perhaps she thinks it'll be a laugh."

"I doubt that," I said, shook my head, and turned back to the files.

After going over the story yet again, I switched to autopilot and began thinking about how odd it all was. Was the girl really linked to the killer? If not, then who was she? And this questioning... it felt like a test. More like she wanted to find out about *me* than the prisoner. I didn't care for that at all.

I turned over the last page, and a file fell onto the desk. It was the one Ms Weston had told me to return to the archives—and I recognised it as the same file I'd fetched for Mr Clark. The bloodrock research he'd been reading the day he'd died.

I opened the file. "PROPERTIES OF BLOODROCK"

read the page's header. Below, a standard list for logging offworld substances. I'd seen them before, as it was required to fill out one of these files for everything brought to Earth from offworld. The Alliance were sticklers for keeping paperwork up to date. This particular file was twenty-five years old. And the name of who'd logged the information leaped out like a neon sign.

LAWRENCE WALKER.

I held the paper carefully, willing my hands to stay steady. A creeping feeling crawled up my spine, and I glanced over my shoulder. No one else was here, as Markos had left the office to hand the papers he'd been filling in back to Ms Weston. *Calm down, Kay.* This didn't mean anything. My father was one of the eminent members of the Alliance, for God's sake, even if he'd left Earth years ago. His name was probably on half the files in the archives. Like Markos had said.

Shaking off the momentary unease, I carried on reading.

"SUBSTANCE: POWDERED BLOODROCK (EARTH NAME). ORIGIN WORLD: UNKNOWN. THIS SAMPLE IS FROM ENZAR (L2D63-9), REGISTERED UNSTABLE)."

The word 'unstable' was crossed out, replaced with 'DANGEROUS'.

Enzar. I frowned at the page. That was one world I knew

next to nothing about. The Alliance had cut itself off from the Enzarian Empire after a war between those with magic and those without had begun to drag in other nearby worlds, too. It was too dangerous to interfere in full-scale magical warfare. But the nature of that warfare remained a mystery, at least to me. The Alliance hadn't posted a single notice about it since the declaration of noninterference. Twenty years ago.

Perhaps something had happened to merit a cover-up. It wasn't uncommon, as far as dangerous offworld substances were concerned—hell, the Alliance worked hard to make sure this kind of information didn't fall into the wrong hands.

I checked the time on my communicator, tempted to make for the fifth floor and the archives—but Ms Weston had said I had to talk to the prisoner. Yet I couldn't shake the feeling that this was important.

Later, I told myself, turning back to the file and flipping over the page. It listed the qualities of this bloodrock substance: negligible on Earth, but on high-magic worlds, it could function as a substitute for virtually anything magic-related.

Jesus, I thought. No wonder it was listed as rare and unstable. In conjunction with other magic-based substances, it could act as an energy source. It could destroy whole universes—even knock the entire Balance out of sync.

Why in the Multiverse would the head of admin search out this?

I continued to read. "As the whereabouts and extent of this source are unknown, bloodrock is to be treated with caution and samples are not to be removed from storage."

Had Ms Weston read this file? It didn't seem like something a novice should be allowed access to. The Academy sure hadn't covered offworld magic-based energy sources. The Alliance was understandably paranoid people would get stupid ideas. Even well-meaning scientists looking to save the planet. You couldn't carry an unknown substance from one world to another and expect it to function the same. I could just picture idiotic teenagers getting hold of this bloodrock and using it to make fireworks or something. Not hard to imagine, because I'd *been* one of those idiotic teenagers, and hadn't even known I was a magic-wielder until I'd first set foot in the Passages.

And this is why we don't teach you about magic, kids. It was unbelievable how many people on Earth still believed in the inaccurate versions of magic popularised by TV and the media, even with the Alliance out in the open the past thirty years. Outside the Alliance and the Academies worldwide, knowledge of magic was minimal, and other worlds guarded their own secrets well enough that I could only imagine what was possible in high-magic worlds. It wasn't like there was an official guide to magic, even an unauthorised one. The Alliance prized confidentiality above everything else.

Natural magic-wielders rarely surfaced independently. Yet it was possible. In the Alliance, magic-wielders who made Ambassador were often the first picked for missions. I'd prefer to keep it under wraps until then. If Aric kept his stupid mouth shut. Though I never intended to use magic again, I could at least use it to my advantage.

There was one page left in the file, and it was almost blank. Apart from a handwritten scrawl in the corner.

Recognition grabbed me. I knew that handwriting, though I couldn't read the words—it was just a meaningless string of letters and numbers. But it brought back the reminder that even though he'd been on a distant world locked in stasis for the past five years, my father's presence still lingered over my shoulder like a goddamned Cethraxian shadow-monster.

I flipped over the page, focusing on calming my breathing. No one had seen this. I never should have opened the file in the first place. It didn't tell me anything useful. It sure as hell didn't explain why Mr Clark had been murdered.

I closed the file, suddenly tired beyond belief. *Focus.* Time to get my head back in the present. I checked all the forms were in the right order—again—and looked up to see a woman glaring at me across the office. I hadn't met her before, but her badge told me she was called Saki, and she was one of the Alliance's nurses.

"You're Kay Walker, right?"

"Yes…" Why did she keep looking at me like I'd drowned a kitten in front of her?

"You arrested the prisoner?"

"I did, yeah."

"She attacked me." *Oh.* "You might have warned me. Your report only said *potentially dangerous*. She could have killed me."

"You seem okay." Wrong thing to say. Her eyes flashed. Well, she didn't have a freaking footprint across her face, did she?

"Potentially dangerous? She made for the door as soon as her handcuffs came off. I thought she was injured."

"What?" I blinked at her. "She's a prisoner. I'd be surprised if she *didn't* make an attempt to get out, given the opportunity."

Saki just glared harder.

"How the hell is it *my* fault?" I said.

"Someone removed her handcuffs."

"Not me." I stood. "Does Ms Weston want me to talk to her now?"

"I don't have a clue." Saki's glare could give the new boss

a run for her money. And then she turned her back and stalked out.

What the hell was up with her? I shook my head. Everyone on the first floor of Central had officially gone batshit insane.

I turned back to the file. *Stop looking at it as if it's going to burst into flames.* It might not seem to contain any clues, and Ms Weston had told me to return it to the archives… but something about it still nagged at me.

Could there really be a connection between Mr Clark's research and his death? It just seemed *odd* that a killer would target someone so innocuous. If they could get into Central undetected, which was supposed to be impossible, then surely they would have gone after a more senior Alliance member. And the killer hadn't left a trail of bodies behind as they sneaked inside. They'd only targeted one person. There was nothing random about this murder.

Right now, I just wanted the damn file gone, put away, so I didn't have to carry what felt increasingly like incriminating evidence. I scanned it again to make sure I had it memorised, and my communicator buzzed in my pocket. I found the blunt message: "Prisoner is awake. Please proceed immediately down to lower corridor, first staircase on the right from the entrance hall."

I sighed. No time to get rid of this thing now. Instead, I

left it on the desk with the other files. No reason to get anyone else wrapped up in Kay's Conspiracy Theories.

Time to talk to the prisoner.

CHAPTER NINE

ADA

The world was hazy when I woke up. For an instant, I thought I was at home, safe in my box-like room. But then the blank, starless ceiling of the cell confronted me, and the cold, horrible pressure of the handcuffs on my wrists and ankles returned.

I managed to push myself to a sitting position on the bed. My limbs felt floppy, and my depleted energy hadn't returned. What the hell had they drugged me with? The back of my throat was dry, and my body ached from the battering it had taken yesterday. Would they at least let me change clothes? Blood had soaked through my jeans from where I'd skinned my knees on the pavement, and my T-shirt was spattered with blood too. I wasn't sure if it was mine or Alliance Guy's.

Holy hell, I assaulted a guard. I wished I'd paid more attention to Nell's lectures on the Alliance's rules. They changed them every so often, and the actual punishment for, say, assaulting someone with magic wasn't commonly known. I'd spent so much time around offworlders who came from places where one wrong word could lead to execution, it had made me distrust all authority. Whatever the Alliance's reputation, this was twenty-first-century Britain. There was such a thing as the Universal

Declaration of Human Rights. Maybe I'd get a trial. But it wasn't like I had a lawyer or solicitor on standby. Nell and I shouldered all the risks ourselves.

I stretched my neck, assessing my options. Should I say nothing, or tell a modified version of the truth? They hadn't seen me use the Passages, and it had been so confused in there, they might not have spotted Skyla fleeing. Alber had been miles behind. I could say I'd gone in there alone, looking for a bit of fun. Nell had told me *that* wasn't punishable by death. I had no clue where she got her information, but she'd told me that some of the kids at the Academy sneaked in there for thrills when they were too young to be allowed to. She'd learned that from one of our sources a couple of years ago, when the Alliance had upped their patrols near the Academy after something had happened in the lower-level Passages involving students there. That seemed likely, from what I'd heard of Academy students—they were all privileged rich kids who'd been brought up knowing about the Multiverse, probably even getting to travel offworld. Lucky bastards.

It looked like a partial lie might be my only option. Not like there was much else I could do locked up here. The cuffs were loose enough not to rub against my skin on my wrists and ankles, but now I'd slept a little, it was clear that they'd drained the magic out of me. It was something I'd always taken for granted, even if I knew it shouldn't be here, even if I knew I couldn't use it to its full extent. Like a sense I'd been half-aware of had been abruptly cut off. It hurt.

I sat bolt upright as the door opened. Alliance Guy—Walker, whoever he was—entered the room. I stared. The image I'd had in my head was of a lean and menacing black-clad Alliance guard with pitiless eyes—this guy, dressed in standard office clothes, a plain dark shirt and trousers, looked surprisingly ordinary. And it threw me off to see the imprint of my own combat boot in vivid bruises across his face. I completely forgot what I planned to say.

"What do you want?" I asked, hoarsely.

He ran a hand through his dark hair. "I'm supposed to question you."

"Ask away," I said, shifting against the wall. "I'm not going anywhere." But my gaze still darted over to the door. He saw and closed it behind him, not taking his eyes off me. To my own annoyance, a part of me couldn't help noting he was pretty good-looking, under the bruises.

But we were alone in here, and I was cuffed, powerless. A shiver broke out across my skin.

"I'm not going to hurt you," he said.

Sure you aren't. My entire body went tense, and I fought the urge to shrink back. I couldn't afford to let him know how intimidating it was to be trapped like this. But he didn't take a step closer to me. He remained by the door, his gaze steady.

"What were you doing in the Passages?"

Straight to the point, then.

"Like I'm going to tell *you*, Walker."

His eyes narrowed, just slightly. "Don't call me that. My name's Kay. What's yours?"

I blinked. So we were exchanging names, now?

"Ada." And that was all he was getting out of me.

"You're some kind of natural-born magic-wielder, aren't you?"

I stared back, unable to hide my surprise. Of all the things to focus on, I hadn't expected that.

"Is that such a strange question?"

I couldn't read his expression at all. He was far better than I was at hiding what he was thinking. "Considering Earth's so low-magic? Yes."

"I don't think you're from Earth," he said.

My blood ran cold, and I shifted back against the wall.

"I don't think my life's any of your business," I said, and then cursed my own idiocy.

"You *are* from another world."

"I didn't think it mattered," I said. "You've already arrested me."

"On the contrary, it does matter. If you're from offworld, then we would need to speak to a representative from your homeworld and refer to the relevant section of the treaty to ensure our disciplinary actions didn't contradict any of your laws."

"Are you a lawyer or something?" The offhand way he'd recited all that sounded like someone reading from a textbook. *I get it.* The sophisticated speech, the total assurance of authority, the way he'd chased me down, hadn't hesitated for a second before zapping me with that Taser... this was an Academy graduate, all right. And I had reason enough to hate him already.

"No, I'm not. You probably need one, though. How did you come to be on Earth?"

I clamped my mouth shut and gave him my best Death Stare. He didn't even blink. I guessed Alliance guards were used to hostility.

"Easy way or hard way, Ada. I doubt my boss will be as lenient as me, so the more questions you answer, the easier it'll be on you."

"All right!" I snapped. "I get it."

"So, tell me where you live."

"Cockfosters," I snapped.

He raised an eyebrow. "It'd be nice if you took this seriously, Ada."

"It is a real place."

"I know that."

"Then why not believe I lived there?" I hadn't lied, though technically I lived just outside the area. It'd be worth it to wind up these Alliance guys, though. Because maturity was totally worth it at this point.

Kay took a step back, gaze darting to the door and then back at me. Maybe he thought I was trying to distract him so I could make a run for it. Not like that was happening while I was still chained up.

"All right. Who do you live with? Alone? With parents?"

I turned away, examining the opposite wall.

"Come on, Ada. There was at least one other person with you in the Passages, wasn't there? You were coming back to Earth. So you're based here. You sound like you were raised here in the UK, in London… but you're not originally from Earth. You grew up here, I'd guess. Adopted?"

Damn those cutting eyes. I clenched my jaw, leaning back against the wall.

"I have to admit, I can't figure out which world you're from. Your hair's dyed and you're wearing contacts, aren't you?"

I stilled, my heart plummeting. How could he tell? No one had ever questioned whether the pale blue of my contact lenses was my real eye colour. There was no reason for me to worry about it. But if the Alliance knew, if they made me take the lenses out—it was the biggest giveaway of my homeworld.

"Well?"

"Well what?"

"Which world are you from?"

"You still think I'm going to answer your questions?"

"I hope you will, yes. It'll save a lot of time and paperwork." Was that sarcasm now? What next? Sure, he'd said he wouldn't hurt me, and he hadn't tried to get me back for kicking him in the face… but that didn't mean I'd trust him in a million years. Not bloody likely.

"Afraid you're going to be disappointed," I said, closing my eyes.

"I'm more than willing to wait."

I opened my eyes again at the sound of footsteps. But he hadn't come near me. He was pacing the room, door to wall. Back and forth. He'd pulled out his communicator, though I had no idea what he was doing with it. Surfing the Internet? What right did he have to walk in here like he owned the place? Academy graduates. They thought they owned everything.

"That's really annoying," I muttered.

"There's not much in the way of entertainment in here, is there?" He glanced at the cuffs on my hands. "Hmm. I heard you attacked the nurse."

What was he doing, guilt-tripping me?

"It was worth a try," I said, shrugging. "The door was open."

There was the slightest twitch in his jaw, almost amusement. "I don't doubt the logic there. But you know you'd be out of here faster if you just answered my questions." He paused. Slid the communicator back into his pocket. "Did you kill Mr Sebastian Clark?"

I inhaled sharply. "You what? You think I'm a killer?"

"I asked you if you murdered him." His manner was more serious now. If that was possible.

"No." I shook my head. "Never. I've never killed anyone." I glared at him. "Bet *you* have."

Kay blinked. "I fail to see how that's relevant."

He had a point. But I'd taken him by surprise. Maybe I could press my advantage. Talk my way out of here. But I had a feeling Kay Walker would be difficult to trick. He'd got the measure of me in about half a second. As for *him*, all I could see was that he was younger than I'd first thought. He couldn't be one of the senior Alliance members. So why had he been sent to question me?

"For the record," he said. "The Alliance doesn't kill people. Not from Earth, anyway. You're under our protection."

"Yeah, that's reassuring," I muttered. "Almost makes up for being locked in here. How long am I stuck here?"

He frowned. "I have no idea. The murder complicates things. Ordinarily, we'd refer to the usual procedure for someone trespassing in the Passages. If that's all you were doing."

"Is it so hard to believe it was?" I said.

"Perhaps. You just decided to take a trip into the between-world? Looking for thrills, or a glimpse of another world?"

"You say that like it's unusual. I bet loads of people have done it."

"They have," he said. "But there was a wyvern loose in there. Those things don't wander in by accident."

Oh, he knew the Passages all right. Did the Alliance's guards ever get to have any fun in the between-world, or was it all routine patrols for them?

"I don't know," I said. "It was just there. It attacked...me."

"And your friend." I glared. "I saw," he added. "Someone created a diversion, but at least one person was spotted fleeing the Passages. Was it you who pulled the trick with the firework?"

I clenched my teeth together, not responding.

"You know you're going to have to answer these questions either way, right? If you're not a killer, there's no reason to keep you here indefinitely. The faster you cooperate, the faster you get out."

Damn him for speaking sense.

"Okay. Fine. There were… two of us. It was all my idea. The wyvern wasn't."

"Did you see where it came from?" There was something other than detachment in his tone now, like he genuinely wanted to know.

"No idea. Appeared out of nowhere." Well, it wasn't like I'd had the chance to ask Skyla or Alber what had happened. At least they'd got away.

"I'm going to have to ask you to give me your friends' names. And your full name, too. How old are you?"

Oh, he thought I was a minor. Fan-freaking-tastic. Blame my Enzar heritage for ensuring I continually got mistaken for a sixteen-year-old.

"I'm twenty-one," I snapped.

He raised an eyebrow. That gesture was starting to get on my nerves. "You look younger."

"Was that supposed to be a compliment?"

"Just stating a fact. Your name?"

"Why does it matter?"

"Well, it'd make it a tiny bit easier to file your report…"

"I don't give a crap," I said. "You think I'm going to turn my friends over to the likes of you?"

"If you're as innocent as you say you are, then it shouldn't be a problem," he said. "That was no normal firework," he added. "It was magic. You shouldn't be messing with that."

"Wait, is this a safety lecture now? I thought it was supposed to be an interrogation."

"Well, it would be helpful to know who taught you magic. Because they didn't do a very good job teaching you the risks."

Don't even go there. No one insulted Nell and got away with it. "What the hell do you know?" I snapped.

"Well, for one thing, what you were doing is not something an Earth native would know how to do. Not unless they had a connection to the Alliance, or training from an offworlder with an appropriate qualification."

"Are you trying to talk me to death?" I said.

"Just making sure you're aware of the facts. Magic is a force, not a toy you can throw around. You could have hurt yourself."

I glared mutely at him. It had been so chaotic in there, I wasn't sure what had caused the place to light up, but it sure as hell wasn't me. He was trying to trick me into admitting how much I knew. Like I'd fall for that one.

He took out his communicator again, tapping the screen.

"Looks like our time's up," he said. "It's been a pleasure talking to you, Ada." The sarcasm made me blink. Had he been putting on the serious-questioner act the whole time? I really couldn't tell.

He left without another word. Great. I tried to shift position, but it was impossible to get comfortable with my hands and ankles cuffed. I'd been stuck here for hours. When did they plan on taking these things off?

I jumped as the door slammed against the wall. What now?

A woman came into the room. She was probably around thirty-five or so, with her dark hair clipped to chin-length and an expression on her face that could freeze water.

"Ada Fletcher," she said.

My blood turned cold. How did she know my last name? I hadn't told Kay. She approached me, slowly, not staying near the door like Kay had. The hairs rose on my arms. This woman, I had reason to be afraid of.

"You have been accused of a serious crime," she went on. "A colleague of mine was murdered two days ago. You were sighted trespassing at Central on that same night, and yesterday, you were caught in the Passages, which are strictly off-limits to anyone without a permit who is not an Alliance employee."

I was kind of tempted to ask if *she* intended to talk me to death. But I clamped my mouth shut. Insulting this woman would not be a wise choice.

"You are not an Earth native," she went on. "The deception was quite well done, but we checked this…" And she pulled my provisional driving license from her pocket. Crap. They'd taken my purse from my coat—and my phone, too. How could I have forgotten that?

She saw the understanding in my eyes. "This is a fake," she said. "Along with all your birth documents, I don't doubt."

"You went through my things." Stupid Ada. Way to state the obvious.

"Yes. We did. We have not yet managed to unlock your phone, but I'm sure it will tell us more."

Not likely. I felt a flicker of pride for Jeth's tech skills. No one could get into that phone but me. Even the Alliance couldn't crack it, apparently. And if they did, it was programmed to wipe itself clean. They wouldn't be able to get my contact details, or any of my friends'.

Didn't mean they had the right to take my freaking phone, though. It was the most expensive thing I owned.

"You have nothing to say to that?"

"When are you going to let me go? I didn't kill anyone."

"You have broken several laws, Ada Fletcher. These forgeries are a concern too…but a human on Earth with inherent magical ability—it's unheard of."

"So what, it's illegal for me to exist?"

"I did not say that. In fact, if your innocence was proven, you could be valuable to the Alliance. But there is the matter of your origin world. We don't want to run up against any problems."

"Seems like you have plenty of problems on your hands," I muttered.

She raised an eyebrow, as if to say, "Go on".

"Well, you haven't caught the killer. I'm innocent. Maybe it was the same person who set the wyvern loose in the Passages."

"Wyverns," she said, "are not native to the Passages. They're from Cethrax, and only come into the Passages when lured there. And you also used magic in the Passages, Ada. Magic always leaves a trace. We might not be able to pinpoint the user, but it's plain to see that it was not one of our stunners."

The Tasers?

I could do no more than sit in silence, hardly daring to breathe.

She continued, "Kay told me that he believes you have an internal magical source. Having examined all the possessions you carried in the Passages, we've concluded that the source is not external. On Earth, the low levels of magic in the atmosphere make it a physical impossibility for a person to be born with that ability. The way the cuffs affected you wouldn't have happened to an Earth-born magic-wielder, so the only explanation is that you were born offworld."

They knew too much. Far too much.

And then came the punch line: "We are currently testing a sample of your blood to determine your origin world."

My blood. It was all I could do not to make a sound. I couldn't meet her eyes anymore.

There was no hiding my own DNA. Soon, the Alliance would know I came from Enzar. And it was one small step from there to the rest of the truth. If I came from Enzar, someone had smuggled me out. Everything that Nell had worked her whole life for, everything we'd risked ourselves a thousand times over, and the countless people we'd saved— would be in danger.

The silence crushed me with its weight, and my skin was clammy all over. I could feel my composure—or what remained of it—cracking like fake glass.

"In the meantime, Ada," said the woman, "we are not so unkind as to leave you here indefinitely. An escort will take you to the bathrooms in order to clean yourself up. You will also be given new clothes, and your cuffs will be removed. If you attempt to escape, it goes without saying that we'll be reinstating them."

That figured. Swallowing, I nodded. The door clicked open again, and I looked up to see two guards enter the room. Neither was familiar to me. I wondered how many employees the Alliance actually had. No matter. I was completely, hopelessly outnumbered.

I hated feeling weak. Hated the way the guards smirked at one another as they hauled me to my feet, and uncuffed my wrists and ankles. I was tempted to use my *I know how to kill a man with my bare hands* line, but these guys would probably laugh at me.

"Don't let her out of your sight," said the woman. I got a glimpse of her name badge under the light, "Ms Danica Weston: Supervisor". "She's a magic-wielder. Not from Earth."

The smirks faded from the guards' faces. Now they were all business.

Thank God none of them followed me into the bathroom. Not that I had an opportunity to escape either way—there were no windows, and Ms Weston herself stood guard at the door. I had a quick wash in the sink, as I was covered in grime from falling in the road and my knees were a mess of matted blood. Could be worse. The bruises weren't too painful, anyway. I'd half expected them to give me black faux leather to change into, but the T-shirt and trousers were made of soft material.

Even without the cuffs, I was still weaker than I'd have liked, though I walked upright amongst the guards as though they didn't intimidate me. My mind raced every time I saw a gap where I might be able to make a run for it. There had to be a way…

I absently reached up to tuck a strand of hair behind my ear, and stumbled forwards. The guards moved closer to me like they expected me to run, but I carried on walking obediently. Hoping they couldn't hear my pounding heart.

My fingers had brushed against something metal behind my ear, something invisible. Something I thought I'd lost.

The earpiece from Jeth's Chameleon.

CHAPTER TEN

KAY

Ms Weston cornered me as soon as I came out of Ada's room. Or cell, really.

"Well?" she demanded. "What did she say?"

"She wasn't very responsive, but she's fairly easy to read. Has a temper, but she's not a killer."

"She could be a practiced liar," said Ms Weston. Her expression challenged me.

"I'm sure she is, actually," I said. "But she gives too much away with her body language. She's hurt and angry, and not used to being under pressure, I'd guess." That much I could read. But unless she started talking, we were no closer to finding out what she'd been doing in the Passages.

Ms Weston sighed. "You should have pushed her harder."

"How so?" Come on, she didn't seriously expect me to threaten someone who was cuffed and powerless. Or maybe she did. *Should've sent Aric, then,* I thought, and was glad she hadn't. It was bad enough that they'd left the cuffs on. I didn't particularly care for the memories it stirred up, of the last night I'd spent in a similar cell. I'd known warning her about magic would get a defiant response, but I'd at least had to try.

Ms Weston muttered something. I caught the word, "disappointing." I knew it. She'd been testing to see what the youngest Walker was capable of. Well, tough shit. I'd rather be a disappointment than a sadistic bastard who'd get a kick out of tormenting a prisoner, guilty or not.

Using my calmest tone, I told Ms Weston everything Ada *had* let slip, including my suspicions that she came from offworld.

"Any idiot can see that," she snapped. "She has inherent magic-wielding abilities—she's either from one of the outer worlds, or…"

She trailed off. Her eyes cut right through me, and I was seized by a cold, horrible suspicion. I blinked, determined to meet her stare. "Or what?"

It can't be. She couldn't know—couldn't know Earth had once been involved in magic-related experiments. It was impossible. How long ago had she joined the Alliance? Could she really have been there when…?

No. I was still shaken from what I'd read in that file. That was all.

Ms Weston drew in a breath. "I am going to talk to the prisoner. You go and finish filling out those files. Don't disappoint me again."

So she was going to interrogate Ada now. I wondered how *that* would go down. Not that it was any of my business.

***

Annoyance at the whole universe made it impossible to concentrate on anything all afternoon. I went in search of a caffeine fix, and took out my frustration on the vending machine.

"Watch out," said Markos, passing by. "It might hit you back. Like the door."

"Yeah, very funny," I said.

"What the hell's up with you?"

Where to bloody start? "Ms Weston," I said, retrieving my espresso from the machine and heading back in the direction of Office Fifteen. "Also, the prisoner." Markos on my heels, I went back into the office. "And Saki. Did someone send out a memo telling every woman in Central to yell at me?"

"I didn't get it," Ellen said, glancing up from the paperwork she was filling out. She smiled at me. At least one person wasn't looking at me like I was the freaking criminal.

"Oh, poor you," said Markos. "Weston's terrorised almost everyone on the floor. I could hear her yelling at Aric from all the way over here."

Well, that was the first bit of good news I'd heard all day.

"It was scary," Ellen said. "I gathered he attacked the

prisoner yesterday or something."

"Yeah, because he's a moron," I said. "He tried to choke her. I stopped him, and that was when she tried to get away."

"And kicked you," Markos added.

"I wondered what happened to your face," said Ellen, wincing. "Ouch."

Would I never hear the end of this? I shrugged, took a sip of coffee. "We got her back to Central. She's locked up now."

"And you talked to her, didn't you?" asked Ellen, eying me curiously. "Markos told me." She held my gaze slightly longer than necessary, but not in a particularly unappealing way.

"Yeah. Couldn't get any answers out of her."

"It's suspicious that she was in the Passages," said Markos. "Right by Central."

Suspicious. But we couldn't rule out coincidence.

"She might just have been sneaking onto another world, when that wyvern jumped her." That didn't seem right, either. From her defensiveness, I figured she'd had a purpose of some kind. Something to hide.

"Maybe," said Markos. "I heard Aric talking to Ms Weston about Academy kids sneaking into the Passages, when he could get a word in edgeways."

Shit. "Yeah, it's not uncommon," I said.

"You broke into the Passages?" From Ellen's tone, I knew what answer she expected. If Aric was putting it about, it was only a matter of time before the whole freaking office knew. Great.

"This is strictly off record," I said in a mock-conspiratorial voice. "But yeah. A few times."

"Ha," said Markos. "Who is the girl, anyway? What's she like?"

"Her name's Ada. I don't think she's originally from Earth…this is off record too, by the way," I added. "Ms Weston might not be thrilled to hear us talking about it. We're supposed to leave it to the Law Division."

"Oh, screw them," said Markos. "I think we can do a little investigating of our own."

I hesitated to share my suspicions with the others—partly because they weren't based on much more than paranoia. And partly because I wasn't a freaking detective. I just wanted to do my job. Ever since I'd driven into Central for the first time, it seemed like everything had conspired to prevent that from happening. "What did you have in mind?" I asked.

"I don't know yet," said Markos. "But my ideas are spectacular."

Ellen rolled her eyes. "So modest," she said.

"Kay Walker?" Alan opened the door to the office.

"Yes?"

"They've changed the rota. You're on the next patrol. And you, Ellen. You're with Carl and Aric. Oh, and they think there's a chalder vox on the loose."

Well, damn. "All right," I said, and downed the rest of the coffee in one. I was going to bloody need it.

**

At least going out on patrol snapped me back onto full alert. There was no long safety lecture from Carl this time, though he did take the opportunity to remind us not to harm any *person* with the stunners. With a significant look at Aric and me. Clearly, he knew about our little altercation last night. If Ms Weston did, though, she hadn't mentioned it.

"Right. This is a tricky one, but it's nothing you Academy graduates can't handle. The creature's around the same place the wyvern attacked yesterday—something's up in Cethrax, I'd wager. But we want to bring the chalder vox down as swiftly as possible. No fancy tricks, and try not to hurt it unless you're close enough to deal a fatal blow. Remember— they're pain-tripping masochists. They get stronger the more damage you deal them."

"We know," Aric interrupted. "The Academy drilled us on this a hundred times. Both in simulation and real life. I could do it blindfolded."

I could tell the cocky bastard was trying to rebuild his ego from when Ms Weston had stamped all over it. Moron.

"Arrogance," said Carl, giving Aric an irritated glance, "is what gets people killed. Your stunners will paralyse it for a moment, use them instead of the daggers, if you can."

Carl led the way, and I walked alongside Ellen, keeping one eye on Aric. We moved in complete silence this time. Even in the daytime, no one came near this back street, and the sounds of traffic and human noise were a distant hum. When we entered the Passages, any other sound was cut off as the door slid closed behind us. This time, we took a different path, one that led down a sloping corridor with fewer doors but more of a static buzz in the air that usually meant magic was high. Something about that observation struck me as off. Since when could I feel the difference in levels of magic? That was new. And not entirely welcome.

Then came a noise, like a faint breeze. But I picked up on it, and so did the others. Without a word, we moved into formation. This was more like it. A situation I knew how to handle.

Chalder voxes moved stealthily as living shadows, but we were quieter. Stunners in hand, we advanced down the corridor, the faint scraping noise growing louder with every corner we turned. This wasn't a Passage I'd patrolled before.

One last corner.

Oh, it was a monster, all right. Six feet of concrete-like skin, four stumpy legs and two arms, huge ears, and an ugly, jagged-toothed smile—all materialising from the shadows. And a gaping wound in its shoulder. Great.

We got within two metres when it spotted us. I prepared to sprint after it, but instead it ran *towards* us, limbs flailing. Damn, it was stoned. Carl hesitated, clearly taken by surprise, but recovered in time to duck its flailing fist and zap it with the stunner.

Then footsteps came out of a side tunnel, loud, hurried steps. There was more than one of them.

Of course—it never would have engaged an entire patrol alone. Stupid assumption to make. I cursed myself for letting the events of the past few days distract me to the extent that I'd forget something as basic as that. The formation broke as Carl jumped at the first monster, stunner in the air. And then the second beast was on us.

I spun to face it, stunner at the ready. Of course, the first instinct was to aim a punch at it, but that would give the monster an advantage—a mistake, the Academy had warned, which had cost more than one guard their life. Tackling it head-on did more damage to you than the enemy, even with the impact-absorbing uniform.

Instead, I jumped. I used its bulky arms for leverage and

pulled myself onto its back. Their one weakness was ridiculous, an indentation behind the ear or on the back of the neck, easy to pick out. I held on one-handed, forced to duck as it moved under a lower part of the ceiling. Its discordant bellows echoed around the Passages, magnified by the magic thick in the air. The stunner thrummed in my hand. I could paralyse it... but it was rabid. It'd only wake and go on a rampage later on.

I had to kill it.

I switched the stunner to my left hand and used my right to pull the dagger, flicking out the blade. It was much more streamlined and smoother than the ones used in drills at the Academy, my hand fitting the handle like it was meant to be there. As the monster bucked and tried to throw me off again, I lunged for its weak point. The blade went right in, and shadows flowed out instead of blood. Its knees buckled, and Ellen, who'd been fighting the second beast below, leaped out of the way as it fell to the ground. Carl and Aric were also dodging attacks from the second beast, which was in an even more rabid state than this one, drool hanging from its curved teeth, spittle flying.

My hand twitched on the dagger. No, I'd never killed a person—whatever that girl might have thought of Alliance guards, the Academy trained us to incapacitate, not kill—but I knew too well that that was a line easily crossed. It took more self-control than I'd expected to let Carl finish off the second monster with a stab to the back of the neck. Danger averted.

"Cethrax really needs to keep better control of their pets," said Carl, referring to the beast's origin world. The Cethraxians were one of many who'd been denied entry into the Alliance due to their blatant disregard for human or cross-species rights… or any kinds of rights, really. Unfortunately for a world which wanted nothing to do with the rest of the Multiverse, theirs was ridden with entrances to the lower-level Passages and generally anything monster-related could be traced back to them.

"Odd, though," Carl said, frowning at the chalder vox's prone form at his feet. "This is nowhere near the doors to Cethrax. They weren't heading our way, either."

I glanced at the other monster's body and the tunnel it had come from. Wait…

Though it had been months since I'd looked at the map, it was imprinted on my memory. And now I thought about it, this particular tunnel wasn't covered by the Alliance's patrols. It supposedly dead-ended.

So where was that light coming from? A faint stream of gold light, not at all like the blue radiating from the Passage walls. Like a staircase…

"That tunnel." I jerked my head in that direction. "Is that

to the lower level?" But that didn't fit right with the map I had in my head. "Because there's light coming from somewhere down there."

Carl skirted around the monster's body and came to stand in the tunnel entrance. "Damn. You're right."

There was a pause. Then a high-pitched screech sounded, reverberating through the Passages.

"Shit," said Aric. "That was a wyvern!"

"Oh, hell," said Ellen. "Sounded like it came from that way." She pointed ahead, to where the corridor divided.

"That's off our route," said Carl. "We'd never get there before it got through…shit." He tapped the screen of his communicator. "We need backup. We suspect there's a wyvern on L1, around the junction of Doors 12B-F."

A buzz of assent from the other end, and then silence. Carl indicated we follow him, leaving the tunnel with the strange light behind.

"We're going to do a full search of this area," he said. "Sounds echo, so it could be anywhere in this sector. We can't afford to risk it breaking through one of the doors."

No one dared argue, even Aric. He just nodded, serious for once. And no one spoke as we followed Carl.

I ignored the magic, though it was stronger than ever, like a live current running through my veins. There was definitely more of it in the Passages than before. That must be what attracted the wyverns. But it didn't happen of its own accord.

The Balance must be tipping. Towards Earth.

*****

"Well, that was a waste of time," said Ellen, as soon as Carl was out of earshot. We stood in the Alliance's entrance hall following our report to the head of the guards—two hours combing the Passages and not so much as a wyvern claw to show for it. The sound had been unmistakable, but nothing appeared.

"You're telling me," I said. "There's not normally this level of activity in the Passages, is there?" And wyverns were the rarest monsters of all, even on the lower level.

Ellen shook her head. "I forgot you're new here." Her eyes flicked up to meet mine, a smile playing on her lips. I couldn't help noticing she'd somehow avoided getting any dirt in her hair. Skill.

"Yeah. Hell of a week." I smiled back.

"It's not always this exciting. You were *amazing* against that chalder vox, by the way."

And I totally wasn't checking her out in that tight faux leather uniform despite it being way below the line of 'professional behaviour'. If I wasn't mistaken, she'd been doing the same to me. "I don't suppose you have plans later…?"

She looked startled, but flushed. "Not that I know of. Wow, that makes a change."

"Sure does." I laughed softly. I needed a distraction. "How about a drink? I'm not familiar with the local scene—only moved here a week ago."

"I'll show you around. Give me time to get ready. I'm covered in tunnel dust and God, do I want a shower. I'll call you, okay… Kay?" She laughed.

"You've no idea how many times I've heard that one," I said.

"I can guess. See you later."

Today wasn't a complete bust after all. No reason to dwell on prisoners and murders and hidden Passages…

I spotted Carl coming out of the guard office, and strode over to him. "Did you tell them about that light?" I asked. "Because I know that place backwards, and that tunnel's supposed to dead-end."

"How do you… ah. You're sure about that?"

"Of course. I have a copy of my grandfather's map, I memorised it."

Technically, it was my father's, and I'd stolen it before he'd left five years ago. But Carl didn't need to know that.

"Right. I'll pass that onto the others."

That was one thing taken care of, at least. I was done

with it. None of my business.

As I left the building, my communicator vibrated in my pocket. Incoming call from the New York Alliance branch. I crossed the car park to my vehicle, and hit the touch screen to accept the call.

"Who is it? It's the ever-elusive Kay Walker."

"Simon," I said, leaning against my car. It figured my old friend from the Academy would want to know the details. Damn, had it really only been less than two weeks since graduation? "Guess you heard?"

"Heard things went apeshit at Central? The whole *world* knows. Haven't you seen the news?"

"Dude, I've been *living* it. I arrested the suspect."

Simon sucked in a breath. "Well, shit. I can't say I'm surprised, but damn, Kay. You've been there what, three days?"

"You won't believe it," I said, "but Aric's here, too."

"Thought he was transferring to the States," said Simon. "Shit. Isn't Tara…?" He cut himself off, too late. "Sorry, man. Too soon?"

"It's been two years, Simon," I said, but my hand strayed to the scar on my left arm just the same. Simon usually knew better than to go poking at the past with a rusty nail. Of the three people who knew what had really gone down at the Academy, he was the only one I was on friendly speaking terms with. Though seeing as the other two were my ex and Aric, that wasn't saying a whole lot.

"Two years. Jesus. Aric's still being a conceited dickhead, then?"

"Yeah. He has zero professionalism. I *know* there must have been bribery involved for him to get in here—but there's too much going on at the moment for anyone to pay attention. I'm hoping he gets himself fired before…"

Before anything happens like two years ago. Simon could fill in the gaps easily enough. He cleared his throat. "How's Central, anyway? Apart from all the craziness? They working you as hard as at the Academy? Because no shit, I don't think I've had more than four straight hours of sleep since I transferred here."

"Yep. Same here. It's all paperwork and questionings, and occasionally kicking monsters around."

"You got to fight already? Not fair. Just don't go tangling with any more wyverns."

"There was one in the Passages the other day, actually, but it got taken care of."

"Damn." Simon whistled. "You do have a knack for getting yourself knee deep in crap, don't you?"

"You're telling me."

"Three days and you've got the place in chaos. Well done."

"What, you've not brought a plague of swamp rats down on New York yet?"

"Watch it, you. Anyway. Is Central as swanky inside as outside? What're the other employees like?"

"All right, I guess." I glanced up at the building, which gleamed against the surroundings like a particularly potent middle finger.

"Yeah, it's weird after five years knowing all the same people. Still, the girls here are drooling over my accent. Kind of awesome."

"Bet it is."

"What about you? It's been three days, so I'm predicting you have at least one admirer."

I rolled my eyes, even though of course he couldn't see. "Yeah, right."

"Anyone caught your eye, then? I know you, Kay. Don't dodge the question."

"Okay. Maybe." I meant Ellen, but another face kept intruding. A pretty, stubborn redheaded prisoner, who intrigued me more than I wanted to admit to myself. The way she'd glared at me when she'd asked if I'd murdered anyone… she genuinely thought the Alliance were cold-blooded killers. That *I* was one. And it bothered me more than it should have.

Quit that. I rested my forehead on my knuckles, holding

my communicator with the other hand.

"Well, that's something," said Simon. "Man, this place couldn't be more different from Central. Did you know they have a Passage door right in the middle of the city which is open to the public? Seriously. I mean, it's a bit dull because there aren't any monsters, but instead you get to meet people coming in from offworld. It's pretty cool. They run, like, shelters for people escaping from their homeworlds for whatever reason. London doesn't have any of those."

"Yeah, Central needs to get on that," I said. With Central being Earth's first Alliance headquarters, they were neck deep in bureaucracy when it came to offworlders wanting to settle on Earth. Some of the other Alliance branches worldwide were more lenient.

"Pity I can't come back and visit until I get my permit. I already figured out how to get to London's Passage door from this side. A two-hour walk's quicker than a flight."

"True," I said. The Passages were arranged in such a way that using them as a shortcut across Earth wasn't usually possible unless you wanted to navigate through ten layers of different worlds' security, or trek through the lower level and risk getting eaten by one of Cethrax's monsters. Flying was definitely a safer bet. "London's under lockdown at the moment, anyway."

"Crap, I suppose it is. They barred all the Passages?"

"Yeah, otherwise I'd have used my own permit by now. It's only open to patrols."

"You be careful. Wait, you're not going to listen, are you?"

"I can give it a try."

"Talk to you later, you lunatic."

"Sure, asshole," I said, and clicked off the phone icon. I looked up at Central, where a crowd of people had gathered outside. Guards, mostly, but also office workers.

Damn. I crossed the car park quickly, in time to see a pale-looking supervisor raise his communicator and project his voice across the crowd.

"There's been another murder, this one in the elevator from the fourth floor. Alan Gregory from Office Fourteen."

CHAPTER ELEVEN

ADA

I hardly dared breathe as I ran my hand over the device, searching out the button that would put me on speakerphone with Jeth. Even though the guards had left, it was risky. He'd be at work right now, and there was no guarantee he'd have the Chameleon on him. Did he carry it everywhere? I'd never asked. But I had to try.

Now the cuffs were off, I could move around my room. I peered out the door and couldn't see any guards, but I knew they'd be there somewhere. I drew in a deep breath, and went back over to the bed, the part of the room furthest from the door. Then I flicked the switch.

"Jeth," I whispered, loudly as I dared. "Can you hear me?"

Silence. I waited, counting to sixty, then flicked the call button again. "Jeth, please. It's me, Ada."

Nothing. I tried again, every five minutes. At least it helped me keep time. Though I had to stop and sit back innocuously when the guards brought me food, and then there was another bathroom break. By what must have been late evening, I was starting to give up hope.

"Jeth. Please answer me. It's Ada."

Finally, there was a sharp intake of breath. *"Ada. Is it really you?"*

"Course it is, you idiot," I said, relief seeping through me. "I'm at Central. The Alliance caught and arrested me." All the panic and fear bubbled up in my throat again. "They think I'm a murderer, Jeth."

"Holy shit, Ada." He paused. *"Okay. If the Alliance is on full alert we won't be able to walk in there and get you out. I'll think of something."*

"I was so worried. Is Nell okay? Did Alber and Skyla get away?"

"They're fine," he said. *"Well, Nell's frantic of course. Skyla knew right away the Alliance must have you, but there was no way we could check."*

Trapped on all sides. "What should I do?" I whispered. "I'm locked in here. I forgot I was still wearing the earpiece. They're bound to find out soon. For all I know, they're listening in."

"Don't panic. Let me think for a second. They haven't hurt you, have they?"

"No…some of the guards are pretty rough, though." *Not all of them.* "I'm fine."

"You said they think you're *a murderer? That's messed up."*

"They've no evidence otherwise. It happened while I was here. Two people have questioned me, and… this woman." I swallowed. "She knows I'm not from Earth—they both know. I have no idea how they figured it out." And my contacts were starting to hurt my eyes. I couldn't keep them in forever. But removing them wasn't an option.

"Hang tight. You had your ID with you, right?"

"Yeah. They saw through it. They know it's fake. They have my phone. But they couldn't get into it."

"Good. Listen, Ada. I've got an idea. I'm going to need you to get hold of a communicator."

"Huh?"

"Any communicator—you know everyone at the Alliance carries one. And *I* know how to hack into them."

I exhaled, almost laughed. "Of course you do."

He recited a short code, and I did my best to commit it to memory.

"Right. That'll get you emergency access to any device. Every communicator comes fitted with an alert button. Hit that, and it'll be like breaking the glass on a fire alarm. Everyone will panic, they'll think they're being attacked. If you escape then, we can meet you at the back gate. Alber already knows how to get in. Think you can manage that?"

"I'll have to run fast," I said. "But yes."

This was no different from one of our usual schemes.

Right? But there was a new tightness in my chest, and it was hard to suppress a shiver. Too much at risk...

"Okay. I'll call Nell. She'll probably send Alber, though she might come herself. We'll have someone watching the place, anyway. Wait for your opportunity, then get hold of a communicator."

"Right, I will." But I didn't know if I could wait too long. The desire to get the hell out of there burned within my very skin. Maybe it was a reaction to the antimagic cuffs...

Wait. I wasn't wearing the cuffs anymore.

"How quickly can Alber be here?" I asked. "I think—if I use magic, I should be able to escape this room. Within an hour."

"Perfect," said Jeth. "Ada, I'm sorry that happened. We'll get you out. Promise."

"I'll hold you to that." I swallowed. "See you soon."

I hoped so. God, I hoped so.

I breathed, in and out, calming myself, reaching for the magic I knew so well. It wasn't like when I'd come out of the Passages with magic buzzing through my veins like adrenaline. I felt drained. But I *could* do this. I had to. It was the only way to escape, the only way to get back home... To get back to what I was supposed to be doing. Helping people. I couldn't be locked up for a murder I'd had nothing to do with.

Shouts rang out from the corridor. My heart leaped in my chest. I ran for the door and pressed my forehead to the window, trying desperately to see what was happening outside. But the bars were in the way. People dashed by, panicked shouts echoed, but I couldn't see the reason.

Like the panic had kick-started it, magic flooded my veins. I could see, as though through a veil, the faint magic present on Earth. More than there usually would be—and enough for me.

I didn't hesitate to debate whether I was making a huge error. I pulled on the magic, let it flow into my hand and released it. A stream of purple-red energy hit the floor, and I shifted aside to avoid the rebound striking me. Instead, it sizzled through the lock on the door. The sound was lost in the general confusion. I rammed the door open with my shoulder. I turned left for the way out, headed for the stairs. I had to get a communicator off a guard, before everyone spotted me—they must have all left for the entrance hall.

Thud. I slammed into someone, who grabbed my arm, tight. Damn. Of all the guards to run into, it had to be Kay Walker.

"Going somewhere?" His eyes flashed. I'd have done my best to kick him… were it not for the communicator sticking out of the inside pocket of his faux-leather guard jacket. Inches away.

I feinted a kick, fast, darted forwards and snatched the communicator. His eyes widened as I spun around and ran faster than I ever had in my life. I had the advantage—I was much shorter than most guards, and easily wove in and out of the gathering crowd. I had a decent head start before I heard the shouts of, "Stop that girl!" and "The prisoner's escaping!"

You won't catch me this time.

As I ran, I tapped the touch screen of the communicator and put in the key Jeth had given me. I wheeled around a corner, nearly dropping the device when it vibrated in my hand. Following Jeth's instructions while running for my life was an obstacle I hadn't seen coming—I was lucky not to trip on the stairs, though the narrow stairwell slowed the guards down, too. At least enough for me to locate the emergency button, and hit it. A high-pitched, siren-like noise reverberated through the air, making my ears ring. I pounded up the last few steps and out into the entrance hall of the Alliance. Too many people to count ran in all directions, came down staircases and poured out of the elevators.

Except for the one at the far end. A gleam of red caught my eyes, reflected in the glass, I couldn't help glancing in that direction...

The world tilted under my feet. That was blood. A lot of it.

Someone else was killed.

I had to get out of here. I shot towards the exit, but someone barred my way. Kay, white-faced with fury, blocked my path. His hand caught my arm, making me skid to a halt. Cursing, I pushed down the instinct to draw on the magic buzzing under my skin, as it'd be too risky in a place with so many people. But it put me in a major dilemma. Unless…

"I'll take that back," he said, snatching the communicator from my outstretched hand, "and I'll be taking *you* back downstairs."

"Like hell," I said, twisting to free my hand, but only getting my arm locked. I bit back a scream, but he'd already caught my other hand. When I dug my heels into the ground, he lifted me into the air.

"Put me down, you bastard!"

My shout drew attention, and I cursed myself for stupidity. Within seconds, several other guards descended on me. Conflicting orders bounced around the entrance hall, but Kay didn't let go of me once, no matter how I twisted and kicked. Finally, they agreed that locking me back downstairs was the best option.

I screamed at them, dignity going clean out the window. "I'm not a murderer!" I yelled. "I didn't *kill* anyone, I haven't even committed a crime. You people are a bunch of blind fucking *morons!*"

"That's very flattering," said Kay, tugging on my hands, "but you're creating a scene. I did tell my supervisor you were innocent, you know. You're not helping your own case."

"Screw you!"

I screamed my throat raw, but he still managed to get me out of the hall and downstairs. Again. There was no chance I was getting that communicator off him now. But he hadn't zapped me with a stunner. There was a surprise. Wait—was he even armed at the moment? Not that it'd help if he wasn't, seeing as I wasn't either.

"You're locking up the wrong person!"

"Stealing an Alliance member's communicator is a crime," he said. "As is breaking out of your room."

And he shut the door on me. Again.

Helpless tears threatened to intrude, but I furiously blinked them away. Damn him. Damn them all.

***

KAY

I shut the door on the girl, noticing that there was a smoking hole where the lock used to be. *Hellfire*. She'd used magic to break out, all right. I positioned myself in case I needed to hold the door. If I'd had some of those cuffs, I'd have had to use them. But I was unarmed. I'd handed my weapons in. The Alliance really needed to look into that. If employees had been allowed to carry weapons inside Central… then Alan Gregory might not be in bloody pieces all over the inside of an elevator.

What the hell was I supposed to do about Ada? My mind was blank, everything I knew about how to deal with emergencies wiped out by the horror of Alan's death. I didn't know him, only that he was one rank above me, from the office next to ours, but whatever attacked him had torn him to pieces. Inside freaking *Central*. A human couldn't have done it.

Ada had been running from this corridor when I'd caught her—she definitely wouldn't have had time to get all the way over to the elevators. She wasn't the killer, but to have melted the lock off the door like that was second level magic. There either had to be a small crater in that room which I'd missed, or she'd somehow absorbed some of the backlash herself. Which was another matter entirely.

I couldn't stand guard here forever. But neither could I let her get away again. I studied the lock. She must have used something else to absorb the backlash. The problem with magic was that it was damned impossible to use it safely even if you did know what you were doing. The odds of accidentally hurting or killing another person were too high. You couldn't stop the backlash, and even if you had the forethought to dodge it yourself, there was no guarantee no innocent bystander wouldn't walk into it.

I glanced up at the sound of footsteps on the stairs, and my gaze fell on a clipboard discarded on the floor, like someone had dropped it. Ada's name leaped out from the top of the page, and there were notes clipped underneath. Pages of notes. Whose were these, Ms Weston's?

Another word leaped out: ENZAR.

Of course. No wonder I hadn't been able to tell which world she was from—Enzar was listed as out of bounds, and no contact with other worlds was allowed. As far as I knew, the Alliance had started out trying to reach a peace treaty between the two warring sides, but it became clear it'd only get even more people killed, so the council had issued a blanket noninterference statement and closed it off. Plainly, this girl had been smuggled out.

Why? Because she was valuable? She must be mageblood, a magic-wielder, which explained the way she could use magic here on Earth. Not that she'd be able to go above second level—at least, I thought not.

The Alliance wasn't out to imprison magic-wielders, especially from places like that, despite the council's statement—hell, it contradicted the Alliance's first principle, for a start. There had to be a way around it, if I could convince Ms Weston she wasn't a killer. And convince Ada herself that we weren't *blind fucking morons*. I had to smile at that. The public might view our headquarters as a flashy nuisance, but I'd always had the impression there was a general agreement that the Alliance was a force for good, even if most people didn't know the extent of it. Ada, though, had clearly been brought up in an environment that had taught her they were something to be feared.

That didn't have to be the case. Not at all.

I hid the file behind my back as someone came downstairs. Carl.

"There you are. You're needed upstairs."

"The prisoner's in there," I said, in a low voice. "She melted the lock." I moved closer to the door again in case I had to brace it shut.

"Damn. Okay." He paused, glanced up and down the corridor. "Do not tell anyone you witnessed this."

And he pulled a stunner from his pocket, jamming it into the hole where the lock used to be. Magic sparked from the tip, but it remained in place.

"She won't be able to touch it without getting zapped," he said. "It's too strong to break through. You can't unlock it now, but I'll tell Ms Weston. She'll have the girl relocated soon as we sort out this mess." His face was grim. "Alan dead… I've never seen anything like it." He glanced at the lock on the door.

"It wasn't her," I said. "She ran into me back there in the main corridor. She was coming from this direction. She wouldn't have had time to get to the lifts. There's no other way there apart from the stairs."

"No," he said. "Her room was guarded right up until the alert went out, after they found him. I'll wager she took advantage of the confusion." He gave the stunner a tap. To be authorised to seal the door like that meant he must be a magic-wielder. Well, shit.

He noticed me looking. "You can use it, too?" he asked.

I nodded. Aric was bound to tell everyone sooner or later, and besides, it was an advantage here, even if I didn't have any intention of ever using magic again.

"I'll put that on record. Might get you a promotion."

That was unexpected. "Cheers," I said, following him upstairs, all too conscious that we were leaving Ada locked in her room, with no way out.

We have to be certain, I reminded myself. But that didn't make me feel any better about it.

CHAPTER TWELVE

ADA

That night was the longest of my life. I could almost feel the oxygen draining from the room, now that the lock was stuck. Permanently. It was so hard to breathe, I had to sit and put my head between my legs for a good five minutes.

I'd never had a panic attack in my life. But then again, I'd never been magically sealed in a room and left there overnight.

To make things worse, the Chameleon was dead. I thought so, anyway, because I couldn't get a message through. I tried every hour—no way was I getting any sleep—but never heard Jeth's voice on the other end. Never heard a single sound.

Morning. I imagined the sun rising over the tower blocks of central London, the hum of traffic picking up, the noises as people went about their days. Ordinary people going to work, school, tourists visiting the sights, others passing through to get to the airports and the rest of the world. Millions of lives, barely aware of the other world standing in their midst, untouchable, all-powerful.

"Jeth." My voice was a whisper now. My throat hurt from

screaming, and my eyes stung and itched with the contacts. I was in so, so much trouble. I let tears fall down my cheeks, knowing no one could see. No one in this stupid building cared enough to even check I was still alive.

"Jeth, *please.*"

Silence. I hated the quiet. At home, I always had music playing, or there were people around, people to talk to. Strangers to share stories with. Nell. She'd be able to handle this situation. Nell could deal with anything.

By now, Jeth would have told her where I was. Her, and Alber and Skyla, and everyone else who could get me the hell out of here. Maybe even Delta and his family. I hoped they were still helping the refugees. Didn't look like any of them would be able to come to Earth for a while.

Guilt choked me. I needed to be out there helping them. I was no use to anyone here.

*I should be able to get my*self *out of here,* I thought. I'd run without thinking and paid the price, and now I'd acted like a total lunatic in front of those guards, they had even more reason to think of me as a crazy murderer.

I walked back over to the door, another idea taking shape. I'd used magic to bust the lock already. Could I take the hinges off? It was apparent that magic *did* work in the Alliance's headquarters—the walls might be magicproofed, but even antimagic wasn't enough to keep it out altogether.

That was how I'd broken in, after all. The door looked like ordinary Earth steel to me. Magic wasn't supposed to work here at all, and I doubted every inch of the place was equipped to hold a magic-wielder from somewhere like Enzar. Even Alber, an average magic-wielder by Enzar's standards, couldn't use magic on Earth… but *I* could.

The magic wasn't as potent as in the Passages, but enough for me to break through this door. At least, I hoped.

I focused on the thin film over my vision—it never really went away, though it had dimmed over the past day—and found the place in the room where it was thickest. Then I readied myself to push on it. This confined space was a risky place to try this. But I was all out of options.

Crash. The door opened, and Ms Weston came in again. If it were possible, she looked even more severe than last time, her mouth drawn into such a thin line it almost disappeared.

"Ada Fletcher," she said. "It seems that prior to last evening's disturbance, the results of your tests came out. The magic you used to break out of this room confirms our results."

"Your blood tested as originating in Enzar, central world of the Enzarian Empire, and identifies you as a nonmage. However… you have magic. It turns out that the Alliance have a copy of the Royals' records. Twenty-five years ago, we were in negotiations to make Enzar part of the Alliance, though as you know, that ended badly. However, the records remain. Your blood identifies you as of the Royal line, heirs to the Empire."

My breath caught in my throat. I knew it already, of course, but it was horrible beyond belief to hear those words coming from the mouth of a stranger. Royal. Did she have any idea how many people had died in that name?

"It seems you were to be one of the potential heirs, and were implanted with magic, in a way. You're named as... Adamantine."

Implanted? If breathing had been hard before, now it was like my lungs were caught in a vice. The Royals had done *what?*

"Implanted?" I said, my voice a hoarse whisper. I'd always known that the Royals were one particular extended family of nonmages who had somehow turned the tables on the magebloods and turned every one of them into slaves for their empire. Nell had never said *how* they'd done it, when the magebloods were the ones with magic on their side. I'd assumed they'd had some kind of weapon.

And I'd always known there was something odd about how I could use magic when I wasn't supposed to have any. The one theory I'd had—and Nell had refused to say otherwise—was that I must be part mageblood somewhere.

Certainly not that the Royals had... *implanted* something in me.

Nor that the Alliance had any information on the war, let alone my blood family. And my real first name, Adamantine. It was supposed to be a reminder of my true world. To ensure I never forgot. Hearing it from Ms Weston's mouth... I couldn't say a word, and I knew she saw every tremble, every moment of weakness. Her words had exposed my very core.

"We don't know how they did this. In any case, it worked. You can use magic the same as a mageblood. I believe this is how the Royals upheld their Empire and ensured that they were the ones who had control of magic. They would have given the Royal-blooded enough magic to overpower regular magebloods."

Wrong. Wrong. The words coming from her mouth had an unmistakable current of truth. How could this woman know so much? *How could she?*

The real question was... did Nell know?

I was hardly aware of the door closing until I was alone again. Alone with my thoughts. And my tainted blood.

***

KAY

"This is going to be the death of me," Markos

announced, as I walked into the office the next morning. "I swear the Alliance is trying to run us into the ground. How in the name of all gods are you so wide awake?"

"Caffeine and human souls," I said, with my best deadpan expression. Or, years of pulling all-nighters for Academy drills. Whichever worked.

Markos laughed so loudly everyone in the office looked in our direction. "You're going to get us all arrested," he said. "Save the inappropriate humour for after the investigation."

"At this rate, there won't *be* an 'after'," I said, checking my communicator for updates. And at this rate, the staff might as well take up permanent residence at Central. If nothing else, it'd save on petrol. I'd barely had time to do more last night than eat, shower and crash. After waking with a killer headache, I had even less patience for a day of being grilled to death by Ms Weston. I could already hear her telling me all the ways I'd mishandled the situation yesterday. Well, I'd done my job. I'd locked up a defenceless girl in a room no one could get out of, and Ms Weston hadn't deigned to respond to my message asking when they planned to move her to another room.

"The dragon's gone to breathe fire somewhere else," said Markos. "Leaving us all this paperwork. Enjoy!"

"I swear this crap multiplies when we're not here," I

muttered, picking up a sheet of paper. "What even is this?"

"Don't ask me, I haven't a clue. It's probably all our obituaries."

"Don't say that," said Ellen, from the corner. "They should have evacuated the building. Maybe relocated us to West Office."

"They couldn't transfer all the staff at Central over there," said Markos. "Besides, half the council's offworld. It's terrible timing."

"Damn right," I said. "*Two* murders—both on this floor."

"Technically, Alan was halfway between third and fourth… well, bits of him were."

"Markos!" Ellen's face went greenish-white. "Cut that out."

"Sorry, sorry." Markos went back to the papers.

"I'm going out for a bit," said Ellen. "I can't think in here."

She stood, and I saw her hands trembling as she walked to the door.

"Oh, gods," said Markos. "See, this is why I was never a good Ambassador."

"I'll go talk to her," I said.

I caught up to her outside. "Sorry about last night," I said. "Guess our tour of the neighbourhood will have to wait."

"Not a problem." She managed to smile back at me. After the crap I'd seen over the past twenty-four hours, it was more than welcome. "I just... I've known Alan two years. He was the first person to say hi to me when I came here. It's surreal. Who'd kill off people in our office?"

"God knows," I said.

Ellen shook her head. "I've got to go anyway—patrolling in an hour." She yawned. "If I can stay awake. Tempted to take a nap in a cupboard, but I don't want Weston on my case."

"I'm surprised she's not around," I said. "She can't still be with the prisoner?"

"I forgot about that. Did she really get out again? I'd literally just left Central when I got the call."

Like I wanted to remember. "Yeah, she used magic and melted the lock on the door." I didn't mention the communicator incident. I had to preserve some dignity.

"Clever," she said. "Must be a powerful magic-wielder, then."

Yeah. She is. And I was probably on her hit list. Not that she'd be getting away again.

"Yeah, the timing was pretty crappy. Right after they found Alan. Place was in chaos already."

"She didn't kill him?"

"No, she escaped after the alert went out," I said. "It *looks* bad, though. You should go get ready for your shift, right?"

"Yeah, sure. I'll see you later."

"Did I just hear what I think I heard?" said Markos, as soon as she'd disappeared. How in hell had he managed to hide himself behind a cabinet?

"If you were eavesdropping, then probably," I said, rubbing my temples. Damn headache.

"I feel it is my duty to warn you I saw her talking to Aric earlier, and he was talking about you."

And there went the brief reprieve from the universe's crap. "That figures." I raised my head to face the ceiling, like if I stared hard enough, whoever up there was laughing at me would fall out his seat and get a concussion.

"Using my highly developed intuitive powers, I've concluded that something happened at the Academy involving you, Aric, and a girl."

"And I've concluded that you're a nosy bastard." Not my best comeback. But damn if I didn't want the day to be over already.

"I like to know my colleagues." His expression changed, becoming more serious. "I overhear a lot of things. I saw Alan leave the office before he died. He was carrying a bunch of papers… said he was going to the archives."

God. No.

"That file," I said, my throat dry. No—there was no way.

"I reckon so, human."

"Damn," I said. "Damn it all to hell." If *I'd* been the one to take the file to the archives—if I hadn't been interrupted—and yet it wasn't my own life I feared for. Maybe it should have been, but perhaps I hadn't reached that level of paranoia yet. That, or as Simon had frequently said at the Academy, I had no sense of self-preservation.

How could I walk away from this now? If it wasn't for Ms Weston's invisible presence, I was on the brink of heading back to the archives and having a closer look in the section where the bloodrock research had come from. Because that was the one connection between the two deaths. I couldn't risk telling anyone.

"Don't go doing anything rash, human."

I glanced over my shoulder, making sure no one else was close enough to hear.

"I read the file," I said in a low voice. "There was nothing incriminating in there. Nothing I imagine anyone would murder someone over." But then, I didn't know a whole lot about bloodrock. Only as much as the file had said. A substance with the potential for limitless energy. I could see why the Alliance would keep it a secret…

Hell. Did I really just consider that someone in the *Alliance* might be responsible for the murders?

"Interesting," said Markos. "Well, I wouldn't normally get

involved, but a notice went out to the higher-ups earlier—I heard them talking on the stairs. Turns out something went missing from the stores the night of the murder." He paused. "Someone stole a bunch of bloodrock from the Alliance's storerooms."

Wait. "Someone... that girl. We saw her."

"It wouldn't surprise me."

"Bloodrock," I said. "She stole bloodrock?"

"That's what went missing. Several bags of it. Carl was talking to the head of the guards. Seems he was supposed to be watching the back door, but the killer threw everyone off."

"The girl broke in *after* the murder." Unless she'd already been here. But I knew how to tell when someone was lying. She'd been angry, defensive, but her body language told the truth. When she said she'd never killed anyone, she'd meant it.

The question was, when we'd caught her in the Passages... what had she been doing?

"So she's a smuggler. Or an offworld trader. She stole from the Alliance—well, that takes guts."

"Too true," I said. "Actually, that makes sense. It fits with what she told me, or didn't tell me. Well, that changes things. If bloodrock's valuable, then that's a whole different ball game to breaking and entering..." I stopped, realising I was thinking aloud.

"Yes, there isn't a standard protocol for thievery. It just

happens so rarely." The centaur frowned. "I have to admit, I admire the girl for courage, even if her timing was terrible. She'll get the worst of it, for sure."

"Yeah." She would. And yet that just didn't feel right, even though she was the one who'd broken the law, whatever her reasons. It was my job to stop that from happening.

Blind fucking morons.

The bloodrock...

"Where are you going?" said Markos.

I turned back from the entry to the stairs. "I'm going to talk to the prisoner again."

And I left him staring after me, bemused. Okay, I was definitely acting out now. But if no one else had made the connection... I had to make sure.

On the way downstairs, I saw that someone had cleaned the blood from the left elevator, but it was still out of use. I shook my head to push the image away. It wouldn't do any good to dwell on the horrific way Alan had died. Not when I could be the next victim. If it really had something to do with the bloodrock, then it wouldn't be too big a leap to figure that I'd had the file. Unless they went after Ms Weston next. And no one had seen her all morning.

I couldn't get downstairs fast enough, and only when I'd reached the corridor to the prisoner's room did I stop. No one seemed to be around, but a door was open farther down. Not the prisoner's, of course—that was closed, but not locked, and I could hear the muted sound of voices within. Ms Weston.

I hesitated a second, then continued down the corridor like I'd intended to go that way all along. I knew what was behind that other door—it was the nurse's room, because last night, I'd put Ms Weston's clipboard back in there before heading back upstairs. Of course, Ms Weston would have all her notes with her, but it couldn't hurt to take a look.

"You again," said a voice as I walked in. The nurse, Saki, glanced up from behind a row of test tubes containing what looked like blood. "What do you want?"

I gestured towards the test tubes. "Is that—did you take blood from Ada? The prisoner?"

"Yes, after a fashion," she snapped. Still angry, then. "What are you doing in here, Walker?"

"Could you please not call me that?"

She blinked. "You know, I don't think I ever heard old Walker say 'please'."

So that's it. She had some issue with my father. Well, I didn't need to ask.

"Believe me, the name's all we have in common," I said. "Did you work out which world Ada's from, anyway?"

She blinked again. "Yeah, I did. Never would have guessed, but the tests don't lie. She's from Enzar." She shook her head. "Not mageblood, either."

I stared. "What? But she can use magic. How can she not be mageblood?"

"I don't know, but it's… look, you can't say a word about this to anyone, Walk… Kay. I shouldn't even be telling you this. But I've never, ever seen anything like this in all the years I've worked here. She's got some sort of anomaly in her blood. Someone… someone tampered with her."

I stepped back. And again.

Tampered with her.

It hit too close to home.

The image flashed before my eyes before I could push it back—the gleam of a needle, point shining with a black sheen unlike anything on Earth.

I had to get out of there.

Ignoring Saki's startled expression, I spun around to leave and came within inches of colliding with Ms Weston.

Damn.

CHAPTER THIRTEEN

KAY

"What were you doing in there?"

Words failed, for a moment. It was like listening to a distant recording to hear my own voice say, quite calmly, "I was just curious about the prisoner's test results. It intrigued me that I couldn't guess where she was from."

Her suspicion faded somewhat. Right answer. Not that it helped.

"Yes. Enzar. I never would have thought I'd get to meet an Enzarian, let alone a Royal."

"She's… Royal?" I asked.

"So it seems," said Ms Weston. "It somewhat complicates matters, because royal status would guarantee her protection under our roof."

The Alliance… damn. I could only imagine what having Enzarian royalty at Central would mean. If nothing else, the Alliance couldn't ignore Enzar's conflict any longer, whatever the reasons for blocking all contact.

"I heard she stole from the storerooms," I said.

"You seem to have heard a lot of things, Kay."

I held her stare. *What do you know? Is the bloodrock really connected with the murders? Is someone covering something up?*

I had firsthand experience of how quickly the Alliance could fabricate a cover story or just make evidence disappear entirely. Hell, the Alliance itself was founded on secrets—that was how they'd remained hidden from most people's sight until they'd gone public thirty years ago. Even within the Alliance, certain information was allowed only to the higher-up members, and with good reason. Like whatever was happening on Enzar. Like the details of most Ambassador missions, even the ones where people were killed.

Like…

An image—the gleam of a needle. I pushed it away.

No one knew. But there had to have been others at the Alliance involved, even if the instigator was long gone.

"Let me talk to her again," I said, surprised how steady my voice sounded. "Is she still resisting questioning?"

"I just told her the truth," said Ms Weston, not giving any sign of our silent exchange. "That ought to occupy her while I confer with the Law Division. Keeping royalty imprisoned reflects terribly on us, but she's dangerous, if not the killer we're looking for."

"You believe she's not the killer?"

She inclined her head. "The matter of the theft, we still have to deal with. But we have our suspicions. Carl told me about your report on the other night. It seems we have an unmapped

Passage."

"That staircase," I said, getting it. "They sent someone back to investigate?"

"Not yet, but we will. I would hazard a guess that this girl and whoever her accomplices are were using it to transport the stolen goods. A clever operation. If you want to talk to her, I'm sure she'll be more inclined to discuss the matter with you, especially anything concerning illicit activity in the Passages."

What the hell? How could she possibly know that?

"Your fellow graduate certainly had strong opinions on illegal trespassing," said Ms Weston. "If it wasn't for these sorry circumstances… but I need to go and meet with the Law Division. I'll give you half an hour, then I expect you back upstairs."

Damn. What the hell had I landed myself in now? So Aric had told my boss about the *incident.* I couldn't even wrap my head around that one, not after everything else. I was starting to feel like the world was shifting out from under my feet, slowly, inch by inch.

Dammit, Kay, pull yourself together. I drew in a deep breath, and headed for Ada's room.

***

ADA

The last thing I wanted was to talk to Kay Walker.

"What?" I said hoarsely, as he came into the room. There was no hiding that I'd been crying, and I thought I saw a flash of pity in his eyes before his expression blanked again.

"I wanted to ask you something," he said. He didn't say Ms Weston had sent him, but I wasn't an idiot. What was he, her lapdog?

"I'm not in the mood," I said. "You *locked* me in here overnight, sealed the place shut."

"You didn't give us an option, Ada!" He seemed edgier than he had before, though I could tell he tried to keep his voice steady.

"Yeah, I don't want to hear it," I said. "I am *through* with this shit."

"Sorry," he said, and for once, he met my eyes with something other than blankness. Like a person, not an Alliance guard. "I'm sorry I locked you in."

I blinked. Was he trying to catch me out by apologising? Implying it was my own fault I'd been locked in?

"Ms Weston—my supervisor—she's gone to plead your case to the Law Division."

I stared. "You what?"

"It's true."

I shook my head. I'd had it with the mind games here.

"I just wanted to know," he said, "why you stole bloodrock from the store rooms."

They know?

Like things weren't bad enough already. I slumped down, not even caring that he was watching. "They found it was missing."

"Why did you take it? It's important."

He didn't say to whom. Why would anyone want to know that? Perhaps... perhaps Kay Walker was just genuinely curious. But there was an urgency in his voice now, and although he assumed a casual stance, the tension in his shoulders gave it away.

Something had spooked him.

"I don't understand why it matters to you," I said.

"You didn't have it when I arrested you," he said. "So where is it? Did you sell it? Is that why you were in the Passages, you're involved in illicit offworld smuggling? Because bloodrock's a severely dangerous substance to be taken offworld, especially in the Passages."

Oh, he was back in condescending dickhead mode again.

"Please. Don't talk about what you don't understand. There are people who needed that stuff more than the Alliance does." Did it matter if he knew? There was no way it could be traced to all the places I'd taken it, least of all offworld.

"Enlighten me," he said. "Bloodrock is classified as a highly volatile magic-based substance for good reason. You're aware of the Balance, I'm sure? Even untrained magic-wielders know that there's a reason for our offworld trade laws."

"Oh, gods, shut up already," I said. "Yes, I'm aware of the freaking Balance. I'm not trying to destroy the Multiverse, I'm trying to protect my family." I stood, hands curling into fists, and glared. "Don't you have anything you care about? Wait, don't answer. I honestly couldn't give a shit. There's a whole Empire tearing itself to pieces out there and you bastards won't even lift a finger to help." I fought back angry tears. "I would do *anything* to protect my family. If you had a heart, you'd understand that."

Something flashed in his eyes. Through clenched teeth, he said, "Don't you assume *anything* about me, Ada."

His tone was calm, too calm. A shiver broke out on my arms. I'd really pissed him off.

And then I jumped out of my skin when a sudden vibration pounded against my ear. Kay's eyes widened. Oh, shit. The earpiece.

"Ada? Are you there?" said Jeth.

I froze and glanced at Kay, panic rising in my chest. He could hear.

My last chance to escape had gone.

"What is that?" he said. "Where did that voice come from?"

"Ada!"

"I'm here, Jeth," I said, dully. "I couldn't get out. I'm sorry."

Kay stared. "Is that what I think it is?"

"Jeth," I said. "I'm going to make a run for it now. Is there anyone outside?"

"Yeah, Nell is. We've been taking turns. Skyla stood out there half the night. Wait a minute and I'll give her the signal to create a diversion."

"Sure." I looked back at Kay, who still stared, completely bemused. "Really sorry about this," I said to him, and reached for the magic.

Boom.

The blast knocked me off balance before I'd had the chance to attack. The air rippled like someone had thrown a hit of magic and it had come spinning back at them. From Kay's expression, he hadn't been responsible, but he went for his communicator all the same. Calling for backup, maybe? It was too late for him, anyway. I was done. He was between me and the door and that was reason enough to hit him with everything I had.

Next thing I knew, I was pinned in a restraining position, flat on my stomach with my hands behind my back. "Stop that!" I gasped. "I use magic, I'll take out both of us."

"That's kind of the idea," he said, resting his knee on my spine. "Didn't you hear what I said? Ms Weston's pleading your case. You won't have to stay here much longer before you're free. You won't have a criminal record. You won't have to submit to the Alliance, not if you don't want to. Hell, you don't even have to tell me why you wanted that bloodrock so badly—

194

but two people have died for it already and I'm not going to let you escape and put more lives in danger."

The air trembled again. I could see the threads of magic pulsing, purple and red as sunset, which made no sense, because it wasn't supposed to be visible on Earth.

"What the *hell* is going on?" Kay said. "Whatever your friends are doing, tell them to stop it before someone gets hurt."

Then Jeth's voice in my ear. "Who's there? Who was that? Is he *threatening* you?"

"I'm trapped, Jeth," I said, the side of my face pressed into the carpet. "Look—maybe I was a bit hasty. They know I'm not the killer. I think. Apparently, they might let me go the legal way…"

"I wish you'd told me that before I gave Nell and Skyla the go-ahead to bust you out of there."

A pause. "Oh," I said.

Another blast rocked the room. Now I could tell what was happening. Someone had caused such a magical disturbance, it had a ripple effect on all the other magic in the vicinity. But my arms were held above my back and Kay wasn't budging despite the trembling floor. I wriggled, trying to grab for the communicator still in his hand.

Boom.

This time, the blast shook one of my hands free, and the split-second advantage was enough for me to touch the communicator. My skin buzzed with the magic, so strong it blanked out my thoughts, and before I could hesitate and think about how stupid my plan was, I'd already sent a bolt of magic into the communicator.

Kay swore and let go of me as the magic exploded. The device burst in a shower of bright, purplish sparks and sent both of us flying back. But I was ready. The door didn't have a lock on the inside, and I ran for it.

"Ada!" Kay's shouts followed me as I pelted out the room and upstairs. Again, I found myself weaving through panic. Guards ran everywhere, and with every step, the noise grew louder. Purple sparks flew overhead, and I picked up speed, cursing the stairs for slowing me down—hands grabbed for my feet. and I kicked out—like hell was I going to be dragged back now.

And then I was out in the entrance hall. I ran flat out for the exit, my heart lifting when I saw the silhouette of a familiar figure, one I'd missed more than I'd ever thought possible.

Nell.

A beam of red light whizzed over my head, and sparks ignited the air. Skyla. She was throwing magic, and each blast triggered a backlash that made the air vibrate. *Hell—that's second level!* Guards ran about, dodging the blasts, and it was easy to strike out a path through the centre—to freedom.

Nell and Skyla stood back to back by the exit, and a few

unconscious guards lay around them. I laughed with relief and sprinted the rest of the way out the door.

Nell's hair straggled loose from its bun and she'd acquired bruises on her face, but appeared otherwise unhurt. "Skyla, that's enough!"

Skyla laughed. "God, I've always wanted to do that. Okay, okay. Let's run."

And damn, did we run. Nell must have taken out an entire guard patrol. I recognised one of the fallen guards as Aric. Ha. We skirted the building and made for the gate, while shouts and bangs from Skyla's magical assault echoed in our wake.

"Thanks," I gasped between breaths. We turned and headed down the road. "I mean it—thanks."

"We're not safe yet," said Nell, who as usual was several strides ahead of me despite us being the same height. "We need to find a crowded place."

We aimed for London Bridge, running out of a tangle of side streets, and saw the tube station ahead. Crowds of commuters poured in and out of the station, and the streets were clogged with people. I half expected Nell to order us to run out into the road.

"I'm not going to get mowed down by a bus!" I said, clutching at a stitch in my side. "At least use the crossing like normal people."

Nell shot me a glare. "Normal people don't break out of

prison and escape through the middle of London!"

"Fair point."

Skyla laughed between gasps. "This is the most fun I've had in months."

"I'm glad to hear you two find this amusing!" said Nell. "What you did in there, Skyla, was dangerous—*so* dangerous—you shouldn't be playing with second level magic, even on Earth!"

"Lighten up, Nell," said Skyla. "It was all I could think of to get her out of there."

"And it was amazing," I said.

"Thank Jeth," said Nell. "Did you know you were wearing the earpiece?"

She knew me too well. "Don't ruin my victory, dammit!"

The lights changed and we hightailed it across the road. I was riding high on adrenaline and though the fear of being followed hadn't quite dispersed, this was one of the most crowded parts of London. Still, I went tense again as we queued to ride the tube—Nell had had the foresight to bring my Oyster card. It'd be ridiculous to get apprehended for not paying train fare after breaking out of Central.

The train was rammed, so we didn't get a chance to talk until we'd disembarked and were hurrying from the station, heading home.

Home. I could have cried. At last. I practically skipped to the front door, realising belatedly that I didn't have my key. In fact, the Alliance still had my purse and ID and phone, too. Good job I'd used a fake address.

"Crap, my stuff's back at Central," I said, stepping back to let Nell unlock the door. "Is Jeth around, by the way?"

"The earpiece's battery ran out," said Nell. "That's why it took him so long to answer your call."

"Glad we got to trounce Central, anyway," said Skyla, grinning. "That was fun."

"Holy freaking crap," said a voice, and I almost tripped over the doorstep as Alber tackle-hugged me.

"Alber—I can't breathe, you idiot!"

"You're the idiot," he said, voice muffled in my shoulder. "I thought—dammit, Ada, don't you do that to us again!"

Nell shoved me from behind. "Get in the house, people will come outside to see what the racket's about. Honestly."

I couldn't stop smiling. *We won*, I thought. *We beat the Alliance…*

But Nell wasn't smiling. A cold feeling grew, masking the happy buzz. Did she know what the Royals had done to me?

Was that really a conversation I wanted to have with her right now?

Tainted blood. Something had been *implanted* in me, when I was a baby, back on Enzar. Something that gave me the ability to use magic…

I'd never thought of it as unnatural before, but it chilled me to think of someone doing that to a baby. Even though I knew what the Enzarian Royals were capable of. I'd long since accepted that I could do nothing about my heritage. But now it gave me a bad taste in my mouth. I wished I'd stayed ignorant.

"We need to leave," Nell said. "As soon as Jeth gets home. Alber, Ada, go and pack a rucksack for a few days away."

"Wait, what?" I asked.

"We can't risk staying here. People have seen us, and the Alliance will have circulated our names and faces within the day. All three of us. It'll only be one step to finding where we live. We'll go and lie low at one of the shelters."

Alber, like me, gaped at her. "You can't be serious," he said. "They don't know we live here."

"They're clever, and there are far more of them than there are of us. Once our photographs get into circulation… well, it looks like we'll be needing to get some of that bloodrock back."

My heart lurched. "You mean, change our own appearances. Like the refugees."

Nell had never wanted to do that to me. Yes, I had to wear coloured contacts, but nothing else about my appearance screamed *offworld*. Same with Nell. Obviously, safety came first, but if I was honest with myself, I always wondered what it would be like to be able to walk around without my real eyes hidden. Sometimes I even slept wearing the lenses, and I certainly didn't remove them anywhere other than home. Most people would run screaming from diamond-white eyes with pitch-black circles around the pupils. I could keep the lenses in for up to a day and not notice, but by now, it was like a constant itch. I had to take them out.

"We don't have a choice, Ada," she said quietly. "Every second we waste here gives the Alliance more opportunity to strike. One bag, each. Skyla, can I have a word?"

Skyla was peering through the letterbox. "Sure."

I could hardly believe this was happening. Would I ever see my comfy box-sized room again? I grabbed a rucksack, giving myself a mental kick, and started filling it. Clothes. A battered sci-fi paperback. All the knives I had (sheathed, of course). After changing from the outfit the Alliance had given me into my own clothes, I stuck one in my boot. Too bad I'd have to leave my last spare pair behind—those combat boots didn't come cheap. But carrying them would only slow me down.

I ran to the bathroom to pick up other essentials—toothbrush, towel, spare contacts. Getting the old contacts out was a relief to my sore eyes. I'd have liked to leave them out, just for a short time, but I hated even Nell seeing my real eyes. Hated that they marked the difference between me and her, that they were a reminder that she'd been a slave and I'd have been—what? A soldier? I didn't like to think about it. Magic-wielders tended to have an odd quality to their eyes, like Skyla's glittering black ones. But mine were practically transparent, while my pupils were like gleaming dark orbs. They'd have creeped me out on anyone else.

I was used to being different. But not like this. Not knowing there was something… alien in my blood. Whatever they'd done, I had no memory of it, but I'd only been a year old when Nell had brought me here.

Nell.

I went back into the hall to find Alber already packed and waiting, and Skyla hovering near the door. A rucksack lay at Nell's feet, too. My throat closed up with unasked questions.

"Nell," I said. "Where are we going, exactly?" *Coward.* But I just couldn't ask with Alber and Skyla standing right there.

"To the Knight family's place. It's the nearest, and they have bloodrock in stores."

I knew that because I'd been the one to deliver it what felt like a lifetime ago.

Nell's phone buzzed. "That'll be Jeth," she said. "He's almost home."

The minutes stretched into awkwardness, no one wanting to acknowledge the humongous elephant in the room. Eventually, Alber asked, "Did they mistreat you? Because I'll kick the ever-loving shit out of them if they did."

"No…" I hesitated. "Some of the guards were douches, but I *did* try to escape a few times." And then there was Kay Walker. I had no idea what to even think about him. Let's face it, I'd been a total ass. He might be annoying, but he was only doing his job. He'd said his supervisor was going to try to get me out…

I shook my head. I wasn't going to think about the Alliance, not now I was free.

"Bet you gave them a run for their money," said Alber. "Come on, give us the details."

Nell flashed him a warning look, but the silence was really getting to me, so I gave him a rundown of my capture, and the times I'd tried to escape. I didn't mention Ms Weston's assessment of me. I'd confront Nell in private, later.

Skyla listened with detached interest. "Good on you for fighting back," she said. "Did they really not plan to let you go?"

"I don't know," I said. "See, there was another murder when I tried to escape the second time. I couldn't have done it, and they knew that, but it slowed everything down. The woman who was interrogating me—Ms Weston—she was going to take my case to the Law Division. But then Jeth contacted me."

"Weston?" said Skyla. "She interrogated you?"

"You know her?"

"I've eavesdropped on enough patrols. She has a reputation."

"That figures," I said, with a slight shudder. "She's scarier than you, Nell. No offence."

Nell glared. I smiled benignly back.

Then there was a click of a key in the lock, and everyone

jumped about a foot in the air—Nell ran to the door and slammed the person into the nearest wall.

"It's only me!" said Jeth, hands raised, as Nell came within inches of getting him in a chokehold. "Jesus Christ, Nell." As she stepped back, he saw me, and grinned. His fair hair stood on end like he'd been running his hands through it. "Holy shit, Ada. You're alive." He wrapped me in a bear hug.

"Cheers, Jeth," I said, swallowing the lump in my throat. "It's... it's good to be home." Dammit, I'd shed more tears over the past twenty-four hours than in the previous year. I stepped away from Jeth and looked at Nell. "Guess this is it?"

"Gimme a sec to get my stuff," said Jeth.

"You are *not* bringing any computers," Nell shouted after him.

"But my Xbox," said Alber. "Seriously, Nell, is this *really* necessary? We just disappear? My friends will wonder what happened to me."

"And my coworkers," said Jeth. "But safety first, right? I hoped this wouldn't happen, but well, you know, we're in a risky business."

"You're not," I said. "It's my fault. I brought this on all of us."

"Don't you ever say that," said Alber. "Seriously, stop talking, now. It is *not* your fault. Blame the dickheads at the Alliance."

"Yes," said Skyla. "This is all their doing. If it wasn't for them making life so difficult for us…"

"Enough," said Nell. "Jeth, are you ready?"

"Sure." Jeth emerged from his room wearing a camper-style backpack. "All right. Where to?"

"Tube station. We'll head west. Pretend we're tourists."

"Easy," said Alber, eyeing Jeth's backpack. "All right. Let's go."

No one was outside, and the street was quiet. We moved in a tight-knit group, not speaking. We passed by the broken-down pub by the alley that led to the Passages.

A whisper sounded—the only warning we got. They came out of the shadows like ghosts, but solid and grey and covered in armoured scales. Nell attacked so quickly her arms became a blur, knocking one to the ground with a series of blows. I spun around and delivered a kick to another that sent it sprawling. The rucksack on my back slowed me down, but I moved to kick another away from Alber. But they kept coming. Dreyvern, or 'goblins', were not like the small, crafty creatures from fairy tales. They were vicious killers.

And some had knives. I ducked a blow from one of them and backed into Jeth. The five of us now stood back to back.

A much bigger creature lumbered out of the alleyway, tusks bared and spittle flying madly. Oh, hell. A chalder vox—and high on pain. I screamed a warning. Nell kicked a dreyvern flying, and it got up, its natural armour having absorbed most of the blow. The chalder vox shifted towards us, its heavy body knocking pieces of brick from the alley walls, and I had a brief, stunned moment to wonder how it got out of the Passages before its fist came at my face.

CHAPTER FOURTEEN

KAY

"She did *what?*" Ms Weston's shout could have shattered the windows. "You let her escape *again?*"

"It was that or kill both of us," I said. "She somehow directed a magical charge into my communicator and destroyed it. The energy in that thing—it was impossible not to let her go. Level two at least."

Ms Weston stood across from me, behind her desk, wrapped in a thundercloud of rage. I'd already mentally braced myself for those dreaded words, the ones that would exile me from the Multiverse forever.

I didn't even want to contemplate what came after.

Ms Weston gave an impatient sigh. "I don't know what to do with you, Kay, to be quite honest. We have lost a valuable prisoner, and if you hadn't taken it upon yourself to interfere, it might not have happened."

"She would have escaped sooner or later," I said, aware that this was no excuse for fucking up like I had. "She had accomplices—and at least one magic-wielder among them."

"Yes, it seems we might have a group of rogue magic-wielders on our hands. At any rate, there were witnesses, and we know the faces of her two companions."

"There were more," I said. "She talked to someone. She had a communication device, an earpiece, but I couldn't see it. She was stripped down, right?"

"Yes, she was searched quite thoroughly. However, judging by the technology employed to lock her mobile phone, it's safe to conclude that she has skilled friends out there somewhere."

As if we didn't have enough to worry about. After Ada had fled, it was chase her or subdue the smoking communicator, and common sense had won out. I didn't want the device she'd blasted with second level magic destroying half of Central.

"What she did with the communicator," I said. "She released pure magical energy into Alliance technology." Dangerous—and a damn good idea, too. I was kind of impressed, though I'd have been less so if I hadn't dropped the thing before it burned my hands off.

"That she did," said Ms Weston. "I'll arrange for you to receive a new one."

She's not firing me. I could breathe easier again.

"However, this situation is out of hand. The murders aside, we have good reason to suspect there might be an underworld of illicit magical activity here in London itself. Even within the Passages."

The Passages. "The untracked one must be the one she

used. If we can find it, it'll lead us right to her. It *must* be near where she lives, or at the very least, the place where these illegal immigrants from offworld are sheltering."

Ms Weston nodded. Her anger had all but evaporated now. "Excellent. We'll need to send in an investigatory team. Would you be willing to lead?"

I stared. Didn't expect that, not after I'd been deemed *disappointing,* let alone the total clusterfuck of Ada's escape. "Of course," I said. It was a chance to make up for the fiasco earlier. To redeem my position in the Alliance. And find out what was really going on with Ada. Why she'd stolen bloodrock.

Someone tampered with her.

"Good. Unfortunately, a number of novices were attacked earlier, as I'm sure you know."

Yeah. Aric had been one of them. It was the shining light in an otherwise-craptacular day. Though it raised the question: who on Earth had the training to kick the crap out of a bunch of Alliance guards? There had only been two of them. I'd missed it all thanks to that communicator and the magic energy flying around the entrance hall. Two people had launched a *direct magical assault* on Central. What the hell were we up against?

Even two stunners didn't feel like enough, but it was as many as they'd give novices going into the Passages. My team was assembled in the entrance hall. No one I'd spoken to before. Lenny was hiding in the office, having been taken off the patrol rota, Ellen had left early. I made a mental note to call her later, and then remembered my communicator was fried.

Carl came over to me before I led the team out. "Here," he said, handing me a new communicator. "This one's all set up. Just type in a new pass code."

"Cheers, man," I said.

"Good luck—you'll need it."

Tell me about it. But I gave orders to the novices with as much authority as I could summon. Judging by the looks some of them gave me, the Walker name's reputation preceded me. Well, at least it'd make it easier.

There's a whole Empire tearing itself to pieces out there, and you bastards won't even lift a finger to help. I would do anything to protect my family. If you had a heart, you'd understand that.

Her anger carried a ring of truth. One I understood too well. Damn it all. Ada was beyond reach now. And yet... she'd been dead right that the Alliance had overlooked the war in the Empire for too long. Obviously, interfering in magical warfare was suicide, but it was like I'd said to Markos. There were other options.

And I had reason enough to challenge the noninterference stance. It sure as hell didn't come from the entire Alliance. Just the council, or one name in particular. Twenty years ago. There were only three council members present at Central right now, and none of them had any ties to the Walker family.

I hadn't wanted to get involved with them. I'd joined the Alliance intending to stay far away from the politics which had got my mother killed offworld thirteen years ago—not to mention avoid magic at all costs. So far, I'd failed on all counts. But if I could just do this one thing…

A wild scheme was forming in my mind—totally batshit crazy. Like the insanity of the past few days had unhinged me, I thought it might actually work. My name alone would make the council sit up and listen. That much I could count on.

My rational side hoped I wasn't about to do something I'd regret.

Into the Passages. The same route Carl had led our team around before, down the sloping corridor to the lower level. No one said a word, but we kept in formation ready for an attack. This was the same place we'd found two chalder voxes, after all. My hand twitched on the stunner, the slight buzz of magic against my fingers like a building charge.

The chalder voxes' bodies were gone, but the stench remained, and so did the green-lit side corridor. I indicated to the others to keep behind me and led the way towards the light. A faint gleam, like sunlight through an open door just out of sight. A staircase, and it led down to the lower level. I led the way, stunner at the ready. This was Cethrax's stomping ground. Even the Alliance hadn't mapped out this place. Blood streaked the walls. Wyvern blood. So it *had* come from down here.

The echo of footsteps was the only noise that sounded in the warren of corridors. And there were no doors, no stairs. Not yet. But the wyvern's blood must be a clue. Ada had got into the Passages somehow, before she'd been chased. Not through the Alliance's entrance. Which meant only one thing.

A knife swung through the shadows. I reacted instinctively, grabbing the owner's hand and snapping the wrist. A squeal of pain, and then the dreyvern fully materialised, howling. Its ugly body was covered in grey scales, and its now-useless arm dropped to its side as I took the knife. It wailed, threatened by its own weapon, and turned to run. I kicked it in the ribs, and it slumped over on the ground—but there were more of them ahead.

And a door, open wide. Unmistakable. On the other side was a brick wall. This was our hidden door, all right. A group of dreyverns was clustered around it—I counted at least twelve of them. My heart rate kicked up, and adrenaline surged through my veins, heightened by the magic.

The obvious thing to do would be to back off as quickly as possible. But the cry of the fallen dreyvern caused the others to turn in our direction. There were eight of us, but we were still outnumbered.

A knife flew towards our group, and pandemonium took over. I prepared to fight for my life.

***

ADA

I ducked the punch and grabbed onto the underside of the chalder vox's massive arm. It roared, trying to shake me off, but I moved fast. As I climbed, I spotted a jagged wound in its side like a knife strike, but since its skin was like concrete, whatever cut it had to be something seriously strong.

My own knife was in my hand. I had to get to the weak point–

"Ada!"

Claws brushed my leg. A dreyvern had followed me, and its claws digging into the chalder vox's skin sent the monster into a frenzy. I was forced to hold on with both hands, still clutching the dagger, while avoiding swipes from the dreyvern's own knife. Cursing, I let go before it impaled my leg, remembering to duck and roll as I hit the ground. The chalder vox bellowed and ran back into the alley, hitting the walls on either side, totally out of it.

Jeth was trading blows with another dreyvern, using the massive backpack to absorb its knife strikes, while Alber and Skyla took on another pair of them. And Nell had moved to the front of the group, a blur of strikes and slashes with a dagger. We were no strangers to fighting Cethraxian monsters. But I couldn't use magic. There were too many of us to risk it.

I kicked the dreyvern into the nearest wall, my thick boot muting the impact of its armour. It slashed back, face stretched in a manic grin, and I kicked at its weapon hand. It moved like a shadow, and I cursed. I'd forgotten they had the same irritating disappearing trick as the chalder voxes.

The knife came down, drawing a line of fire on my arm. I gasped from the pain, my own weapon slipping in my sweaty hand. I stabbed at its arm but missed, and was forced to back up a step—into the path of another dreyvern.

My injured arm moved like it was weighted. Time slowed down. And then Nell was there, delivering a flying kick to the dreyvern's face. There was a satisfying *crunch* as the blow connected and the creature fell.

The second dreyvern stabbed at her. I whirled in, ignoring the stinging pain in my arm, and brought my boot down on its clawed foot. It yelped, and I took the opportunity to stab its weapon hand. Blood spurted, and the knife clattered to the ground. I dived to retrieve it.

Another knife came flying out of the shadows, past me, and struck Nell in the shoulder.

Time seemed to slow again. I was aware that several voices screamed, *"Nell!"* A roaring in my ears drowned all other sound. The dreyvern grinned a crooked smile.

I kicked it, again and again, driving it into the wall. Adrenaline surged in my veins. *You hurt Nell. I'll kill you.*

I screamed in pure rage, stabbing my dagger into the dreyvern's exposed neck.

Blood spurted in a fountain, more than I'd expected. I fell back, weakness pulling at my limbs. Jeth and Skyla fought side by side, three fallen dreyverns at their feet. And Alber was crouched over a fallen body. Nell.

"God, no." I pulled the dagger out of the monster's neck, shuddering. I'd never killed so violently before. So much blood... "Nell. Please. Be okay."

"Holy *shit!*" Jeth yelled, and I threw myself over Nell as brick exploded above our heads. The chalder vox was back. And raging mad.

I jumped to my feet, willing my legs to stop shaking. Now wasn't the time to panic. The chalder vox roared and flailed its four branch-like arms, knocking huge chunks out of the alley wall. It saw us, and cold horror seized me—it was preparing to charge.

"Get out of the way!" someone shouted.

My mouth fell open. Kay ran down the alleyway, caught the back of the monster's arm, and used it to launch himself into the air. He landed on the creature's back. A dagger flashed, the chalder vox screamed—and fell.

"I said, get out of the way!" shouted Kay, leaping clear of the falling monster. Alber and I pulled Nell aside, and the chalder vox came down like a ton of concrete.

A sudden current of magic made the hairs stand up on my arms, and two dreyverns ran past the fallen monster. Kay swore, reacting to intercept one of them—a *snapping* sound, and the dreyvern fell. Skyla kicked at the second, her face a mask of fury. She kept kicking it even when it was on the ground.

"Skyla! Stop." Jeth went over to her. Alber remained by Nell, pale and staring, arms at his sides. "People are watching…"

I turned to where he was pointing. My heart dropped. I should have guessed we'd draw an audience. People had come out of the nearby houses—old and young, teenagers, families—and all wore varied expressions of shock and terror, like a horror movie had played out right in front of them. I supposed it had. None of them knew about the

Passage, after all, and most people preferred not to acknowledge the monsters that lived a heartbeat away.

"Where are *you* going?" Jeth demanded. He was talking to Kay, who'd moved back into the alley entrance.

"I have to check on my team, make sure there aren't any more dreyverns in the Passage." He appeared remarkably unruffled for someone who'd just been in a fight, and his dark eyes seemed to shine with contained excitement.

"Oh, shit. He knows." Alber swallowed, looking sick. "Nell..."

"Is she...?" My voice choked. She lay very still, blood soaking her shoulder.

"She's breathing."

I sighed, relief seeping through my aching limbs. My arm throbbed, blood dripping from the wound, but thankfully it was only a shallow cut.

"Come on. We need to get her out of here," said Jeth, coming back over with Skyla. "Shit. We can't use the Passages now. We don't have any of the bloodrock solution, either, we gave the last of it to that Enzar family..." He looked helplessly at Nell. Like it had just hit him how much we depended on her guidance.

"You need to move." Kay was back. "There's a full guard patrol back there, and there's not much I can do to stop them arresting all of you."

"Then get on with it," I said, wearily. "You win." Nell's injury had shaken the fight out of me.

"I'm not going to do that," he said, and for a second, I thought I'd misheard. "Your friend needs medical attention."

"Yes, but our faces will be plastered over half London by now," I snapped. "Thanks to the Alliance. Besides, we have friends who can help."

"That's foolish," he said. "She'll die before you get to wherever you're planning to take her."

"I'll call an ambulance, then. Oh, wait, you dickheads *stole my phone*."

"I'll call," Jeth said quickly, digging in his pocket.

"You can't be serious." Skyla shot Kay a look of contempt. "He works for the Alliance. You're not going to let him order you around?"

"Nell's in trouble," said Jeth, dialling. "Hello? We need an ambulance…"

"Where are you going?" Alber said to Kay, who'd half retreated into the alley.

I stood up and followed him. "Wait! You're running off?"

"I'm ordering my patrol to clear up this mess," he said, indicating the bodies of the fallen dreyverns and the massive lump that was the chalder vox. Shadows still streamed where he'd stabbed it, and blood spattered the ground. "I think there might be complaints if we leave them here, though they do add a certain character."

"It's not funny," I snapped. Seriously, he chose *now* to demonstrate a sense of humour? Then again, he was an Alliance guard and an Academy graduate to boot. From what I'd heard about Academy students, they got unimaginably bored unless there was a threat of imminent death.

The image of the dreyvern's blood spraying out replayed before I could stop it. I shook my head, determined not to dwell on the fight. Nell needed us.

"And then you're taking me back there. Right?"

He looked at me, hesitating for a moment. "You know you shouldn't have run, Ada. If you come without a fuss, we might be able to get you a trial. Ms Weston thinks you could be valuable to the Alliance."

"You're joking," I said. "What makes you think I'd ever work for you?"

"You might change your mind." He pulled his communicator from his pocket, keeping one eye on me like he expected me to grab for it again.

"Is this it? You're reporting us?"

He glanced down at the communicator, then back at me. "You know I don't have a choice." His gaze moved to Nell, just for a second, like he hadn't been able to help it. Then he flicked the touch screen. Looked like he was typing something. Probably an order.

"Oh, for heaven's sake," I said, desperately. "Do we look like career criminals? I told you, I'm protecting my family. You arrest us, that's it. We lose everything. Nell probably dies. We get deported back to a war zone. Everyone loses, except you, and I hope you're bloody happy about it."

"You won't be deported. You're under the Alliance's protection, like I told you. At worst, you'll have to register as offworld immigrants and maybe pay for damages to headquarters—not that you did much damage. That place is pretty tough. If you tell me why you stole from the Alliance, I can clear your name, too."

"Yeah. A likely story."

"It's true. I'm not trying to trick you, Ada. I don't know what you've heard about the Alliance, but we're not heartless monsters. It's our prerogative to help, offworld or otherwise."

There was the tiniest hint of bitterness in the way he said *heartless monsters* that puzzled me. Made me pause.

"The bloodrock," he said. "All we want to know is what you were planning to do with it. I just heard your brother say something about… a bloodrock solution? Something you need. To escape."

I could see him piecing it together. He'd heard Jeth. But if he knew what bloodrock could do already, why ask? And the guards hadn't materialised yet. What had he typed into the communicator?

I shook my head. "It's just a disguise. That's all we use it for."

"You're wearing a disguise?" He frowned.

"Uh. No. It's for…"

"Enzar. There are more of you."

No. I took a step back, too stunned, too shaken to hide what I was thinking.

"Ada, I'm not going to arrest anyone. If there's anyone else in the same situation as you, they're under the Alliance's protection by default."

I gave a humourless laugh. "Nice try."

"It's true. Human rights come before the noninterference law. First principle of the Alliance—you must know it."

I *did* know it. The Alliance's mandate. And none of the refugees had broken any laws except running from a world where they'd otherwise have died or been forced to fight in a war.

Exactly what the Alliance worked to prevent from happening.

"Yeah," I said, finally. "I know the laws."

"So you make disguises? For people from Enzar?"

Damn him for being so bloody perceptive. "Nell does. The Alliance forbids any contact with that world. There's no other way to do it."

"So that's what you stole the bloodrock for?"

I crossed my arms defensively. "Why's it so hard for you to believe?"

"People have been killed over it," he said.

I shook my head again. "That's… that has nothing to do with us. We only steal the bloodrock because we need it, the refugees need it. Not like there's a legal shelter anywhere around here."

"No." He glanced down at his communicator, looking preoccupied. "There aren't any in London at all."

"I know that," I said. "What's it to you anyway?"

"Because I know there's one run by New York's Alliance branch. They've a whole network set up—it wouldn't be too far out there to link it to Enzar."

"What?" I couldn't be hearing this right.

"Honestly, most of the Alliance employees at Central don't know how bad the situation in the Empire is—even I only know the basics. People are really escaping? Like you?"

I didn't want to talk about that. He seemed to notice, and said, "Okay. I know how you feel about the Alliance. But I can at least put you in touch with someone who works at US Central. Once this mess is cleared up."

No freaking way. "Yeah, right. I'm not going back to Central."

"I'm not tricking you. I can pull strings in the Alliance.

Help the others from your homeworld."

He might as well have sucker punched me in the chest. "That isn't something to joke about."

"You think—" He cut himself off, running a hand through his hair. "I don't know what more I can do. I'll talk to the council. You don't have to believe I will, but I'm not your enemy, Ada. And I don't lie."

I gaped. Who the hell *was* Kay Walker? I didn't dare believe him. The very idea that the refugees could get out legally—could have a genuine chance to build new lives—it was the one thing we could never have. Nell had drilled it into me so often it was inconceivable to assume otherwise. But she was lying on the ground, close to death, the world had upended itself, and never mind the freaking Balance. Reality itself felt like it was out of sync.

I couldn't deal with it. And I couldn't even look at the man who'd torn my life apart and then promised me something I'd never, not for a second, conceived of as possible.

A way to keep everyone safe.

If he was lying, I'd tear him to pieces, and yet I knew it would never, ever be enough. If he had any idea what those words meant...

Maybe I should just stop assuming anything. Accept what happened as part of a wacky, stress-induced hallucination.

There was no other way it made sense.

Kay was speaking into his communicator. I hadn't even heard, like the shock had muted all sound. But now he put the device away. "I have to take care of this," he said, his tone flat. Emotionless again. "We can't leave corpses in the middle of the street. I doubt the local council will be happy about it."

"Yeah." I drew in a shuddering breath. "But if your team comes in, they'll arrest me—arrest all of us. Right?"

"I delayed them," he said. "Told them to clean out the dead dreyverns in the Passages. But I can only keep them back for so long. Go in the ambulance. I'll come and find you later."

"You know where we'll—right, the hospital."

"I'll find you," he said. "You go back to your friends, okay?"

This was surreal. He was actually letting us go. What the hell had got into Kay Walker? I didn't know, and God, I was so scared for Nell, but for a moment, at least, we had a plan.

The ambulance didn't take long, and Kay, who'd remained at the alley entrance, moved back into the shadows and was gone in an instant.

CHAPTER FIFTEEN

KAY

What had I got myself into?

Once my team had cleared out the monsters' corpses, I then had to come up with an explanation for Ms Weston as to how Ada had got away. Again.

I'd lost it. I'd really lost it. Helping a former prisoner? And what the hell had I been thinking offering to call Simon? Like anyone else needed to be dragged into this mess. But this was different. Maybe it was proof of my naïve idiot stupidity, but what bugged me most about the way things had gone for me at Central was the sense that it was damned impossible to do anything remotely *useful*, even to solve the murders that were happening right there in the office. Let alone the crap-ton of problems out there in the Multiverse that Ambassadors like my mother had given their lives trying to solve. It might be idealistic to think I might be able to make the slightest bit of a difference, but I could at least use the blasted Walker name for something decent. For Enzar.

For Ada. I'd seen it in her eyes. She'd not lied. Her story matched the facts. And yet, whether she'd stolen from the Alliance didn't seem important anymore. *We lose everything,* she'd said. Because of the Alliance.

Because of me.

She hadn't believed me about the shelter. I should never have expected her to. Her distrust of the Alliance ran so deep, nothing I said would change her mind. There was a good chance she'd scream the place down tomorrow. She wore a defensive shell I recognised all too clearly.

Idiot, Kay.

So Ada had agreed to come back. The fact remained that I'd let her and four others, walk free, including the two people who'd assaulted half the security team. But I'd known from the look on Ada's face that the injured woman had been important—like a mother figure. I couldn't take her away now. I refused to believe that there was no one in the Alliance who would have made the same choice. Ms Weston was just going to have to deal with it.

So I'd given my orders. Cleaned up the Passages, arranged for other teams to come and check out the hidden entrance. There was no clue as to where these other shelters might be. I'd leave that for later.

Back to Central and Ms Weston's wrath.

But she wasn't there. Gone home, I guessed. It was late evening by this time. *So it's postponed until tomorrow,* I thought, delivering my report to Carl. He didn't ask too many questions.

"Bring on the weekend," he said, putting his communicator

away. "No bloody overtime pay for dealing with this mess… no matter. You go home."

"Sure." Except I wasn't going back to my apartment, I was driving across London to make sure Ada kept her word, because I'd officially lost it. And tomorrow, I'd probably lose my *job*. If I brought Ada tomorrow, then maybe…

Like redeeming myself mattered, I thought as I drove through late-evening traffic. The truth was, I'd seen that look before, the total devastation when Ms Weston had dropped the bombshell on her. Even through those coloured contact lenses, I'd seen the fear that whatever had happened to her—had been *done* to her—had made her something other than human.

And God, did I wish I could have said something. But I could just picture her reaction.

There's a whole Empire tearing itself to pieces out there and you bastards won't even lift a finger to help. I would do anything to protect my family. If you had a heart, you'd understand that.

I tightened my grip on the steering wheel, willing the goddamned traffic to move faster, and switched on the radio to drown out my own thoughts.

***

ADA

Nell was taken in for surgery immediately. With nothing else to do, we sat in the waiting room, numb with shock. Alber barely said a word, and Jeth wasn't very conversational either. Skyla left shortly after Nell went in, saying she had to get home, but she'd call later.

I took the opportunity to check my bag for damage. Somehow my possessions had survived intact, though the bag was clawed up from the dreyvern attack. But my clothes were okay. I hurried off to find the ladies', unable to stand another minute sitting there covered in blood. Luckily, the cut on my own arm had stopped bleeding. Shallow wound. But when Jeth spotted it, he told the doctor so I could get it bandaged. Few other people were around, and no one else was in the waiting room. It had that hospital-bleach smell I hated, and every time a nurse passed by, I went tense. I looked out the window instead, but there was nothing to see but a car park and the sinking sun. I was worn ragged, and if not for the worry for Nell, I'd have curled up on a chair and fallen asleep. I started shaking all over, whether with the adrenaline drain or the fact that I hadn't slept or eaten in over a day, I didn't know. Or maybe it was shock. Too much had happened at once. I just couldn't process it. I leaned on Jeth's shoulder and closed my eyes, and he patted my head absently.

"Hang in there, Ada. Nell's tough. She'll be fine."

Alber swallowed. He sat on the opposite seat with his feet up, the colour leached from his face by the harsh fluorescent lights. "I hope so," he said.

"Why did that Alliance guy let us go?" Jeth asked no one in particular. "I don't get it. Is he reporting us?"

I lifted my head from Jeth's shoulder. "I said I'd go back. Listen—the Alliance thinks I'm important. To them." I paused. The secret was seconds from slipping out.

"Important?" said Jeth, giving me a sidelong look of confusion. "Because you're a magic-wielder?"

"It's... more than that." I glanced at Alber. "They tested my blood. I'm not—I'm not mageblood. I'm Royal. Someone *did* something to me back on Enzar. I was only a baby, I don't remember. But it changed me. Somehow. It's why I can use magic." I closed my eyes. "I was going to ask—to ask—"

I swallowed against the lump in my throat.

"Nell," said Jeth, and put an arm around me.

"*Did something* to you?" said Alber, fists clenching. "Who hurt you?"

"I'm not hurt," I said. "It's just—a shock. I'm related to, to..."

"Not another word." Alber came over and hugged me, too, creating a weird group hug.

And then out of the corner of my eye, I saw someone

enter the room. I glanced up.

Kay stared at the three of us like we were aliens. Under normal circumstances, I'd have laughed. His dark Alliance guard uniform made him look out of place under the bright lights.

"You came?" I said, shifting away from the others. Alber stood, fidgeting awkwardly.

"She's in surgery," Jeth said flatly. "None of us are going anywhere until we know she's okay."

"That's fine," said Kay. "I wanted to talk to Ada."

"Talk away," said Jeth, glaring.

Kay didn't look away from me. "We need to discuss matters which are confidential to the Alliance."

"Good God, you're a pretentious dickhead, aren't you?" said Jeth.

He might as well have spoken to a brick wall. "Ada?"

I sighed, standing up. "Sure, whatever." Jeth and Alber exchanged surprised glances, but I was too tired to argue.

Outside the waiting room, Kay said, "I sent in my report, but I haven't heard from Ms Weston yet. She's not likely to be pleased that I let you go."

"Oh, what a shame," I said. "Does anything matter more than your job?"

"If it didn't, I wouldn't be here," Kay said quietly. "Any other guard would have brought you in. But what you said—

about the refugees—you're right. The Alliance needs to do something. Half our council's offworld at the moment, so I can't promise it'll happen quickly, but I'll do what I can."

What? How could he change the minds of the council who'd ruled noninterference? I didn't need to hear this. Not with Nell possibly dying in there.

"You—"

"You don't have to believe me, like I said," he interrupted. "Just give me a chance."

Huh? I shook my head. Playing mind games with Kay effing Walker was not what I needed right now.

"I did have one question, actually," he said. "When you were attacked, the dreyverns came from the hidden Passage entrance. Has that ever happened before?"

I hesitated. Oh, what did it matter? "Never. It's on the lower level of the Passages and sometimes there are monsters down there, but none of them have come close to getting out. We're the only people who know about the door." I drew a ragged breath. "Guess this is it. All the refugees from twenty-odd worlds use that Passage. I've been helping people since I was eight years old."

"You have?"

I bit my lower lip, but it was too late, like I'd switched on a faucet. The words just wouldn't stop coming. "Yes. Nell brought me to Earth when I was a baby. I don't remember it.

But she built us a life, all of us. And that's what I want to do. Help people like she did me. I never wanted any of this to happen."

There was no point in hiding it from him now. I'd never said so much to another person, let alone a stranger. *I'm not your enemy, Ada,* he'd said. But the Alliance had destroyed my world, almost got Nell killed, and to add insult to injury, strongly implied she'd been lying to me all my life. I didn't even know how to deal with that. It was too messed up.

Maybe that was why confessing to him felt like part of the horrible weight on my shoulders had lifted, just a little.

"You know, the Alliance does more than police the Passages," he said. "We help people too. Offworld."

"Only if their worlds are approved members," I said. "I get it. The Alliance isn't all bad. Look, you can't expect me to just start trusting you people after what you did to me."

"I don't expect that," said Kay. "It's your decision. You said you'd speak to us, I'll hold you to that, but if you were to join…" He paused, like he expected me to interrupt with a *hell, no.* But I didn't. Call me crazy, but the part of me still clinging onto sanity was curious to know how this would play out.

Join the Alliance. Like Delta had said. Like, up until the Alliance had caught me, I'd dreamed of. I couldn't deny it. The Multiverse called to me. It was in my blood—literally, as

I knew now. But after how they'd treated me? After accusing me of murder?

"Don't pile this on me now," I said. "I can't think straight. Nell doesn't trust any of you, but I... I always wondered. I want to go offworld. See the Multiverse."

Kay looked at me for a second. "Same here."

"You've never been?" I assumed he was in a position of authority, but I guessed not everyone at the Alliance got to go offworld.

"Not yet," he said. "I've only technically been employed there four days. And in that time there have been two murders, a trespasser, two chalder voxes—including one getting onto Earth—through an unknown Passage, no less."

Four days? Seriously?

"Damn," I said.

He smiled crookedly. "I know, right?"

I didn't even know how to respond to that. It explained *some* things, but at the same time, all the questions exploding in my head were drowned out by the urgency of Nell's being near death. I glanced back at the waiting room.

"Do you normally hire criminals?"

His smile faded. "This isn't exactly a usual situation. Your friends could have done a lot of damage. Who was using magic in Central?"

Crap. "Not Nell," I said quickly. "She's not mageblood.

My little brother is, but he's never broken any laws. Neither's Jeth." Aside from the trespassing, which seemed trivial by now. "You're not going to charge us for criminal damage, are you?"

"I'd be more worried about those guards she knocked out pressing charges."

I winced. "Nell doesn't do things by halves. But…" The last thing I wanted was to confess our dire financial situation to someone who could probably buy out Nell's whole business.

Apparently some of my alarm must have shown on my face, because he said, "We'll worry about that when we come to it."

Like I could ever *not* worry about it.

"I don't understand what was up with those dreyverns," I said, scrambling around for something unrelated to talk about. "It's not like them to work *with* a chalder vox. Someone set them up. Set them to ambush us."

"You think that?" he said.

"I don't know what to think. It seemed so… calculated. They were waiting right there, as if they knew we were coming."

"There was another chalder vox in the Passages the other day," he said. "That's how I found the hidden tunnel."

"*You* found it?" I said, whatever curiosity I'd felt swiftly evaporating. "Let me guess. You reported it."

"If I hadn't then, I'd have to now," he said calmly. "When any offworld creature escapes onto Earth, there has to be an inquiry. Though the Alliance is knee-deep in inquiries at the moment already."

"The murders," I said. "Honestly, it has nothing to do with any of us."

"I know that," he said. "The two victims had one thing in common, and I'm the only person who noticed it. They both got hold of a certain file from the archives, containing information on bloodrock."

"Bloodrock?" I echoed, wondering why he'd told me that—by the expression on his face, I guessed he was wondering the same.

"It's dangerous and classified for good reason," said Kay. "But I can't see why someone would commit murder over it. You said you use it for disguise?"

"Yeah, Nell makes this formula," I said. "That's all we use it for, I swear. So why's bloodrock classified, then? Seeing as you're supposed to be the expert."

"Not on that," he said. "I've read the archives, and there's barely any information. But it mentioned Enzar."

"It does?"

"Yeah. I don't know what it means. I'm guessing it's connected to the murders. Started as paranoia, to be honest—hell, maybe it still is. Too many coincidences."

"Or it could be a cover-up," I said.

For an instant, I swore there was an odd gleam at the back of his eyes, but perhaps it was a trick of the light. "For what?"

I shrugged. "Depends who filed the information, I guess, and who stored the stuff at Central. I did look when I took it, but there wasn't any record. It was just labelled as bloodrock."

"How did you even know there was bloodrock in the stores at Central?" asked Kay. "We don't exactly broadcast offworld substances."

"I—good question. I'll have to ask Nell, when she wakes up." I winced at the tremble in my voice. "I think it has something to do with this family we know. The Campbell family. My friend Delta lives with them on Valeria. They know people in the Alliance there."

"Valeria? You really do have contacts," he said.

"Yeah, Delta's family are like mine. I guess he's probably worried about me, I haven't called him in a while."

"Your phone," he said. "I'll get it back for you tomorrow, okay? Who locked it? The tech team couldn't get into it."

"Jeth." I jerked my head in the direction of the waiting room. "He's a genius."

"Hmm."

"What now?" I asked. "We're sticking here till Nell's okay, but, well, that could be a while."

"Then I'll call Simon at US Central," said Kay. "See if we can make an arrangement."

"Now?" My heart beat loudly in my ears. He—he couldn't be serious.

"Might as well." He pulled out his communicator. Must have got a new one, I thought, wondering for the first time since this mess had started what life was like for Alliance employees outside office hours. He didn't have to be here, let alone *helping* me. To think he'd arrested me a few days ago. It was surreal.

"Simon," he said into the communicator. "How're you doing, asshole?"

In answer, I heard something along the lines of "you lunatic."

Despite everything, I stifled a giggle. Who would have guessed that Kay Walker would turn out to be a normal guy?

I went back into the waiting room while he paced outside, talking to Simon, whoever he was. Jeth and Alber both stared at me as I closed the door behind me.

"What in the world were you two chatting about?" asked Jeth.

I shrugged. "Everything, really. Just making sure we're on the same page."

"He works for the *Alliance*," said Alber. "Nell's going to be pissed."

"Yeah…" Speaking of, there was movement outside the door. I stiffened as a nurse entered the waiting room.

"How is she?" Alber asked immediately.

"She's fine, the surgery went well. She won't come round from the anaesthetic for a while yet, but she'll recover. She's a survivor."

I let out a breath, lightheaded with relief, and sank into a chair.

"Thank God," said Jeth.

That still left the obvious question of where we were going next. Jeth had had the presence of mind to retrieve our packed rucksacks from the carnage of the fight, but none of us had a lot of cash. We could either hole up in a hotel for the night, or risk going home. But we might be attacked again. Was anywhere really safe now?

"I'm not leaving," said Alber, when I brought this up. "I'm staying with Nell."

"I'm not letting you stay here alone," said Jeth. "Look, after visiting hours close, we'll just have to go home. Nell was being paranoid, but the house is pretty secure. You know it is. Ada, you're really going to the Alliance tomorrow?"

"I guess so," I said. My chest tightened at the thought.

And yet… it might be my chance to make a difference. For real. I might even find out what had really happened to me on Enzar, too.

At that moment, Kay came back into the room, stowing his communicator in the inside pocket of his leather-style jacket. I wouldn't have minded owning one of those. It was pretty snazzy, not to mention it didn't have so much as a mark from the fight earlier.

"What was that about?" Jeth asked, eying him with distrust.

"Just made a phone call," said Kay. "There's a safe house run by the New York Alliance. You can get there through the Passages. If you know anyone who needs somewhere to stay, I can just ask."

My mouth fell open. "You're serious?"

"Of course."

"Wait, *what* is going on?" asked Jeth.

"The Alliance branch over in America has a safe house for refugees," said Kay. "I don't expect you to believe me, but here." And he handed me his communicator. My eyes practically bugged out, and it took a moment to focus on the screen. Contact details. I scrolled through, disbelief building by the second. Photos. Of… people from offworld. Karthos. Zanthar. This place was legit.

"Thought you might have been listening in," he said. "I

can ask Simon to talk to you directly, if you need any more proof."

"That's…"

I jumped when his fingers brushed mine as he took the communicator from my hand before I dropped it. I hadn't even realised my grip was slipping—hell, I was losing my grip on *reality*.

"You're kidding," said Alber, staring at Kay. "He's tricking you or something."

"So little faith," said Kay. "What are you doing now, anyway?" He directed the question at me.

"I don't know. Staying here, I guess. Nell needs us. Well, she will when she wakes up."

"That won't be for a while," said Jeth. "They might kick us out first."

"Then I'll camp out on the floor," said Alber. "Ada's with me, right?"

"Um…" Central was miles away from here, and Kay's watching me didn't make it any easier to think clearly. "Maybe we should go home. I'll catch the train to Central in the morning."

"The house… I don't know," said Jeth. "I'm tempted to be over-cautious and go to the Knights' place or something. They're still secure."

"Yeah, but they're miles away," I said. "It'd be a pain to

get to Central from there."

"You could always come back to my place," said Kay, directing this at me.

Wait, what?

He read my expression before I could speak. "It's the only place I can think of where we can stay under the radar. Someone attacked you, and if you travel across London on your own, it might well happen again. I can drive you there, and I have authorised access to Central any time. We can get this mess sorted as soon as the council check in, before it draws any more attention—I'm pretty sure you don't want another spectacle. There are enough rumours already."

I shook my head. Started to speak, then realised I didn't have a clue what I intended to say.

"No freaking way," said Alber. "I bet you're planning to murder her. Well, she can kill you with her bare hands."

Kay actually laughed. "I don't doubt that," he said. "Just a suggestion, that's all."

"Where do you live?" I asked.

"Ten-minute drive from Central."

I bit my lip. Of course he wasn't a serial killer, but did that mean I was willing to trust him? He worked for the Alliance.

He'd offered to help me, help the refugees, in a way I'd never thought anyone could, even after I'd acted like a total ass, insulted and attacked him. What the hell was this?

Alber interrupted the silence. "Jesus, Ada, I know you have bad taste in guys, but this is ridiculous."

My jaw dropped. "You did not just say that." I punched my brother in the shoulder. Hard.

"Ouch! I was just messing with—gah!" I had him in one of Nell's infamous headlocks in a heartbeat.

Kay, who hadn't reacted at all to Alber's comment, now looked amused. Which made me even more annoyed. "Don't flatter yourself," I shot at him. "I'm not interested in Alliance guards. My brother's a total ass who's going to apologise right now, aren't you?"

"Gah—all right! I'm sorry. Jesus." Alber rubbed his neck. "That was uncalled for."

"So was that a yes or a no?" Kay inquired. "For the record, I'm not at all interested in magic-wielders." Huh. I'd expected him to say *criminals,* not magic-wielders.

"Good." I glared at him. "What're you going to do if I say no?"

"Absolutely nothing."

"And if I say yes?"

"What I said. Drive you back with me. Not murder you in your sleep. No offence, but you look like you're about to crash."

"That *was* offensive," I said. "But all right. Fine." Maybe I was tripping out from sheer tiredness. I hadn't slept all night, and it had been a hell of a long day. One freaking bombshell after another.

Maybe I just wanted this whole fiasco dealt with. Like he'd said, I'd made a pretty big spectacle of myself already. Everyone would know who I was, who my family were. They probably thought I was a lunatic, if not a criminal. If I could really clear my name, clear Nell's, then things could go back to normal. I didn't *have* to join the Alliance.

I really did have a choice in the matter.

And okay, maybe one percent of me was the tiniest bit curious to learn about the Alliance guard who'd gone from enemy to possible ally within the space of only a few hours.

***

This had to be some bizarre dream. I sat in the front of Kay Walker's flashy red car as he steered through late-night London traffic. I hadn't a clue what to say, and Kay seemed content to drive in silence—apart from occasionally cursing at particularly idiotic drivers.

"Damn city drivers," he muttered, tapping his fingers on the dashboard.

"You're not from the city?"

"I grew up on the outskirts," he said, not elaborating.

"The Academy's… south of London, isn't it?" I said. "I've never been, but Nell used to talk about it." I bit my lip. Shouldn't have mentioned Nell. I looked down, but Kay's eyes were on the road anyway.

He nodded. But didn't say a word.

Gotta love awkward silences. I fidgeted, watching the traffic instead, the ordinary streets, shops, chattering people boarding red buses, thronging the pavements. People who had no clue what insanity was happening so close by. Outside the Alliance, did anyone know at all? Nell had got all our information from contacts, like Skyla, who relentlessly spied on Central. Back before all this craziness, that was all I'd known—secrecy. I could never tell anyone who, what, I really was.

Kay knew. More than I'd ever intended to tell anyone. And it was only now occurring to me that I knew nothing about him. At all. Including why the hell he'd taken it upon himself to help me, after everything that had happened. I glanced at him out the corner of my eye. He looked… tired? Sad? I couldn't tell.

Before I could think of anything intelligent to say, he stopped the car next to a row of apartments.

I didn't know what to expect of Kay's house. Living in central London wasn't cheap, and Academy graduates were usually loaded. But his studio flat was pretty modest. Top

floor, up four flights of stairs. I was about ready to collapse
by the time we reached the room, but I didn't say a word and
followed him into the apartment. First time I'd ever been to
a guy's flat, seeing as most of the guys I'd dated had still lived
with their parents. As for my two brothers, Alber's room was
a no-go area, and Jeth's was the kind of organised chaos only
a tech geek could achieve. Kay, though…his one-room
apartment was spotless. Almost too clean. The fitted wooden
furniture was bare, save for a flat-screen TV on the desk,
couch in front. Kitchenette off to the side, bathroom
through another door. Nothing lay on the floor, no
discarded clothes or anything. No girlfriend, I thought. A
handful of boxes were stacked in one corner, next to a
punch bag.

"Don't you have…anything else?" I said, lamely.

"It's a new apartment," he said, shrugging off his jacket. "I
just moved in a week ago, I've been at Central most of the time."

I felt a rush of homesickness for my own cupboard-sized
room, stars on the ceiling and all. Would I ever get to go back?

"Wow," I said, not sure what else to say. I dropped my
rucksack to the floor. "Damn. What a day."

"I was going to order takeout Chinese. Want some?"

"God. Yes."

As he dug in his jacket pocket for his communicator, I saw a
mark on his left arm that I thought at first glance was a tattoo—

245

but it was a scar, a deep line that ended in a jagged mark on his forearm. What had done that? It wasn't recent, though it looked painful. As he moved, I saw it was on both sides of his arm, like a sharp claw had stabbed right through it.

Ouch. I turned my back and nosed around some more while he dialled the number, peering into boxes. Books, mostly. Offworld dictionaries? Academy graduation certificate—damn, he really had just graduated. With top grades.

"What are you doing?"

"Being curious," I said, shamelessly. "About what Alliance guards do when they're not beating up monsters or arresting people."

"We're not that interesting," said Kay. "Don't touch that."

Whoa. "I'm touching nothing."

"Good. I have those arranged alphabetically."

I burst out laughing. "Sorry," I said. "Wait—you're not serious."

"Maybe a little." The slightest smile lifted the corner of his mouth.

I turned back to the boxes. "Tell me that isn't the collector's edition of Tolkien's *The Lord of the Rings*. Because I might just kill you if it is."

He was the one to laugh this time. "I'm terrified. That's what I told you not to touch, by the way."

"Really? Hmm. Didn't figure it was your thing."

"Call it a guilty pleasure."

"I lent my copy to Delta—my friend from Valeria," I explained. "Most of the stuff he gives me doesn't work on Earth, though." I stopped myself before I said anymore. For someone who'd spent her life keeping secrets, I was crap at not letting information slip lately.

"Valeria?" Kay said. "You've not been there. No, you said you hadn't been offworld."

"Believe me, I've tried to persuade him to sneak me in a dozen times," I said. "I mean, they have freaking *hover cars*. And hover boots now, too. I'm going there someday, no matter what."

"How were you planning on doing that?" he asked. "Not to judge or anything. I'm intending to get on a mission to Valeria as soon as I make Ambassador. That is, if this mess doesn't cost me my job."

Crap. We were back to that again. Kay looked like he regretted mentioning it. I fell silent, and Kay started pacing the room, like he had in my prison cell—had that really only been yesterday?

I stood, leaving the boxes, and went to check through my bag again.

"You can crash on the bed," he said. "I don't mind."

Well, that was something. And I *did* feel like crashing. I'd been running on pure adrenaline all day.

I jumped at the buzz of static as Kay switched on the TV. He wasn't even watching it, but the familiar background noise soothed my nerves.

The food arrived and we ate in silence, the TV playing some old action flick. I barely noticed, and Kay looked like he was avoiding my eyes. He gave me privacy to go and clean myself up in the bathroom. I'd acquired more bruises, and my knees were scraped raw, but I'd had worse injuries in Nell's intense training classes. Thank the gods I'd had the sense not to pack the blue rabbit-patterned pyjamas. Because that really wasn't a level of embarrassment I was ready to handle—this was awkward enough already.

Naturally, because I was trying not to think about it, I wondered how many other girls he'd brought back home. Wait, new apartment. Where did he live when he was at the Academy, then? It was like a university, so probably campus accommodation. And before then? Who were his parents?

Cut that out, Ada, I told myself. Now was not the time to get overly curious about Kay Walker. We were from different worlds. Though I couldn't help imagining how Nell would react if I started dating an Alliance employee. She'd interrogated most of my exes, actually scared a couple of them off. Kind of depressing, really. Sign up for an overprotective guardian who assumes everyone's a murderer in disguise.

Someone who'd defend me to the end of the Multiverse.

That thought sobered me up pretty fast.

Despite the TV and Kay's constant pacing about—seriously, did he ever sit *still?*—I fell asleep the instant I lay back on the pillow.

***

I awoke with a gasp. I'd been dreaming of fighting the dreyverns again, unable to stop the knife flying out and striking Nell. Disoriented, I looked around the darkened room. Kay sat opposite me, back to the wall, eyes closed.

"What in the world are you doing?" I asked. He couldn't possibly be asleep like that.

One eye half opened. "Meditating."

"As opposed to sleeping?"

"I'm an incurable insomniac." Both eyes opened this time. "Are you okay?"

"Huh? Yeah, I'm fine."

"You talk in your sleep."

I flushed. "Oh, God." I pulled the covers over my head, and he laughed softly.

"You speak Karthonic?"

"Yeah... was I speaking that?" I was about to ask how he recognised it, but he probably knew twice as many offworld languages as I did. Academy graduate.

"Kind of. Didn't make much sense. Who taught you, anyway?" He hesitated. "This is off record. No one's gonna come in here and arrest you."

You know what? I believed him. I let the covers drop from my face. "My foster brother, Jeth. He was originally from Karthos. He wanted to learn from a tutor. I picked up a few phrases."

"What about your other foster brother? Which world's he from?"

"Alber's from Enzar too. But mageblood." I paused. "What about you? Any siblings?"

A shake of the head. "Just me."

"Is it not… lonely here on your own?" Now I was definitely prying.

He shrugged. "Not really. I've only owned this place a few days, and I've been at Central or in the Passages most of that time. Ambassadors don't really settle on one world, anyway."

"What about… your parents?"

His eyes narrowed, barely perceptibly. "Dead or otherwise absent."

I knew it was rude to keep asking questions. "Sorry," I said. "I was just curious. I don't know what happened to my real parents. I never met them. But Royals aren't exactly known for being friendly. They probably started the war in the first place." I sighed. "It's a mess."

"Really?" He paused for an instant. "So who raised you, then?"

"Nell."

"She kicked Aric's ass. I wish I'd seen."

"Me, too," I said, smiling despite myself. "So... you went to the Academy."

"Yeah. Graduated nearly two weeks ago."

How old did that make him, then? A couple of years older than me at most. But he acted older. Not that I was a shining example of maturity, but still. Then again, half the people from my year at school were married and had houses and kids, and the other half spent most of the time drunk and passed out in their own gardens. I'd never really had anyone my age I could relate to, save for my brothers. Even the people who thought the idea of travelling to another universe was awesome would ultimately pick Earth, the familiar, in the end.

Even Nell. I'd lived in a literal shelter all my life, for all the excitement.

"The Academy," I said. "Was that like pre-Alliance training?"

"Sort of. You don't have to go there to get a job at the Alliance, but it lets you skip most of training because you already have the experience. But most people go through an apprenticeship instead. Are you at university, or working?"

"Uh. Neither, at the moment. I used to help Nell at the shelter. Now..." I'd no idea. What would happen to the shelters now?

"I'll talk to the council," he said. "The Alliance could use the help, if New York Central opens that Passage to the shelter over there."

"You're… really going to do that."

"Of course."

I shook my head. It still seemed so surreal. For all I knew, I was dreaming now. I absently glanced about the room. "I still don't get it, you know that?"

"You don't have to," he said.

No. Except… now, I kind of wanted to. Pity magic didn't extend to reading minds.

"If I were you, I'd consider joining the Alliance," he said. "You'd still get to help people, only in a legal way. And Ambassadors get free run of the Multiverse."

"Only if I can still help people from Enzar," I said. "Ambassadors—that's what you want to do, right?"

He inclined his head.

"All right. Well, I know I grew up here, but Enzar is my homeworld, and so many people have died. If I can help people get away from that place, I will."

"Enzar," he said. "The Alliance has kept that one under wraps, which is quite unusual given the scope of the war. I was planning to check their archives in the morning. The connection to bloodrock—it seems too odd a coincidence."

"Yeah, it does. You can never be too careful with magic."

"Nell said that, right?"

"How did you know that?"

"I guessed. Judging by what you did with magic, I don't think safety's first on your list."

I fully sat up, arms folded. "Oh, you're back to lecturing me again? Believe it or not, I know magic's dangerous. I know what I'm doing."

"Look, I'm not trying to lecture you... okay, maybe a bit. At the Academy, there was an incident. Several people got hurt because of magic. Nearly died."

"Ah." I figured he'd been involved. But the careful blankness on his face could have been the calm before a storm, and as curious as I might be, I didn't want to push further.

Is he a magic-wielder? There was no way to tell from looking at someone, not if they were from Earth. Though trying to read Kay Walker was an impossibility. The only time I'd got a real reaction from him had been when...

Ah, crap. I shook my head, annoyed at the guilt rising. "I'm sorry I yelled at you before," I said. "What I said was... awful. I..."

"Don't worry about it," he said, cutting me off. "Really."

The guilt didn't go away. I'd been desperate enough not to care what I said, just to hurt the nearest person, and it happened to be him. And instead of arresting me again, he'd risked his job and helped me. However surreal it seemed, if he'd really intended to help Enzar... *I don't lie,* he'd said, and then handed me proof about that shelter. As for the rest? It might be crazy, but it felt like he'd told the truth. Which made me even more of a bitch.

"Dammit," I muttered. "Why did you have to turn out to be *nice?*" And why couldn't I keep my stupid mouth shut?

"Huh?"

"Nothing," I said. "Just it was easier to hate the Alliance and blame you for all the crap in my life. Now I don't know who to blame. And I feel like the world's biggest idiot."

"You're welcome to blame me if it makes it easier," he said lightly.

"Hmm. Nah, I think I'll blame the Multiverse in general."

"Get some sleep." His mouth curled into a faint smile. But a genuine one.

Yeah. Good idea. No point in thinking about what I couldn't control. I lay back down, heaviness weighing on my eyelids. Tilting my head, I saw him shift slightly. In fact, now I looked closer, I could tell he was only feigning casualness, and his eyes were open, alert. He sat at a slight angle, so he could see the door. Like a trained soldier. Keeping an eye out? Did he expect an attack?

My eyes ached too much to keep open any longer, and the world faded away.

***

My eyes flickered open to the sight of Kay walking past the door, shirtless. I sat bolt upright.

"Holy hell."

"What?" He smirked. "Like what you see?"

"What the—what the hell happened to you?"

Scars crisscrossed the entire left side of his body—long, deep scars like the one on his left arm, like claw-marks. I gripped the bed convulsively. I couldn't even imagine the pain.

"I had a disagreement with a wyvern," he said, absently running his right hand over the mark on his left arm.

"How are you still alive?"

"Lucky." He said this in an ironic tone.

"You're insane." I shook my head. "You're actually insane. You know that?"

"I did wonder." He went into the bathroom, leaving me staring. I rubbed my eyes. Damn. Here I was, getting distracted again. It was morning now. I had to get my head together.

Today was our last chance.

CHAPTER SIXTEEN

KAY

"Why bother driving in London?" asked Ada.

"I hate public transport," I said, amused at her incredulity, as we waited at a red light. She perched on the edge of her seat, short red hair still slightly tousled though she'd dragged a brush through it. She wore black, her own approximation of guard uniform complete with daggers sheathed in those famous boots of hers. Dangerous, and in my book, that equalled "extremely attractive". And the reflection of her low-cut long-sleeved top in the wing mirror didn't help. I hadn't counted on her being so bloody distracting now her defences were lowered around me.

"That figures," she muttered. "People are too slow, right?"

Despite everything, a smile crept onto my face. She was observant, I gave her that. And fearless. If not for the circumstances, last night could have gone very differently. And if I wasn't at least fifty per cent sure she still didn't like me.

That's enough, Kay. Concentrate.

Ada picked at a loose thread on her coat as the towering shadow of Central Headquarters came into view. "You're *sure* they won't just lock me up again? Because I'm placing a hell of a lot of faith in you at the moment. If you're lying, I'm gonna drop-kick you into next week."

"Honestly, the worst that can happen is that we *both* get put on trial," I said, only half paying attention. My communicator kept buzzing. The morning guard had sent an alert that all novices were to arrive clad in guard uniform ready for another search of the Passages. I wore the uniform, but no weapons, and right now, even the ordinary streets of London seemed suspect. No one had a clue what was happening. Even in Central, really. I sure as hell hadn't told anyone I had the prisoner at my freaking *apartment.* Well, what was I supposed to do? It was plain obvious she was a victim of circumstance, lawbreaker or not, and the same went for her family. She probably thought I'd just wanted to keep an eye on her to make sure she didn't skive today's meeting, and maybe the rational part of me had. But like I'd said, she'd been attacked once already. Everything—the killings, the attacks, the threats—hiked my paranoia up to full level. I'd tried my damned hardest not to look at her sleeping when I'd been watching the door, but now she most likely thought I was a creeper on top of everything else. Or a weirdo.

I'd heard worse. I shouldn't even care what she thought of me, and yet, there it was.

I steered the car past the road that led to the Passages. "Trust me, the Alliance doesn't arrest people all that often. This week is *not* typical. By the way, Simon's going to meet us in the Passages later to talk about the refugees. I'll get your phone back for you and you can contact your friends, okay?"

"I—sure." She shook her head. "Why are you helping me?"

"Would you rather I didn't?"

"I don't have a clue what's going through your head at the moment."

Yeah. Neither did I.

As we turned towards the gates of Central, a sharp screech rent the air, and a huge, heavy shape came half running, half flying out of the side-street to the Passages. I saw talons, twin membranous wings, thick-scaled body, lashing poison-barbed tail—before it all slammed together into one image.

Wyvern.

"Shit!" I yelled, braking.

Scaled feet slammed down onto the front of my car, claws digging in. I swerved, killing the engine a second before we collided with another vehicle. My car shuddered to a stop—or what was left of it.

I was already unbuckling my seatbelt and diving for the door, snatching up the tire iron I kept under the seat for emergencies. I rolled over on the pavement and Ada tumbled out as the wyvern clawed its way through the front of my car. Bits of metal flew everywhere, and jaws clamped down where we'd been sitting seconds ago.

Swearing, I threw the tire iron as the beast raised its giant scaly head, striking it in the mouth and knocking several teeth flying in a spray of blood. But I hadn't hit it at the right angle to knock it out, only piss it off even more.

Crap, this was bad. I didn't have my stunner *or* any other weapon—it seemed to me the Alliance was seriously misguided on that one, not allowing employees to carry weapons outside patrol hours. But Ada reached for her boot and pulled a dagger.

"You can't fight it, Ada," I said, backing up. This wasn't a fight two people could win.

"Kay!" Ms Weston leaped out from the car I'd almost hit, and the wyvern headed right for her.

"Son of a *bitch,*" I said, and prepared to kick common sense in the face.

Ms Weston, however, raised her hand and threw her stunner to me. I reacted just in time to catch it, and saw that she had another one of her own and was waving it threateningly.

The wyvern clawed its way through the ruins of my car and spread its bat-like wings wide. It was bleeding, I noticed, from several places its thick armoured scales had been knocked off. But it was still eight feet tall, covered in thick armour, and angry as hell.

I instinctively moved in front of Ada.

"Don't you dare," she said. "It's only fair that I get a crack at the monster, too." She grinned, and ran at the wyvern.

"Get the tail!" I shouted over my shoulder—we needed to cut off the poison barb otherwise odds were, it was game over for at least one of us. I crossed the road in a zigzag to avoid the thrashing tail, which left dents wherever it struck the tarmac. Ms Weston brandished her stunner, but the wyvern seemed undaunted. It screeched, and the claws swiped out. Ada ran for the tail, dagger in hand. And I aimed at the side, stunner at the ready, and jumped. I managed to get a grip on a patch of loose scales and haul myself up, pressing the stunner to a wound in its side.

Magic sizzled through the beast's skin, and it cried out, tail lashing wildly—behind it, Ada screamed.

Shaken from the backblast, I climbed sideways and peered around, my heart stopping when I spotted Ada splayed on the ground, but she jumped up again and made another lunge for the tail.

The wyvern swiped for Ms Weston. She let out a stifled yell as her hand was tangled in its claw, but the buzz of static warned me she'd used the opportunity to fire the stunner. I knew the drill, I'd done it in simulation a hundred times. *Aim for the weak points, the joints between its armour.* Not that it had many of those. I quickly let go and dropped to the ground, the echo of the magic shock vibrating through my body. Ada, meanwhile, had thrown herself flat on the tarmac to avoid the lashing tail and was stabbing wildly with her dagger. I hoped she knew what she was doing. One wrong move could kill her.

Weakened by the double attack, the wyvern staggered sideways. I had a brief glimpse of terrified faces peering from windows of the occupied houses as I readied myself to fire another shot with the stunner.

And did my best to ignore the answering pulse in my veins, the tug of magic that shouldn't even be present on Earth.

The wyvern swayed, knees buckling, and I jumped clear as its side smashed into the metal fence. The tail came down again, with Ada clinging to the underside, inches away from the poisonous barb. Cursing, I checked on Ms Weston, who'd drawn a knife and was slashing at the wyvern's flailing claws, ignoring the blood streaming from her own arm.

"Got a spare?" I ran to her side and joined in the attack, firing another shot with the stunner into the palm of its hand. The beast reared back, its scaly hide trembling, drool and blood dripping from its gaping mouth.

To my surprise, Ms Weston handed me her weapon and backed off, allowing me to take the attack. She'd drawn her communicator instead. Calling for backup. I concentrated on the flailing monster, which was beginning to recover from the double attack.

Then it screeched, a grating cry that cracked the glass in several car windows. There was a heavy *thud*, and its tail struck the ground in a shower of blood. Ada had found her mark. Claws swiped in Ms Weston's direction, and I slashed back with the knife, severing the end of one claw. I struck again, cutting deep into its arm under the damaged armour. Blood poured from the wound and the wyvern flailed back. Ms Weston rejoined me with another knife in her hand and her face a determined mask.

"Let's give it hell, Kay," she said.

Claws swiped, and so did my knife. Several scaled fingers, claws and all, fell to the ground, and before it could rear back, I slammed the stunner into the wounds. This time, the recoil nearly took me off my feet. Magic burned through my veins, and I staggered but kept my balance.

There was a snapping sound, and the wyvern screeched. My eardrums vibrated, and several people screamed inside the houses.

Ada came running around from the spot where the monster's tail had been. She'd cut it clean off. Blood spattered her dark clothes and streaked her face, but she threw herself back into the fight. The three of us moved to surround the beast. It had nowhere to turn.

Shouts rang out, and several guards ran up to join us. The message had got through. Knives slashed, stunners sent buzzes of magic through the air, and the wyvern fell.

Ms Weston stepped back to let the guards take care of it and beckoned to me before I could jump into the action again. Ada had moved back too, gasping for breath, her face painted with the wyvern's blood.

"I need you to run to Central," said Ms Weston. "My communicator's damaged, but this was a calculated attack. And they're planning another one."

I looked from her to the wyvern. "You think–?"

"This would have seemed like an accident, of course. But there are others in danger, too. I want you to go to the medical division and order an evacuation. I think that's the next target."

What the hell was I missing? I shook my head, slightly dazed and breathing heavily from the fight.

"You're absolutely sure?" I said.

"Better to be safe. Go, now."

"I'll stay here," said Ada quickly. "Go on."

Ms Weston looked in her direction. Damn. There went my plan to clear her name. I had to trust that Ada would stay calm. If people really were in danger at Central, then that had to take priority.

Thanks, universe, I thought, running back towards Central. Guards were still coming out the doors and several people stopped to talk to me as I went in.

"What's going on?" asked Carl. "We got a call, but no orders."

"Wyvern attack," I said breathlessly, pointing over the fence. "Mostly taken care of."

"Damn."

I headed downstairs, past the room where Ada had been imprisoned, and saw that the door to Saki's lab was slightly open.

"You again?" she said from behind her desk, as I pushed the door further in. "What this time?"

"Ms Weston's ordered an evacuation," I said, in a low voice. "She thinks the labs are the next target. A wyvern attacked us in the road."

"You're kidding me," she said.

I shook my head. "She really believes it. I don't know why, but I reckon you ought to get out of here."

Saki made an impatient noise. "If you're absolutely sure." She grabbed a handful of papers and came out of the lab to join me. "Ada's blood," I said, as we walked quickly towards the other labs. "You didn't figure out what was wrong with it, did you?"

"Kind of. It's quite similar to what Mr Clark was asking about just before he was killed. This old research project was abandoned a while ago—thirteen years ago, I think…"

Shit. I'd suspected, but I hadn't known for sure. No one

in the Alliance was supposed to know about the brief spell of failed experiments. Because the instigator had relocated to London's West Office immediately afterwards, and had finally disappeared off grid, five years ago, on the closed-off world of Thairon. Leaving his son behind.

His son, who'd also participated in the experiment. Not by choice.

"You have to get out of here," I said. "Is there anyone else down here?"

"Yeah... hold on." She rapped on the nearest door, while I pushed open another. Some were locked. One contained Ada's phone, discarded on the table, and I picked it up.

"Everyone's out," said Saki, who was now surrounded by confused-looking doctors.

"What's happening?" one of them asked.

"Ms Weston's ordered an evacuation," I said. "Follow me."

Though I led the way in silence, the world felt like it was tilting under my feet. Now I had a pretty good idea of the killer's motives. I hadn't thought anyone else was involved, that there'd been any other... subjects. But it made sense.

The question was, who was it?

A tense silence followed us upstairs. No one questioned the order, and Saki and I led the group across the entrance hall. Nothing looked out of place, except the unusual lack of people coming into work, and I knew that was down to most of the guards having gone after the wyvern. It still felt wrong.

Outside. I could see the carnage from the battle even from here, a crowd gathering around the hunched, scaly body of the wyvern. It must be dead, or close to. I knew from experience in the Academy's fight simulations that those bastards were wicked tough to kill. It was probably the same one which had been in the Passages the other day.

Ms Weston crossed the car park towards us. She'd pressed a cloth to her bleeding arm and her usually impeccable uniform was somewhat dishevelled and dust-stained, but she held herself upright. She gave me a tight nod, which I assumed meant "thank you".

"What's the problem?" Saki asked. "Why the evacuation—what happened?" Her eyes bugged out at the sight of Ms Weston bleeding, and beyond that, the torn-up street and wrecked cars.

As Ms Weston spoke to them, I spotted Ada just outside the gate. She'd resheathed her dagger and wiped the blood from her face, which relaxed when she saw me. "That's your boss, right?" she said. "She told me to come back later for questioning."

"She won't arrest you again," I said, pulling her phone from my pocket and handing it to her. "Got this back for you."

"I—thanks," she said, a surprised flush lighting her face. She started tapping the touch screen. "Hell. I've a ton of messages from Delta."

"About that," I said. "This mess is going to take a while to clean up. I can't promise I'll be able to help you find the shelter, but I can give you Simon's details."

"Sure." She shook her head, looking a little dazed, and I rattled off Simon's code number, then mine. She nodded. "Stored. Hang on. There's a quicker way." She dug a hand in her pocket and pulled out—nothing. "It's an earpiece," she said quickly. "Invisible. My brother invented them. That's how I talked to him when I was imprisoned."

I stared at her. "You what?" I'd forgotten all about that, in the wake of everything else. But I reached out and felt something small, metal and solid in my hand. I could see the faint outline if I squinted.

"Clip it to your ear. There's a switch to activate it on the back."

I held the tiny object delicately, pushing it into place behind my left ear. "If your brother wants to apply for a job in our tech department, I can ask," I said.

She smiled grimly. "If we ever get out of this mess, I'll tell him that." She glanced at Ms Weston, who was talking urgently to Saki and the medics.

"I don't understand," Saki was saying. "What part of our research–?"

"What do you mean, experiments?" someone else said. "I've never heard anything about—"

Voices. Dragging it all out, piece by piece. I froze, unable to move away. Even though I knew what was coming. Like it was inevitable.

"That's the point. It was confidential. The subjects didn't have any reaction, so it was judged a failure," said Ms Weston.

She knew. God help me, she knew. The experiment had been a one-off. Earth didn't usually go in for magic-based research, for obvious reasons, but from what I'd picked up on through listening to his conversations with other Alliance members on the phone, my father had been fascinated with the notion of people with inbuilt magic sources, a rarity even in high-magic worlds. Fascinated enough to convince a handful of scientists at Central to inject people with—I had no idea. Distilled magic sources, like a jacked-up version of the temporary-boost implants used on some of the east-way worlds. They'd gone along with it, of course, because he was a council member, and half-crazed with grief over losing his wife in a failed Ambassador mission. At least, that's what everyone thought.

I knew better.

I pressed my clenched fist to my mouth, willing my mind to stop replaying those images. *Stop. Stop that.*

I damn near jumped out of my skin when my communicator buzzed in my pocket. I retrieved it and swiped in the code, seeing there was a new message under Markos's name.

"Lenny's dead."

"Shit," I said, taking a step back. "Oh, shit."

"What?" said Ada.

"I have to go. Ms Weston—someone else from Office Fifteen has been killed. Lenny."

"No," said Ms Weston, the blood draining from her face. "I thought—I thought they'd go for the labs. We have to make sure everyone else gets out."

She marched towards Central. I turned back to Ada.

"You're going?"

"I have to. They're killing people in my department."

"But—but *you* could be their next target."

Yeah. I knew that. And was she actually worried about me? "I won't get killed," I said.

"You bloody better not," said Ada. "I'll wait out here."

I turned and ran back to Central, the buzz of the communicator becoming a roaring in my ears. I flew upstairs and skidded to a halt outside the office. The grey carpet was soaked in blood.

"Fuck," I said.

Ignoring the instinct to get the hell away, I followed the trail of blood. Then I jumped back as a head appeared over the top of a filing cabinet.

"Only me," said Markos, moving around the cabinet, tail swishing anxiously. "I just found him—it must have happened in the past few minutes."

I went into the office. Lenny's body slumped in a chair, blood pouring from multiple stab wounds in his neck and chest. And discarded on a desk was the murder weapon—an Alliance guard dagger, crusted with blood. My hands clenched into fists.

"We need to get out of here," I said, turning back to Markos.

"Yes, I can't say I'm keen on sticking around. But the Law Division will be on our cases if we go wandering off."

"Fuck the Law Division," I said. "A wyvern just attacked us. Ms Weston thinks she knows who did it. We're next."

The centaur's mouth fell open. "You *what?*"

"You think I'd joke about something like that?"

"I think you look slightly mad. Okay, I'm coming."

"Where's Ellen? And everyone else?"

"I was the only person here. People think our office is haunted, funnily enough." But he clip-clopped after me into the corridor.

"Oh, for crying out loud, do you think I'm getting in that bloody elevator after Alan died in there?" I said, seeing which direction he headed in.

"Centaurs," said Markos, with a great deal of dignity, "don't get along with stairs."

That figured.

Someone shouted, "Where the hell are you two going?" Damn. I'd forgotten Aric.

"Out," I said. "We're next on the killer's hit list."

"A likely story." Aric stepped in to block our path.

"For God's sake, we don't have time for this!" I glanced at Markos. "Lenny's dead back there. The killer's targeting our department—hell, they're probably somewhere in here right now."

Aric looked around, like he couldn't help himself. He narrowed his eyes at me. "Like I'm going to fall for that one, Walker."

"Does the blood and carnage not speak for itself?"

"You know," said Aric, taking a step towards me so he blocked the exit, "I think *you're* the one behaving suspiciously. If anyone has the potential to be the killer, it's you, Walker."

That was it. "Out of the way, Aric."

"What, or you'll try to kill me again?"

"Are you still not over that? Get a goddamned life."

"Enough!" Markos's hooves shot out, sending Aric sprawling to the ground. "I'll trample both of you if we don't get the hell out of here."

Aric got to his feet, glaring at Markos. "You'll pay for that."

"He says that a lot," I said. "C'mon." And despite it going against all instinct, I followed him into the elevator.

"Well, that wasn't how I expected to find out the damage," said Markos, glancing at me, as the glass lift descended. "You tried to kill him?"

"Let's just say I got a taste of magic, and got burned. He conveniently left out the part where he set a wyvern loose in the Passages and almost got me and my friends killed."

"Ah," said Markos. "Magic-wielder, are you?"

"Unfortunately." But I'd had no choice in the matter, and running away from it hadn't done me any good lately.

The elevator emitted a screeching sound, and began to slow down.

"Oh, you've got to be shitting me," I said. The screeching continued, until the lift ground to a halt, the entrance hall glittering below, blurred by the glass doors.

"I think we're in trouble, Kay," said Markos, tapping a hoof against the glass.

"You don't say?"

Lights flickered, and the power went out.

CHAPTER SEVENTEEN

ADA

I couldn't believe Ms Weston had let me walk away free. But she was preoccupied talking to the other Alliance members and hardly seemed to see me. I walked towards the gate at first, then broke into a run. I jogged the length of the fence and stopped at the corner to figure out my next move.

"Ada!" someone called from behind me.

I turned around. "Skyla?" She was dressed in her work gear, hair pulled into a messy bun, dishevelled, like she'd run from her office.

"I thought it was you, but... What happened?"

"I—this isn't a good place." Around the corner, half the Alliance's guard was still dealing with the wyvern. "I just left the Alliance, but I was supposed to…" My phone buzzed again. "Delta keeps calling me."

"He won't know about the Alliance taking you in, right?"

"Guess not. I need to talk to him anyway." I answered the call. "Delta?

"Red! You're alive?"

"I'm okay," I said, quickly. "I got arrested. The Alliance had my phone. But they couldn't hack it."

I gave him a quick rundown of what had happened, for

Skyla's benefit too. But I didn't mention Kay's promise to open the New York Alliance's Passage for offworlders. I still didn't quite believe it.

"Red, you rock. You know that?"

"I do my best." I grinned, despite the lingering worry for Kay, who might be in the same building as a killer.

"Wanna come meet me in the Passages now?"

"I—I can't. There's someone I have to meet. Later. I'll come to the Passages later. There's this guy, Kay, he's going to help, uh, with the refugees… it's too hard to explain."

"What? Who's Kay?"

"Kay Walker. He works for the Alliance, but well, he helped me."

"Wait, you met *Walker*?"

"Yes…" I frowned. "Do you know him?"

"Do I–? Ada, it was someone called Walker who cut Enzar off from the Passages twenty years ago. A high council member. The son of the Alliance's founder!"

"No." I stopped, my heart plummeting. "It wasn't him. Kay's only been there a week."

"Must be his son."

"I don't…" Walker. Why hadn't I made the connection before? Nell had probably mentioned the name, but with everything that had happened lately, I hadn't thought about it. I'd mostly tuned out her rants against the Alliance, really.

Now it came back to hit me. Kay was the son of the eminent council member who'd opposed interference, even to help the millions of people dying.

I didn't even know what to think about that. But he'd said not to call him "Walker", I remembered.

"Anyway. Seriously, come to the Passages, if you can. There's a family coming through. Soon."

"What?"

"That's why I've been calling. Rumours, man. I didn't believe you'd really been taken in."

Skyla mouthed, *What?*

Someone needs me in the Passages, I mouthed back.

"It's sort of difficult," I said. "I'm outside Central, but there's been a wyvern attack by the road where their Passage entrance is."

"A wyvern? You serious?"

"Not sure the Passages are the safest place at the moment," I said. "Is there—is there no other way?"

"I can do it alone, but Valeria's temporarily closed its borders because of all the spawn of Cethrax rampaging around the Passages lately."

"Damn." Guess I should have expected the impact to spill offworld. "Look, half the Alliance's guard's gathered in the street. They're dealing with the wyvern. It's dead, but there are terrified ordinary people about, and the other Alliance employees."

"They're distracted?"

"Yes, but…" I chewed on my bottom lip. This was all too much to process. I needed to *think,* and there was no time to do that right now.

"I'll come with you," said Skyla. "Tell you what. I'll create a diversion."

"You sure?"

"Yeah." Skyla nodded. "It'd be my pleasure."

There was nothing to do about Kay now and no way to help Nell, either—and this family needed me, especially with the Passages even more dangerous than usual. So I turned and headed back towards Central. The gleaming exterior of the skyscraper revealed nothing of the chaos that was happening inside, but on the outside, the world had ground to a standstill. Traffic had stopped, and people were leaving the offices opposite Central and driving or just running away. Around the corner, the wyvern had been dragged out of the rubble and guards surrounded it, clearly trying to figure out how to get it back into the Passages. I could see the gleam of the open door at the street's end.

Drawing in a deep breath, I hurried past the guards and the wyvern and the busted, broken-down houses.

I'd almost made it when a shout rang out. "Hey, you can't go that way!"

I ran, glancing over my shoulder to see where Skyla was. She'd disappeared. But a blond woman was arguing with the guards who'd called after me.

Something seemed odd about that, but I had to take the opportunity. I reached the entrance to the Passages. The magic charge was so strong, the air lit up inside with lightning, red as blood.

"I'm here, Delta," I said into the phone. "Which door?"

"This door."

I spun around. There *was* a door opposite, one that hadn't been in use—but now it was wide open. Delta stood in the entrance. Smiling.

Two dreyverns stood on either side of him.

"Sorry, Red," he said.

"Delta," I said, hardly acknowledging the stupid nickname. "What—what the hell are you doing with *them?*"

My heart beat loud in my ears, and even the magic seemed to be telling me to get the hell out of there.

"Don't take it personally," he said. "But my family needs you."

The two dreyverns advanced. Two against one, and I had only one weapon.

I turned around, and ran.

Hands grabbed me around the waist and lifted me into the air. Delta locked something metal around my arms. Twisting my head, I saw that my arms were locked onto his hands, and before I could process that, he'd pulled me back through the door and the world dropped away as we soared into a cloudy sky.

I screamed, squirming in his grip. Below, a city unfolded, skyscrapers piercing the heavens, hover cars swarming the roads between like ants. Next to us, a car hovered in midair, on a level with the rooftops, and as we spun around, I saw the door we'd come through, literally at the edge of a skyscraper. We weren't standing on the ground, but floating. *It just had to be effing hover boots*, I thought.

Another world. At last. But wrong, so wrong. The grid-like city below, crisscrossed by four-lane roads on three levels, the glass skyscrapers, the monoliths set at the four map points of the biggest city in Valeria—I'd only seen it in photos, pictures Delta had showed me.

"Let me go!" I screamed—possibly a bad idea under the circumstances. But whatever held my arms was like a magnet. It probably was, considering Valeria's technology—the boots, as Delta had boasted, also came with oxygen shields. We could fly ten thousand feet and still breathe. And scream, as I did when the pair of us shot into the sky, through a damp mass of cloud. The wind rushed past, making my ears pop.

"Stop! Put me down!"

We wove among the skyscrapers, no one looking twice at us from the offices within or the cars on the high skyways, like this was a normal sight. No one heard my screams.

"Sorry, Ada," Delta said, again, his voice muffled by the roaring wind. "I always wondered what the big deal was with you. Why my family kept sending me out to meet you. I thought it was odd that you could use magic when you weren't mageblood, but I didn't know you were a freaking *Royal*. To be honest, I didn't know much about Enzar, but my family's *very* interested in you."

"What the hell?" I gasped. We'd slowed down, the cold air stinging my face. "I'm not going anywhere with you!" *And how the hell does he know I'm Royal?*

"Skyla told me," he said, like he'd read my mind. "She's a bug, an implant in the Alliance."

"You what? Skyla doesn't work for…"

"The Alliance tried an experiment once," he said, his voice slamming into me along with the stinging breeze. "They tried injecting dormant magic sources into humans. Stopped after the council beat them down. At first, it looked like they were unsuccessful. None of the experimental subjects responded. They didn't realise they needed to take the subject into a high-magic world, or the Passages."

"What the hell does this have to do with anything?"

"Skyla was one of them," said Delta. "She was an experiment. And when she first came into the Passages, she almost killed herself. Third level magic took her over. But she can control it now. It's pretty impressive."

I shook my head, the best I could. Skyla was a magic-wielder, I knew that, but I always assumed she was sensitive to it like some people on Earth were. I'd never had reason to suspect she might be capable of anything more than what I could do—though she *had* used second level magic to distract the Alliance when I'd broken out…

"You don't believe me, do you?" He dropped in the air so suddenly that my head spun and windows rushed past in a blur. "That Skyla's been in the Alliance as a spy? I think she enjoyed it. She's been working there two years, trying to figure out what they did to her. But there's more than that. She was willing to work for my family, to give us information, in exchange for a shot at revenge. And she brought us that information. You. You have a potent magic source inside you, implanted inside you when you were just a baby. You're what we need. You can give us the Multiverse. Never mind Skyla's petty revenge plan."

I was silent. My heart hammered, like I was free-falling all over again.

"Turns out my foster dad's pretty pissed at the Alliance for putting up restrictions on offworld trade. He thinks they need a reminder that they're not the only people with power. We needed a weapon, and now we have one. We have you."

"You don't have me," I gasped, my mind roiling. He was

mad, totally insane, and so was his father by the sound of it. A weapon? Me? And Skyla—she had a life, a job, she'd helped us for years. She didn't have anything to do with the Alliance. Sure, I'd always known Delta's family weren't exactly law-abiding citizens, but this…

We were slowing down, heading for the ground. We hovered alongside the cars on a crowded street where people swarmed in and out of a glass-fronted shopping arcade alight with bright-coloured holographic images. A few people whistled and waved; clearly, hover boots were still a novelty. Delta waved back, laughing.

I tried to elbow him, but couldn't move my arm. I was stuck to him, a reluctant passenger. *Let go!* Anger burned through me, potent and sizzling. Like static. Like magic. Wait. Valeria had a higher level of magic than Earth. I braced myself, and *pushed.* Delta didn't seem affected by the shot, though it was second level and should have shocked him, but I pitched forwards. Delta swore as my feet hit the pavement. I staggered forwards but kept my balance. Magic tingled through me.

Now I had another weapon.

"Oh no, you don't!" he shouted after me, as I whirled around and ran. Stupid, stupid idea. I heard Delta curse behind me. There was a whirring sound, then he was at my side. "Super speed, Red. You can't run away."

I felt for the magic pulsing in the air. It was thick as smoke here on the main road; they used magic-based engines to power their vehicles. There was no shortage of power to draw on. Problem: too many people, swarming in and out of the arcade, waiting in traffic while a series of lights flashed overhead and every hover car glided to a stop. Our altercation went unnoticed for now, but if I used magic, anyone could get caught in the backlash. Plus, the obvious problem. I had no idea how to get back to Earth, and the Passage Delta had used was miles up in the air.

Delta grabbed for me again, and I punched him in the face. The impact bruised my knuckles, but Delta almost flipped over in the air, his hover boots knocking him off balance into a group of shoppers. As they scattered, exclaiming in shock, I lunged and grabbed his foot.

"Stars, Red!"

I tugged, hard, ducking as he righted himself and tried to hit me back.

"Bastard!"

The boot came free, and I stumbled back, turned, and ran for a gap in the traffic, Delta swearing colourfully as a gleaming blue hover-car zoomed across his path. With only one boot, he was forced to hobble, while I pelted through three lanes of hover cars in a zigzag, feet skidding on the odd metal they used in place of tarmac. I reached the other side of the road, tugging my laces undone, and slid my foot out of my own shoe and into the loose metal-plated hover-boot.

Damn, how does this thing work? I fumbled and found a switch on the back. And screamed as the world dropped away, pavements shrinking to grey rivers, Delta to a tiny dot. I let go of the switch and dropped, my yelp drawing stares from passers-by when I flipped over in midair.

Somehow, I managed to right myself before my foot slipped out of the shoe, and laughed at Delta's incredulous expression on the other side of the road, past rows of gleaming hover cars. The boot was a couple of sizes too big, but I could feel a switch under the heel. I pressed down, and accelerated. Now this was more like it. I took control, steering myself away from the arcade, past the green expanse of a city park, and into a cluster of towering office buildings. *Think, Ada.* Swooping around the city at random wasn't the best plan, but I did have my phone back, and it had built-in offworld GPS. Ironically, that had been Delta's idea.

I should never have trusted him. Nell trusted no one at all, and no one ever blindsided *her*. Lesson learned. Even Kay Walker had lied to me. His father had ruled against helping Enzar. I *should* have made the connection.

Cursing the Multiverse, I slowed enough to fire up the 'Maps' tab on my phone and wait for it to connect. A birds-eye view of the city not unlike my own view from the sky appeared on the screen.

Where Delta had brought me in was a platform on the roof of one of the skyscrapers, labelled "Landing Dock." Odd place for a door to the Passages, I thought, turning in that direction. I flew lopsidedly above the crowded roads, like a particularly ungraceful bird. But at least I was moving. It took everything I had to stay upright, and the boot was so loose around my foot that if I performed any crazy acrobatics, I was pretty sure it'd fall off.

Speaking of birds… several black shapes were rising between the buildings, dots growing bigger by the second. Not birds. People. Flying up. Flying right at me.

I hit the switch on the back and sped up, rising higher. *Where the hell is this supersonic switch?* I groped with one hand and pressed another indentation in the heel. The world zipped by so fast my ears popped and my hair streamed back, my eyes aching, a scream jammed in my throat. I'd lost all track of the direction, and when my hand fumbled the switch, I stopped so abruptly I nearly went careening into an office window.

Holy shit. I spun around, the wind whipping my hair across my face. I'd barely kept hold of my phone, and the GPS was telling me to head north. I turned that way, using the switch on the back of my heel to readjust the speed. Okay, this would be seriously fun if I had two shoes that fit. And if I wasn't being chased by men in black.

They surrounded me, dark figures amongst the low clouds. I

recognised a couple of them as Delta's cousins, who I'd met before when he couldn't meet me in the Passages. What were their names? Gregor and… Josef. Though they wore hover boots, they looked like serious businessmen in pressed suits, a sight that ought to have been ridiculous, but was somehow frightening. Plus the material of the suits had an odd, scaled sheen that gave me the sinking feeling it was magicproof.

No way out. I hit the descent button and they followed me in a circle.

"Come quietly, Ada, and we won't have to hurt you," said Josef, smirking. He'd always given me the creeps.

"No way," I said.

A fist slammed into the side of my head, then another. I yelled, losing control of the boot altogether, dropping like a bullet. But they were dropping, too. A fist caught me in the stomach and knocked the breath out of me. I struck out blindly but I was falling, we were falling, far too fast.

And then we reached the ground. Hands caught me before I could hit the pavement. Held my own hands behind my back while one of the other men struck me across the face. My teeth sank into the inside of my mouth, and I spat blood at him, squirming to escape. Someone pulled the hover boot off my foot.

"Let me go!"

"Cooperate with us, girl, and we won't hurt you."

"Like hell."

The next slap hit me so hard, my brain slammed into my skull. The world went hazy.

"Stop, now," said one of the men, presumably the leader. He looked the oldest anyway. His neatly combed hair was streaked with grey. "She won't be any use to us if you hurt her too much."

"Go fuck yourself," I said. "I'm not helping you, not for anything in the Multiverse."

"You don't get a say. We need a weapon. Skyla isn't strong enough, though she's done an admirable job stirring up trouble." He must be Delta's father.

"So what was all that about helping the refugees from Enzar?" I asked, stalling for time. "A cover-up? You're despicable monsters." Josef smirked at me, fuelling my anger. My nails bit into my palms.

"I expect your guardian concealed the truth from you because she wanted to keep you safe," said Delta's father. "As a Royal on Enzar, you'd be a pitiless assassin, or the future ruler of the Multiverse. This isn't just about revenge for us, Ada, it's about stopping Enzar. You think the war will stay on the Empire's worlds forever? They'll find a way out, and they'll destroy what's left of the Alliance. You weren't alive when the war broke out, Ada, and the Royals decimated ten worlds overnight. The Alliance might well have crumbled, were it not for the council's quick intervention."

My heart thudded. I hadn't known the specifics. Hell, I couldn't have. It wasn't like Nell had given a blow-by-blow account of the war. Even Josef's smirk faded as his father spoke.

"The Alliance think they're prepared for anything, Ada, but they're mistaken. The only way to stop Enzar conquering the entire Multiverse is to have an equal force to oppose them. Imagine my surprise when I found out we've had one of their own in front of us all along." Delta's father's mouth curled into a grim smile. "The Alliance need a reminder, I think, of the danger of a full-scale magical assault. The current council is incompetent, so we'll take them out first. Luckily, we already have an implant in the Central Headquarters in London. As a known Earth landmark, a targeted attack will make the worlds pay attention."

Central. *Kay.*

"You want *me* to be your assassin? To kill everyone at Central?"

"I was thinking something a little more dramatic," said Delta's father. "Like a bomb."

Magic. Numb horror pulsed through my veins. He intended to use me as a living bomb. But that level of magic would do more than take out Central. It'd knock the Balance across the Multiverse—magic would go haywire, low-magic worlds like Earth would be overrun, and others would end up like Enzar.

"You can't be serious."

"Ada, I am terribly serious. Adamantine? That was a poor choice of name on your guardian's part."

"Go to hell."

I squirmed and kicked at the man who held me. But he anticipated it and drove his knee into my spine. Agony radiated through my body, and my last thought before losing consciousness was that Nell would be seriously pissed.

CHAPTER EIGHTEEN

KAY

Lights flashed overhead, and I glanced at Markos. The elevator had halted under the first floor, and the entrance hall glittered below. Too far below. Easily the height of a three-storey apartment building.

"Damn," I said. "I can't make that jump if we break the glass." Not in one piece, anyway. Even I wasn't idiot enough to try it.

There was a humming sound, subtle at first, but rapidly growing louder. The stunner vibrated in my pocket, and that unmistakable static meant magic was somewhere nearby. *On Earth?* I scanned the inside of the square glass box, looking for the source.

Sparks jumped out from the corner of the glass box, seemingly from nowhere at all. I took a step back, instinct warning me of a danger I couldn't see.

"What in all gods' name is that?" Markos said.

"Magic," I said, as more sparks danced out. Sparks generally meant a stored energy source. I stepped back, running a hand through my hair, thinking–

"Shit," I said. My fingers had brushed the invisible device clipped to my ear, the one Ada had given me. Chameleon. "I reckon I know what killed Alan. It's a disguised magical device."

"Like a bomb." The centaur's face had gone deathly pale. "Like—firing a rocket in an elevator."

"Or shooting a gun in the Passages," I said grimly.

Without warning, Markos reared up, and kicked at the front doors with two hooves. I ducked to avoid the shower of glass. But there was still a hell of a drop between us and the entrance hall.

More sparks danced across the ground, and I tingled all over like I'd run headlong into an electric fence.

"God." What a way to die. I glanced at Markos. "Sadly, my stunt double's not available. Guess this is it."

Markos cursed. "*Gods,* human, if you mention this to anyone, I'll kill you. Get on my back."

"I—what?"

"You heard me." I could almost see the device now, surrounded by a halo of red light. A warning. Markos didn't have to tell me to get a move on.

"This is fucking weird," I said, vaulting onto the centaur's back.

"Hold on tight," was Markos's response.

And he jumped, clean through the newly shattered doors. I gritted my teeth and hung on for my life. *I'll bet no human's ever done this and lived*—and that was all I had time to think before we were plunging towards the ground.

"Holy *shit*," I gasped, flat against the centaur's back. Behind, I heard a tremendous, earth-shaking blast, and the static grew to a fever pitch. There was a shattering, several crashes, screams, and we hit the floor of the entrance hall with enough force to send my heart slamming into my ribs. I hung on and half lay there, gasping out curses.

"Holy fuck." And I swore in several other languages, too, for good measure.

The centaur shook with laughter. "You can get down now, human."

"Yeah—thanks," I added and more fell than climbed off the centaur's back. I hurt everywhere, like I'd been stuck in a blender.

"I didn't know you were fluent in Aglaian," Markos remarked. "We could have had some interesting conversations."

I mentally tried to pull myself together. *Focus. Someone tried to kill you.*

"Yeah—now's not the time." We had an audience. Faces peered over the balconies a couple of floors up, and several people had gathered near the entrance, too.

"Please excuse me while I bury my dignity," said Markos.

I shook my head, which felt like it had tried to detach itself from my neck. "Okay. I'm taking a wild guess the killer's still in the building. We need to send out an alert." I pulled my communicator out with my still-shaking hand. I managed to open the window for emergencies. "FULL CENTRAL ALERT." I hit the button.

Sirens rang out. The people on the balconies withdrew, probably heading downstairs—hell, I hoped the other elevators weren't rigged with bombs like ours.

"Damn," I said. "I have to tell everyone to use the stairs."

"You don't need to." Ellen stood across from me, surrounded by a halo of shattered glass from the elevator. "I only did two of them."

There was an infinite heartbeat's pause.

"You *what?*" said Markos.

The flicker of a smile crept onto Ellen's face. "You would keep interfering, wouldn't you? I really didn't want to kill you, Kay, but you left me no choice."

"The hell are you on?" I said, feeling more like I was the one tripping on something. Maybe the fall had done some head damage after all.

"Sorry, I never got to show you around, Kay." She smiled a sad smile. And then… she changed. Her poker-straight blond hair turned wiry and dark brown. Her face changed too, subtly, but enough that I looked at a completely different person.

"By the gods," said Markos.

"You used bloodrock."

"I did."

"You're the killer." *You don't say. Intelligent, Kay.*

"I had to stop the information getting out," she said. "I'm damned if I'm going to let them start their twisted crap again."

Something pitched inside me. She didn't mean…

"Their experiments," she said, and dread seeped through my veins like poison. "They used me. I nearly died when I went into the Passages—the magic was too much. But I learned to control it." She smiled. "I've enjoyed working here, more than I expected. I didn't intend to stay this long, only it was convenient to know what was happening in the Alliance. But unfortunately, my two lives couldn't stay separate forever."

"Get to the bloody point already," said Markos. "I'm about a second from trampling you into a puddle."

"The point is, I'm sorry, Kay. I admit you threw me off. You're not like him, not at all. You don't even look like him. But you're still a Walker. And I'm in this for revenge."

What the hell? She was batshit crazy. Small consolation that she'd said I was nothing like *him*. My hand crept towards the stunner in my pocket. I had one shot left.

"Don't you dare," said Ellen, or whoever she really was. She raised a hand, and the charge building in the air fixated itself around her. Hell, there was enough magic in here to power the equivalent of a nuclear weapon.

And she was going to hit me with it. Third level. Almost always fatal. And unavoidable.

"No you don't," said Markos. Before I could blink, the centaur *charged*.

I'd never seen a centaur charge before, but I was bloody glad he was on my side. He reared up and lashed out, and Ellen was sent flying across the hall. She struck the wall and crumpled to the ground.

"I always thought she was a ditzy idiot," said Markos. "Never liked her." He glanced at me. "Kay, are you there?"

I shook off the dazed feeling. "Did you kill her?"

"Nope, knocked her out."

"How could *she* have been the one?"

"Very good question." Ms Weston limped into the hall. "We'll need to conduct an investigation."

Did this not surprise her at all?

"Law Division are going to have their hands full," said Markos. "They ought to lump all the investigations together. It'd save time."

"Ha," I said, shaking my head. *Ellen* of all people—the killer? Not that I'd known her at all, really, but...

"What was all that about experiments?" asked Markos.

"It's classified," said Ms Weston. "But I suppose the

word will get out either way. The Alliance once conducted experiments. It was shut down after concerns about ethics came up. None of the experiments succeeded, anyway. Some scientists within the Alliance believed that they could find a way to inject humans with pure magic in distilled form, to give someone from Earth the same level of ability of a natural-born magic-wielder."

"That's twisted," said Markos, kicking his back foot, face taut with anger.

"On Earth and Aglaia, perhaps, but it's quite commonplace in high-magic worlds—Klathica, for one, where magic-based implants are sold on the streets. It wouldn't cause any lasting damage or side effects, and it's not illegal by any means. The scientists knew what they were doing, and plainly one of the experiments succeeded." She indicated Ellen's unmoving body. "We do have a list of the participants, as it happens. In the lab." She addressed the crowd gathered by the entrance, who were starting to move closer. A mixture of guards and office workers who'd arrived to the chaotic scene. Glass from the shattered lift glittered on the floor, reflecting planes of light. Still more people were coming downstairs and in the other elevators, spilling out into the hall, all staring. The entire force of the Alliance was present; there were easily three hundred people in the entrance hall.

And above everything, magic hung like a red haze. I couldn't shake it away. And nor could I shake off the raw panic that the whole freaking *world* was going to hear about this now.

Not illegal. No lasting damage. And they wouldn't want the instigator's name to get out. God forbid. The Alliance would cover it up. Reputation won out every time, and there wasn't a damn thing I could do. Who would they believe, the eminent council member and one of the most powerful people in the Multiverse—or his magic-wielder son, who was lucky not to be in jail?

Saki volunteered to go and fetch the notes, and Ms Weston directed a couple of guards to handcuff Ellen. She still hadn't moved. But I watched as Carl and another guard cuffed her, prepared to step in if she woke up. I didn't trust her at all, unconscious or not.

"Now the killer is apprehended..." Ms Weston nodded, and I turned to see Saki approaching, clipboard in hand. My heart started drumming in my ears.

Ms Weston flicked through the pages clipped to the board, and nodded. "Three of them—and the other two were listed as missing five years ago. Right. We need to put out a search warrant." She raised her voice. "There are two other rogue magic-wielders out there, the other experimental subjects were sent to go free. They'd have been children at the time, thirteen years ago. With Earth's magic levels unnaturally high right now, there's the chance they could hurt people, assuming they're still on Earth."

My heart stopped drumming and plunged instead. I clenched my fists, fought to keep still and not make a run for it. A search warrant? What had happened to the others? *What did he do—drag in children off the streets?* I doubted they'd been *willing* participants.

I didn't run. If it got me fired, arrested, so be it. I'd deserved as much when I'd used magic and nearly killed Aric two years ago—it was a miracle *that* hadn't got out, too. Magic-wielder. And I'd fought it so damn hard. I'd never used magic since. Not once.

A tall man in a pressed suit approached Ms Weston and spoke to her. She nodded, and they conversed in low voices.

Hell. That man must be one of the council members. I knew there were only three of them present, but it hadn't hit home that they'd be here, right now, because I'd sent out an emergency signal to the entire building.

Any hope of not drawing attention to myself had gone clean out the window. I tried to look unobtrusive instead—a little difficult when you stood next to a centaur, surrounded by a mess of broken glass and an unconscious woman. Carl glanced at Ms Weston. "Should I take her downstairs, or is this a full evacuation?"

She shook her head, wearily brushing back her dust-streaked hair.

"Kay raised the alarm," she said, and turned to me like she expected *me* to give the order.

I summoned what little authority I could. "I'd say we evacuate just to be on the safe side," I said. "Ellen—whoever she is—rigged two of the elevators with magic-based bombs. She was killing off anyone who came close to exposing the research, but she was also out for revenge on anyone else involved." That seemed likely, anyway.

Ms Weston nodded. "Skyla Benson," she said. "Her real name. She has a distinct magic-wielding style, too—I recognise it from when she used it the other day. And I believe it matches the magic used in the Passages the day we found the intruders."

"Wait, what?" I said.

"I have this," said Carl, from beside Ellen, holding up a round metal device. "It can detect traces of magic and see if they match. It wouldn't be half as effective offworld, of course, but on Earth, it could only have been the same person."

Damn. She was one of the people who helped Ada escape. Ada couldn't have known she was the killer—no way—but at the moment, I didn't know *what* to think.

"There are other experimental subjects?" the tall man

asked Ms Weston, as if he'd read my thoughts.

"Two," she said. "Twins. They'd be in their late teens—the experiments were on kids, naturally. There's nothing in the file, they disappeared the same time as Skyla did. We need to consider the possibility that they're working with her. They wouldn't be bound by the same rules as other magic-wielders on Earth—even more so now the Balance has been shifted this way."

I went ice cold all over. She didn't mention me. She *had* to know. It was right there in front of her. But she didn't say it. She didn't name the last *volunteer*. No, victim.

At the time, I'd half assumed my mother's death had pushed my father over the edge, and the experiment was some twisted new punishment, or a convenient way to dispose of the son he'd never wanted. I'd blocked the memory out, just like everything else.

And when I'd first set foot in the Passages two years ago, magic had lured me into its trap and then turned on me and almost destroyed any chance I had of joining the Alliance on my own terms. All because of some sick, pointless experiment. I should have known it would catch up to me.

Get out. I could feel blood dampen my hands where the nails dug in, sweat cold on the back of my neck. I needed to get the hell out of there before I lost it completely.

A buzzing sounded in my ear. I barely stifled my reaction,

and backed away from the crowd as Ada's voice whispered in my ear. "Kay?"

***

ADA

My eyes flickered open. Cold metal pressed into my back, and I realised almost immediately that I was freezing. Passages-freezing. I sat on the floor, my back against a wall. Not tied up. Where in the Multiverse was I? Valeria? Earth? Another world entirely? It was dark, but looked like the inside of an empty warehouse, made entirely of cold grey metal.

Locked up again, I thought. It was becoming a bad habit. I pushed myself to my feet, wincing. Should've checked my injuries first. Nothing was broken otherwise I'd be in far more pain. But the bruises hurt like a bitch, and I was pretty sure there was a fist-sized lump on the back of my head. I still wore one boot. I sighed, unlacing it. At least I'd have something to use as a weapon, though it was ridiculous that I'd lost two pairs in a week. Then again, this whole situation was ridiculous. I took deep, calming breaths to stifle the growing sense of walls closing in on me. I was imagining things. Of course the walls weren't moving. I just wasn't a fan of locked rooms.

I rummaged in the pockets of my coat. Someone had taken my phone away, and the main part of the Chameleon must have fallen out of my pocket at some point. But the earpiece was still in place. I could contact Kay.

First things first. It wouldn't be much use if I didn't know where I was. The warehouse seemed to be cube-shaped. At least, the ceiling appeared the same height as the length of the floor, both ways. And there were no windows. I finally spotted the door, hidden like a door to the Passages. But this wasn't the Passages. I could feel a different kind of magic. More contained, somehow, than the random bursts that came from behind the doors between-worlds. Magic-wielders could tell the difference between levels of magic in the various worlds, I knew, like a sixth sense. It figured that I'd be super attuned to it. *Wish I had built in GPS instead.*

The door didn't have any handle. Sliding door, maybe? I dug my fingers into the edges and only got a broken fingernail for my trouble. Hell. I was going to have to call Kay. Like a freaking damsel in distress.

"Kay," I whispered.

There was a sharp intake of breath. Not me. Then a pause. Seconds passed, more seconds—at least a minute. Then: "Ada?"

"Listen, Kay. You have to get away from the Alliance. There's a spy, I think they're going to try to kill you."

"Already did," said Kay, in a low voice. "We've taken care of it. Turns out my colleague was the killer. Her real name's Skyla—you know her."

"I thought I did," I said. "Delta told me. Skyla was sent there as a spy."

"For who?"

"Delta's family, the Campbell lot," I said. If he knew the Alliance as well as it seemed he did, he'd know that name.

"From Valeria," he said. "Was this your offworld contact?"

"Yes." I swallowed. "He betrayed me. For his family. He brought me here."

"Where are you?"

I drew in a ragged breath, claustrophobia kicking in despite the size of the room. "I'm trapped in a warehouse. It might be on Valeria—I'm not sure. I tried to get away, but his family surrounded me and took me prisoner. They're planning to use me as a weapon against the Alliance. Because of my blood. They want to—to blow up Central or something. Assassinate the council."

I could hear Kay swearing in an undertone, in several languages I didn't recognise. "Shit, Ada. Do you have no idea where you are?"

"No windows. I was in–" I paused, trying to remember the name; Delta had told me enough times—"Neo Greyle. Capital of Valeria."

"I know where that is. Let me get to the Passages."

"Yeah, but it's a whole *city,*" I said. "This is a warehouse. Hang on." I turned on the spot. "About twenty feet by twenty. Like a giant cube? Sorry, that's not much help. The door's sealed, of course. Looks like it's a sliding door, Passages-style."

"Got it. You have nothing on you?"

"Only this headset. It's not much use on its own. You have your communicator, right?"

"Yeah—tell you what, I'll put out a couple of calls. Alert everyone. Though the council are giving me the evil eye right now."

"Huh?"

"I'm in the entrance hall. Ellen, Skyla or whoever she is, tried to kill me. She's knocked out and in cuffs."

"Well, that's something," I said. My heart beat unnaturally fast. *Tried to kill me.* We could both die. "You know what, you tell the council to get out of Central, out of London, even. Don't come for me. When they do whatever they're going to do with me, I'll fight them with everything I have."

"Dammit, Ada. You think I'm going to stay here when you're…" He cut himself off, cursing. "Right. I'm coming. I can locate the Campbell family's residence. If you're not there, then I'll get the information out of them one way or another."

A thrill of nervous horror went through me. I was still trapped for the meantime. But I had one weapon in my arsenal:

magic.

"Okay," I said. "I'm going to try to break out, but if not, well, I'm trusting you to kick the shit out of Delta's family for me. Just don't kill him. I want to deal with him myself."

"Got it," said Kay. "I'll see you later." Was I imagining it, or was there something in his tone that suggested he wasn't only coming to save me for the sake of the Multiverse?

Time to get the hell out. If I could. The lighting was dim, but it was enough that I could see the faint shimmer of magic beneath the surface. I had to be able to break down the door.

I stepped back, getting into position so the backlash wouldn't hit me.

"Interesting," said a voice from right in front of me. "Sorry to interrupt. I've never seen someone have such an intense conversation with herself before."

CHAPTER NINETEEN

KAY

The council member regarded me with a distinct sense of disapproval in his expression. I read his name badge: Wilson Sanders.

"Kay Walker," he said. "I'm glad to see you've decided to rejoin us."

I ignored the sarcasm. "I have a contact," I said, "who has just informed me of a terrorist threat to the Alliance. We need to evacuate. In fact, the council needs to get out of the city altogether."

Mr Sanders's expression changed to incredulity. "Is that so? Danica, I believe Kay Walker is your charge."

"Yes, and he speaks the truth," said Ms Weston, to my surprise. "If Kay says there's a threat, there is one. Tell us."

I summed up what Ada had told me as succinctly as I could, well aware I was confessing to keeping contact with a prisoner, and using probably illegal technology besides. But I was far, far past caring by now. If they fired me, on their own heads be it. No matter what happened, I was getting the hell out of here and going to save Ada. Even if it meant breaking Alliance code.

"I see," said Mr Sanders. "The Campbell family has

connections, strong connections, within Alliances both on Valeria and Earth—they provide much of our technology. There will be repercussions if this turns out to be true."

"We haven't time for speculation," said Ms Weston. "A Royal from Enzar is being used against her will. That's a violation of the Alliance's basic code. Add in the magical misuse and we have a threat to the Balance itself. One step below declaring a war."

Damn. "Listen," I said. "I think I can find Ada. She's a magic-wielder, and so am I. I'll get her away from that madman before he turns her into a suicide weapon."

Mr Sanders shook his head. "That goes against our policy—more than one of them. You know our rules."

"Backwards," I said. "All this–" I gestured at the room in general—"is far off Alliance policy. I can stop them." There was no alternative. I was damned if I was going to stay on Earth.

"This isn't the time to play the hero, Kay Walker," said Mr Sanders. "This is not the Academy. Magic-wielder or not."

"I know that," I said. And looked him directly in the eyes. Unblinking. Knowing that he would have faced the same stare before, from someone nobody dared disobey.

Something in his expression changed, and he looked away. "We will prepare to evacuate." He gave orders to the others, while I stood stock-still, instinctive revulsion warring with disbelief that it had actually worked.

"Earth to Kay," said Markos, tapping a hoof on the floor.

"Time to go and be a hero."

"Don't say that," I said. "I know what it looks like. If I die…"

"I'll keep your secret, magic-wielder."

I nodded to him, suddenly conscious of the dozens of eyes on me. They knew who I was. This was no surprise to them. And yet…

"Wait," said Carl, from behind. "You're not armed, are you?"

Right. This, I could deal with. I had to. "I've only one shot left in this stunner," I said.

Carl handed me a knife. "You don't need that stunner when you have your own magic," he said. "Just remember the three rules. Valeria's high-magic—but I'm sure you know that already. This situation is urgent enough that you're allowed to use it."

Magic. Guess there was no avoiding it now. Not that avoidance had done me much good lately. "Okay," I said. "Thanks."

I didn't look back. Once outside, I broke into a run.

The back road was cordoned off, but I vaulted the metal fence they'd hastily put up and headed towards the still-open Passage entrance. The message had gone out to all the guards, and those watching the Passage nodded to me and let me pass. Not speaking. Magic crackled around me like lightning as I entered the between-world. *Two doors down*, I thought—but the door to Valeria's major city was already open. Good job I paused first, because it appeared to open into the sky, a hundred-odd feet in the air. Opposite, I could see a platform on the side of a skyscraper, impossible to reach by jumping.

Hell. Most of their Passages opened high in the air—something to do with the ocean levels—but it was pretty effective in making sure no one could get in, while the Valerians, with their hover transport, could still get out. I didn't have the time to get to the other door and go through security, and I didn't have a centaur to ride this time. But I did have magic.

Maybe it was the high magic level making me crazy. I knew the three rules. And it sure as hell couldn't make me fly—but I could use the backlash rule.

This was far and away the most dangerous thing I'd ever done, and that was saying a lot. But I tapped into the magic and fired an experimental shot at the ground. It carried me to the ceiling, and I dropped to the ground, landing on my feet. Before I could lose my nerve, I shot a second blast of magic directly at the back wall. This time, icy air slammed into me, and I barely reacted in time to grab for the edge of the platform and hang there, cursing whoever in the Multiverse had thought this was a good idea for offworld security. Hauling myself up with shaking hands, I surveyed the city below, heart drumming and the cold breeze cutting through my jacket.

That was a damn close call. I wondered how many people had fallen to their deaths from here. I could see the city below, the rows of hover cars clogging the streets and skyways in gleaming lines that reflected the sky, the maze of grey metal buildings. Ada was there somewhere. And I had to get down there, too.

The wind roared in my ears, but along with that, the buzz of magic surrounded me. I spun around, thinking hard. A hundred feet to the ground, and no way into the building from here. A few hover cars were parked below at different levels, by parking signs affixed to the building's side. This place was probably an offworld transition point. I scanned the hover cars and spotted one that I could jump for, parked beside a balcony open over the street. Valerian hover cars were smaller than Earth cars, made for one or two people, with transparent covers over the roofs. The one below was open, the driver having just climbed out onto the balcony. Perfect.

I had no idea how to operate one of those things, but I couldn't worry about that now. I jumped, dropping onto the back of the car at a crouch, grabbing onto the back of the headrest to keep from sliding off. Heads turned in my direction from inside the room. I leaped into the front, through the open roof, slamming my foot on what looked like the accelerator.

The hover car dropped so fast, it was all I could do to hang onto the disc-shaped steering wheel. The world rushed past, buildings blurring to grey, the wind striking like a physical force, cold and sharp. I fell back in the seat, lifting my foot from the pedal. The car slowed enough for me to hit the actual accelerator button. Nothing happened.

"Shit," I said, voice muffled by the raging wind. I was starting to go deaf, and the ground was only a short drop away. The hover car was already drawing attention from the people on the street below. I guessed I was violating some traffic law.

I don't have time for this. I left the car parked in midair and jumped, hitting the ground running.

"What the hell are you doing?" a guy yelled at me from a floating, wheelless motorcycle-type thing—a hover bike. Damn, I wanted one of those. Except there were two enforcement-type figures on the opposite side of the road, and they'd seen me.

Goddammit. I ran around the corner of the nearest office block and went for my communicator, navigating my way to offworld maps and opening one of the city. I needed to find the Campbell family's place. They owned a large business, in one of the biggest skyscrapers in the city, shaped like a double helix. First, I had to lose the officers. I made for a main road, weaving in and out of the crowd, and veering into a side street alongside a hover-car transit point. Once I was sure I'd lost them, I stopped at a street corner to check the map again.

There. The Campbell family's business. Just west of here.

The towering, twisting grey building was unremarkable by Valerian standards, but there was no mistaking it from the map. And nearby, two warehouse-style buildings. *Ada.* I had a fifty-fifty chance of getting the right one on the first try. Neither had a door at the front, so I aimed for the narrow gap between them.

They came out of nowhere. Two black-clad figures, hulking, and wielding knives. One at either end of the alley.

Stupid mistake! I cursed myself for it. No time to draw a weapon. I had to use magic.

A knife stabbed at me, and the second guy closed in behind. I went for the stunner while grabbing the wrist that held the knife with my other hand and pushing it back, driving the weapon away from my face. The second guy dived for me, but I kicked the knife out of his hand and shot magic at him. He fell down. At the same time, I tightened my grip on the other guy's wrist and drove a knee into his ribs. The magical backlash hit me at that instant, knocking both of us into the wall. The back of his head slammed against brick and he crumpled. I spun around and kicked the second guy again, before he could get me from behind with the knife. I stamped on his knife hand, hard, and felt bones break. He screamed, going for my ankle with the other hand, but I punched him in the face and he flailed, still screaming. Blood spurted from his broken nose. I kicked him again, crouched beside him and pressed the stunner to his outstretched hand.

I was prepared for the recoil this time. He shuddered and went limp, but I could still feel the charge radiating from the stunner. No, not from the stunner anymore. From me.

I was controlling the magic. Pushing the level higher. He

twitched all over with the same convulsive shudder as someone being electrocuted. The stunner broke apart in my hands as the backlash hit, and I dropped it as it seared my hand.

Third level. Fatal.

Somehow, I had time to think that in the endless seconds before his eyes went blank.

The other guy was half-slumped against the wall, blood pooling around his head. I crouched, felt for a pulse. Nothing.

I'd never killed anyone before. Not a human being. I'd always assumed that I'd feel something other than this numbness, a total disconnection from my surroundings. I took another step back. The roaring in my ears was my own heartbeat, like crashing waves.

Breathe. Breathe, Kay. You didn't have a choice.

I did have a choice. It had been easy. And it had always been easy, because I was a goddamned Walker.

You finally did it, Kay. Stark images quite unrelated to the horror in front of me threatened to break down the walls in my head. The world froze in that moment, the alleyway tilting, like I stood on one side of a gulf with the other side moving farther and farther away by the second, irrecoverable, irreversible. The same, but never the same.

Go. You have to go. Run… no one will know.

Precisely the problem. No one would know.

Ada's face broke through the numbness. *Bet you have,* she'd said, pinning me as a murderer.

I had to find her.

I ran.

***

ADA

I gaped, looking around for the speaker. There was a soft laugh. And then two people appeared, a metre away from me. I yelped and jumped back.

"Hi," said one. A girl. The boy at her side must have been her twin. They were *that* identical. Straight brown hair—the girl's was cut short—eyes dark as black pits. There was something oddly familiar about those eyes.

Where the hell did they come from?

"Hey," said the boy. "You're Ada, right?"

I stared mutely. They'd heard everything. And there was only one way I knew could make something—or someone—invisible. "Chameleons…" I murmured. But they didn't appear to be wearing any devices.

"That's what we call ourselves." The siblings exchanged identical grins. "Pretty neat, right? It was almost worth it. Almost

313

worth what the Alliance did to us."

I shook my head, slowly. "You what?"

"You're an experiment, too, aren't you?" said the girl. "Well, Delta said you were different. Said you were only a baby, and magic was common on your world. You could hide it. We never could."

"Experiments." Crap, what had Kay said? "The Alliance? They-"

"Tampered with us," said the boy dismissively. "This nut-job Alliance-council guy Walker started it. He injected us with pure magic and then threw us out on the streets. It happened when were sixteen." He glanced at his sister. "Then we went into the Passages for the first time. It was like being reborn. Too bad it nearly got us locked up back here on Valeria when we moved here. They're not a fan of natural magic-wielders here. But luckily, Delta helped us. His family took us in."

"Yeah, Delta rocks," said the girl. "You were his friend? Or something more?"

"God, no," I said automatically. Didn't mean the betrayal hurt any less. "So you're what, his bastard father's pet magic-wielders?"

The girl burst into delighted laughter. "You're just like he described you. This is gonna be so much fun."

"What is?" I glared at both of them. "I reckon I can take on both of you. So don't try anything."

The boy laughed. "Yeah, sure you can. We're here to bring out your *potential*. Hit us with everything you've got."

I gaped. "You what?"

"Seriously," said the girl. "It'd be my honour to get beaten up by Adamantine, Royal of Enzar." She snickered. The siblings grinned at one another again and turned back to face me. Creepy as hell.

"I think we're freaking her out," said the boy.

"Brilliant deduction," I said. "Thing is, you're between me and the door." I let magic flow towards me, as a warning. I didn't want to hit them. They acted like little kids, though I suspected they were about Alber's age. Not that I was usually averse to violence, but if it was what Delta and his family wanted, they could go to hell.

"Ooh, she's ready."

"Well, so are we." Magic crackled, sending red lightning streaks through the air. I gathered a palm full and threw it at them. First level, enough to knock them off their feet.

But they were quicker. Hands pinned my arms to my sides, and the shot I'd fired bounced harmlessly off the wall. But the backlash caught all three of us. My back slammed into the floor, and the girl laughed delightedly from a few feet away. "Do it again!"

"Shut up," I hissed through my teeth, climbing to my feet. I gathered magic again and fired it at the floor, angled so the backblast would strike the door. The boy leaped in the way, and the impact sent him sprawling.

"Come on, you can do better than this."

The girl appeared behind me and kicked me viciously in the knee. I was too slow to react, and pain shot through my leg. Swaying on my feet, I aimed a punch at her, but she'd already moved, and the boy caught my arm. He twisted my wrist, hard.

"Delta didn't specify what he wanted us to do," he said. "But you know, being locked up for so long is kind of boring. Delta said your guardian taught you to fight, not to question. Right?"

No. That wasn't it, at all.

"He hit me, sometimes," said the girl, and while I gaped at her, eyes streaming from the pain in my leg, she hit *me*. Agony exploded in my jaw.

I knew how to defend myself in almost every situation—but there was a world of difference between Nell's lessons and *this*. They were kids who thought violence was fun, and the shock of it made my attacks clumsy, weak.

The boy kicked my legs out from under me, and I hit the ground again. My head struck metal and I tasted blood at the back of my mouth. Groaning, I tried to sit up, but the boy pressed the heel of his shoe into my stomach. I whimpered.

"Fight back," the girl hissed, crouching beside me and whispering in my ear. "You're angry. Fight back."

The magic responded, crackling around her, reflecting in her pitch-black eyes. It was in the eyes, I thought. Whatever the experiment did had given them that unnatural spark, like my own eyes reflected my Royal status. Like gleaming purple meant mageblood.

And with a thrill of horror, I knew where I'd seen that colour before.

Kay. His eyes were the same unnatural gleaming dark shade as the twins'. There was no mistaking it. I'd spent my life looking out for these "tells", as Nell called them. Signs that someone was different.

No. It couldn't be true.

Walker...

Who had orchestrated the experiments? Had he even volunteered his own son?

The girl smiled at me. "Bye, Ada."

Boy and girl moved in unison, mirrors of one another, twin fists coming at my face. Something snapped inside. I pulled down on the magic, and it came in a swirling mass, unlike it had ever done before. The boy went flying, over to the other side of the room, and hit the wall with a *crack*. The girl, too, went head over heels. And then came the backlash. I screamed aloud as it flooded my body, expecting it to burn me to cinders.

But it didn't. It fizzled out, becoming mere sparks, which danced over the floor, over me.

"That's more like it!" The girl bounded to her feet, clapping.

"You just needed an incentive. You have to really *want* to use it for it to work. I'm surprised you didn't experiment more."

So was I. But Nell's warnings had stayed me, kept me sane. Whether she knew about this or not, she'd done a good job of warning me of the dangers. And I'd done a bloody awful job of repaying her.

"Oh hey, Eddie," said the girl, calling to her brother. "Rise and shine!"

He didn't move.

Shit. Shit.

"Eddie!" She threw a blast of magic at him, almost playfully. The magic turned him over, but he didn't get up.

I wanted to throw up. But everything seemed to be stuck in place, including me. My chest felt like it was caving in. I wanted to scream and sob uncontrollably. But no tears came. Nothing, nothing, like the boy's, like Eddie's silence.

Dead silence.

"Eddie?"

The shrill pitch of her voice coaxed my limbs into motion again. I stood, no longer caring if movement got me hit, and grabbed the door, shoving at it. I pulled on magic and used its force to drive me, and the wrenching motion sent me flying backwards.

But the door slid open.

"Eddie!"

318

I ran, jerkily. Not looking where I was going. Anywhere. There were several other warehouses nearby. And offices beyond that. The city. An alien city. One I'd wanted to visit as long as I'd known Delta.

Keep moving, whispered a Nell-like voice in my ear. *Don't think.*

Time passed in stop-start motions. Suddenly, I was in an alley between two warehouses with no recollection how I got there. Two bodies lay prone at the end, one surrounded by a halo of blood. *Hell. I didn't do that, did I?*

I didn't trust my own memory. I didn't trust myself. Not anymore.

Run. Ada. Run.

And I did. I circled the block and found myself heading east, away from the warehouses, towards the sound of traffic. This was a secure area, I guessed. Important. Delta's family were important.

Delta's family had turned me into a murderer.

I stopped running. My heart beat fast, too fast. *Don't pass out. Not now.* One foot in front of the other.

"Ada."

I had to be hallucinating. Kay was approaching me, utter shock stark on his face. The ground swayed under my feet, and it took everything I had to stay in the here and now, not give in to the scream fighting to burst from my chest. I couldn't say a word. *I killed him.*

Kay looked papery-white, eyes deep and staring. I must look worse. I steadied myself against a nearby streetlamp before he reached me, hands out like he'd intended to catch me.

"Ada. Come on."

"Yeah," I said. "Come on." Hysterical laughter rose in my throat, and with a wrenching sensation, I shoved it behind a barrier. "Gotta—find the Passages."

"This way," he said, indicating a locomotive track over the other side of the bridge. "There's a ground-level one. We're going to have to sneak onto a train."

After everything I'd been through already, I didn't question it. Kay looked at me with what might have been concern. I walked fast, not speaking, thinking only of the next step. And the next. Ad infinitum.

Kay was speaking again. "We'll have to jump on here." We stood on some kind of platform. I had no recollection of climbing up, but I must have done it. And there was a locomotive zooming towards us. Hovering over the gleaming tracks, like everything in this world. A hover train. I giggled, and Kay's concerned expression deepened.

"Ada, don't zone out on me now. Jump when I say. Okay?"

"Oh… Kay." I pressed my hand to my mouth to muffle another giggle. I was losing it, all right.

But I managed to hold myself together. When the train whipped past, the wind buffeting us, Kay shouted, "Jump!" And

I did. He'd timed it perfectly. Trains here were windowless and we landed in the middle of a packed carriage. Several people gasped, and most backed away from us. I sprawled on a seat, half upside down. I righted myself and fell into Kay as the train picked up speed. His arm wrapped around my shoulder, and he steered us into a newly vacated pair of seats.

I closed my eyes, willing the world to disappear. To fade out.

"Breathe, Ada. Concentrate on your breathing."

Wait, I wasn't breathing? So that's why I felt lightheaded. Seemed good advice to me, so I did as Kay said.

"You're all right. It's going be all right." In my half-dazed state, I thought he was talking to himself as much as me.

Breathe.

We were getting out of here, we were free.

CHAPTER TWENTY

KAY

Ada's breathing steadied. What the hell had they done to her? I couldn't ask, not with all these people around. They probably assumed we were—I cut off the thought before it got to the words *criminals* and *murderers*.

"Where are we going?" Ada looked up at me. She'd lost some of the dazedness in her eyes, though I could still feel her trembling against me.

"There's a Passage entrance in the north of the city," I said. "Easy to get out, nightmare to get back in, unless you live here. It shouldn't be a problem for us. I have my Alliance ID, and by now the word ought to be out that the council's under threat."

Ada made a noise halfway between a laugh and a sob. "You really think of everything, don't you?"

I shook my head. "If I thought of everything, I'd have seen Ellen for what she was. I could have…" I stopped. "Never mind. It's done now. We'll go back to Earth and let the Alliance take care of the rest."

If it's not too late. And the Campbell family wouldn't take our escape lying down. I glanced at Ada, wondering whether it was worth risking a question.

"How were they planning on attacking Central?" I asked. "You said they wanted–" I checked to make sure no one was listening, but the other passengers had done their best to squeeze themselves into the neighbouring carriages, and more than a few had got off at the stop we'd passed—"to use you as a weapon."

"They didn't get that far." She swallowed. "I was supposed to show them what I could do. They tested me—on two other magic-wielders."

Oh God. I knew what happened. Because I'd almost caused similar carnage myself. When magic took control… anyone who stood in the way could get killed.

There was nothing I could say. Adding my pain to her own wouldn't help her, anyway.

Instead, I forced out the question, "How did you escape?"

She took a shaky breath. "Turns out they were in the room with me, can you believe it? Two—two of them. They were mad, totally crazy. They *wanted* me to hurt them." Her hand gripped mine convulsively, making me jerk back in surprise. Her fingers were icy cold. "They were experiments," she said. "The Alliance did some kind of experiment on them a few years ago. They could turn invisible. They had magic, like, inside them. Like–like–"

Like Ada. Was it the same thing? It seemed unlikely, unless of course the Alliance had got the substance from Enzar. But I knew my father had connections with other worlds where magic-based sources were commonplace. I wouldn't put anything past him. He'd just left the other victims to their own devices—let them walk around with a dangerous power and no clue how to use it. No way could he have known the results. He'd never have left me behind otherwise, even though I'd flat-out refused to have anything more to do with him. A magic-wielder with a permanent inbuilt magic source would be a perfect weapon. As was all too clear, someone else had made the connection first.

Ada's hand held mine, tighter, and I realised I was shaking, too.

"They could turn invisible?" I asked.

She nodded. "Like human Chameleon devices." She fiddled with something on her ear. The earpiece. "This is only part of it. The devices can turn someone completely invisible, for a few minutes, anyway. I used it to sneak into Central and steal the bloodrock. That effing bloodrock." She laughed shakily. "It's what made the Chameleons invisible. Maybe that's what they injected those kids with. It's sick, so sick…"

"I know," I said quietly.

She tilted her head back so our eyes met. And… I knew. She'd found out, all right. But that wasn't pity in her eyes: it was understanding.

"I could have stopped them. They…" Ada's grip tightened. I was beginning to lose feeling in my fingers.

"Whatever happened, it wasn't your fault," I said.

Ada shook her head. "You didn't… didn't see…"

"It wasn't your fault." I had to repeat that. No one had said it for me. I still didn't think I'd deserved it. But Ada hadn't chosen this for herself.

The locomotive slowed and most of the people clustering at the edges of the carriage disembarked. I glanced up. "We're almost at north-side. One more stop."

"How in the Multiverse do you know all this? I thought you'd never been offworld."

"I checked out the directions on my communicator."

"What, you have like a photographic memory or something?"

"Habit. Never mind that. There's an entrance to the Passages on the other side of the station. We'll go through there. And then…"

Then I was going to have to tell her. She couldn't go back to Earth, not with the Campbell family out looking for her and waiting to destroy the Alliance.

There was only one option.

But I couldn't say it with her half lying in my lap, her hand clenched around mine. "Wait, what happened to your shoes?"

"Oh," she said. "I stole Delta's hover boot."

"You did what?" Just when I thought she couldn't surprise me anymore. I glanced at the few remaining passengers. No point in debating when the Multiverse might be depending on us right now. "Hey, over there," I called, and several people squeaked in terror, trying to hide behind one another. "For God's sake, I'm not going to hurt you. We need some shoes. It's important."

Ada stared up at me like I'd started speaking another language. But a terrified-looking woman tossed over a pair of shoes. I caught them by the laces and handed them to Ada.

"Thanks," she whispered. "Gods, this is the weirdest…"

"Tell me about it. We have to get off at the next stop, anyway."

The locomotive glided into north-side station. I pulled Ada to her feet and she responded by yanking her hand out of mine and saying, "I can get up by myself, you know."

At least that meant she was recovering from whatever happened back at the warehouse. Good. I needed her to be prepared for what I was about to say to her.

Out into the station, through the sea of commuters, past the ticket machines—ordinarily, I'd have noted everything in case I needed to remember later. But we needed to get out as fast as possible. To the Passages. At least it was signposted. Valeria's Alliance didn't live in the shadows, but out in the open.

Finally, we stood before a security guard, who stared as I pulled out my Alliance pass. I caught sight of our reflections in the opposite wall—in Valeria, all buildings seemed to be made of this strange reflective metal, the name escaped me—and I saw why. Ada's clothes were torn and her face bruised. She was far too pale, dead on her feet, her clothes still spattered with blood from killing the wyvern. As for me... my eyes shone black, even from a distance. A killer's eyes. I turned away and told the security guard in an undertone that there had been a threat to London's Alliance branch, and it was imperative that we be allowed back into the Passages *now*.

For once, luck was on my side. The alert had gone out, and once I'd identified myself by my Alliance codes, he let us through without a fuss. The Passages were all but deserted. I'd never been in this particular area before, but I mentally mapped it out. We were three corridors from the door back to Central. Which made the US branch two corridors the opposite way.

I headed that way, making sure Ada stayed at my side. "I can't believe you did that," she muttered. "You can't go stealing people's shoes..." She bit her lip. I guessed the impact of the other lawbreaking had hit her again. That was the thing about dealing with a shock, or upheaval—it never *stopped* hitting you. But then, maybe it was easier when you'd already long since walked out of a hell to which nothing else in the Multiverse could ever compare. Pretending had become second nature. Pretending I could sleep more than two hours at a time without reliving a memory that ought to be long dead. Pretending I could walk out of the shadow of a name other people would kill to have, without the compulsion to glance over my shoulder at every turn.

I don't lie, I'd said to Ada, but it wasn't true. There was more than one way to lie. Like omitting the truth, because it was easier than facing the fallout.

I stopped walking. "Ada," I said.

"Huh?"

"We're not going back to London. I'd rather not go back to Earth at all, but we don't have the paperwork. I'm going to call Simon at the New York branch and tell him you're coming. You'll have to lie low at the shelter there."

Her mouth fell open. "You're joking. I'm not going anywhere. My family's in London, Kay."

"I know, but the Campbell family won't give up. They want to use you to destroy Central, and they'll be expecting us to go back there. They might have an ambush prepared."

"What, we hide like cowards?"

"I'd rather that than destroy the Alliance, wouldn't you?"

"Don't you patronise me, Kay Walker," she spat. Her eyes gleamed with fury. "My family are more important to me than anything in the Multiverse. I wouldn't expect you to get that, seeing as your father volunteered you as an experiment, but–" She stopped, her breath catching. Her eyes said, *Oh, hell.*

I couldn't move. Couldn't shout after her as she turned around and ran. The roaring in my ears kicked up again, loud and insistent and in tandem with the magic surging in the air, gathering around me like a swarm of moths drawn to a flame.

***

ADA

It was more difficult than I'd expected, running through the Passages in those awkwardly fitting Valeria-style metal-plated shoes. The floor was slippery as hell. Not to mention I'd have a serious disadvantage in a fight if my shoes fell off. Maybe I should have stolen *Kay's* shoes, while he stood there staring at me like I'd just…

Said something unforgivable.

I couldn't think about that right now. Of course, some part of me knew it was stupid to go back to Earth. But… no. That was a line I wouldn't cross. I could never abandon Nell.

I'd been around this area before, Delta sometimes used that Passage, so I at least knew the way back to the doors to Earth from there. The problem was, of course, there had been a chalder vox and a bunch of dreyverns at one entrance, and a wyvern at the other. *Between effing Scylla and Charybdis*, I thought, recalling Nell's reading me Greek mythological tales when I was younger, as much for her own benefit as a non-Earth native as my own.

I had to get to Nell. I had to see if she'd woken up, if Jeth and Alber were okay. So I headed in the direction I'd used too many times to count, when helping people back to Earth. I might not have weapons, but I had magic. If anything attacked me, well, it'd be the worse for them.

Don't think about that.

And definitely don't think about Kay.

I half ran, half skidded into the right corridor, and found the door. Right where I'd left it. The Alliance had cleaned up the mess from where the dreyverns and chalder vox had attacked. All was eerily quiet. The door slid open without a sound. I drew in a steadying breath and walked out into the alleyway. It was only when I stood on my doorstep that I realised I'd unconsciously walked home. I glanced around, but no one was behind me. I didn't have a key, of course, but I'd hidden a lock pick under a loose tile in the yard for this very purpose. First step: find weapons.

BANG.

A blast of magic roared through the air, taking me off my feet. I was too startled to cry out as my back slammed into the fence and I slid to the ground. Three people emerged from the house. All were dressed in suits of glittering black. Delta and two of his cousins.

"I suspected you'd come home," said Delta. "It's easy to get off Valeria, you know. I can't believe you were idiot enough to come here alone."

I jumped to my feet and fired my most expressive curses at

him, following up with a bolt of magic. But instead, I was the one who was knocked to the ground again—had he *blocked* my attack?

"There's someone here who wants to talk to you," said Delta's cousin, Josef. "She's pretty pissed with you for killing her brother."

My insides twisted. I stood again, swallowing back nausea.

Delta shook his head, an awed kind of horror in his expression. "Damn, Red. I didn't know you'd go ahead and do it. That's messed up."

Ignore them. They're trying to distract you.

A footstep behind me. The girl had appeared from thin air, inches away from me. I stepped back instinctively, dread gripping my limbs. Her face was tear-streaked and her jaw set.

"Don't mess her up too badly," said Delta's other cousin, Gregor. "We need her alive. She's our weapon."

"Like hell," I said, and attacked first. The girl didn't bother to block my strike—but she suddenly wasn't there anymore. Invisible again. A blow struck me on the back of the head. I whipped around, kicking blindly. No way to tell where she was.

I stilled, frustrated, looking around for any clue where she might be. Any disturbance. Delta's cousins were both smirking, though Delta himself still watched me, eyes wide.

Fingers touched my face, pressing into the corners of my

eyes. I jerked my head away, squeezing my eyes shut, but Delta's cousins moved in unison, grabbing my arms to stop me lashing out.

"Come on, Ada, cooperate," said Josef. "We want to see your pretty eyes. Your *real* eyes. Janice here reckons it's the key to your magic."

"Stop!" I yelped as fingers dug into both corners of my eyes. I kicked out blindly and Josef cursed.

"Get the lenses out, girl, and we won't have to break you."

"You're planning to use me as a bomb, you psychos!" I hit out and by the pain that shot through my wrist, I could tell I'd struck him in the face. Now I knew where my target was. I kicked blindly and stuck out an elbow when I sensed Gregor come up behind me.

"This is fun," said the girl, Janice, "but you killed my brother. I'm not in the mood for screwing around."

The magic stirred the air a split second before it hit me like an electric current. I was flung onto the ground, and my eyes flew open. Delta's cousins had been sent flying, too, but Janice merely laughed at them and walked up to me. "You're stronger than I am, but you don't know half what you can do." As I sat up, she aimed a punch at me. I rolled over and she missed wildly—but the magic didn't. My spine arched, and every hair on my body stood on end as the shock rippled through me.

Earth should never have such high levels.

"You're going to mess up the whole Balance!" I gasped.

"That's the plan," said Delta. "Attacking Central will swing the Balance towards Earth. Right?" He looked to Josef for confirmation. "It's already happening. When the Balance comes this way, it's drawn away from high-magic places like Enzar. They won't stand a chance when we turn our weapon on them next."

"I'm nobody's weapon," I spat at Delta.

"Pretty girl, you were *born* to be a weapon," said Josef, and I didn't care for the hunger in his expression.

"Yeah," said Janice. "Delta reckons you must have some sort of absorbent in whatever crazy magic's inside you, 'cause that attack should have really hurt. I kinda want to see what you can do. But we've gotta get a move on, right?"

"Yes, we have," said Gregor. "We need to take her back to Central."

"You're not *taking* me anywhere."

"Sorry, Ada," said Delta, "but two of our people are at the hospital right now." He took out his phone. I couldn't help notice his hands were shaking slightly as he tapped the screen. "They're hidden, of course, but one word from me and they'll go after your brothers. I know your guardian's seriously hurt." His voice trembled on the last word, but he nodded to his cousins.

My insides plummeted downwards into icy darkness. "You bastards."

"We need you, Ada," said Delta, with another glance at Josef. "You heard my dad, right? You're a weapon. We can't let you go now. We need your magic."

"I don't," said Janice. "But you're gonna die anyway, so I'm happy to let these guys take care of it. You're gonna kill *worlds*, Ada. And then, once these guys are done with you, I'm coming for you."

"I'm not your weapon. It's suicide, for both of us. If you use me to attack, then I'll be killed along with everyone else. Is that really what you want?"

"I'm not fussed either way, to be honest," said Janice.

"Actually—" Delta began, but Josef cut him off.

"You'll see when we reach Central," he said. "Don't give away our secrets now, Delta."

"We have to go," said Gregor. "Your choice, girl. If you don't help us, your family dies. Delta, dial the number."

"Sure." Delta looked a touch paler, but he tapped buttons on his phone. Valerian technology hooked up to the offworld network, of course.

There was the unmistakable sound of a dial tone and then a male voice.

"Wait!" I said, scrambling to my feet. "Don't hurt them."

I bit my lip. I hated begging, but there was absolutely no doubt Delta's ruthless family would kill Nell, Jeth, and Alber if I didn't obey. It was hopeless expecting otherwise. I knew Nell would tell me to save my own life first, but I couldn't do that to my brothers. Not for the world, not for the Multiverse. Delta had known that. It was one of the few parts of my life I'd shared with him.

One of the few certainties in my whole life.

"Excellent," said Delta's cousin, taking my arm. "If you'd come with us…"

Janice giggled, but when she looked at me, her eyes were full of malice. I shook with anger all over. *Wait till you get to the Passages.* The level of magic on Earth was higher than it had ever been, but in the Passages, it'd be even stronger. There was no time for caution. I'd hit them with everything I had.

Delta looked oddly relieved as he led the way, Janice skipping ahead. He turned back to make sure I was following. I had a cousin on either side, and I knew running wasn't an option. Even if Delta plainly didn't agree with every detail of the plan, he'd do anything his family asked him to. Since I'd known him, he'd always had to ask permission from his father for the most ridiculous things. I'd never thought it odd. I sure as hell never considered he'd kidnap me and threaten my family.

Every step seemed endless as I followed them back the way I'd come, to the Passages. The door slid open. The instant my foot touched the metal floor, magic flowed over me, and I drew it in and unleashed it in a second level blast that ought to have taken all of them off their feet, at least. But instead, I was the one knocked over. The hard floor grazed my elbows. I gasped, the current making my hands tingle and the hairs rise on my arms.

"Magicproof, baby," said Delta, indicating the sharp new jacket he wore. "New patent."

"You look ridiculous," I said, pushing to my feet. Not my best line, but I was all out of imagination. And patience. I fired magic at the ground, instead. I might not be able to hit them with magic, but I could knock them off balance, and it gave me the chance to get a good punch in. Delta's head snapped back with a satisfying crack. But I hadn't put enough power behind it to break his jaw.

"Gods, Ada!" he said, clutching his face. "Don't shoot the messenger. I'm not the one you should be angry with."

"You're joking, right?" I said. "You deserve worse than this." Magic swirled towards me again, urging me to unleash it, but I held off, knowing it wouldn't work.

"I can make the call from in here, you know," said Delta, rubbing the spot where I'd hit him.

"Yes, speaking of calls," said Josef, "our father's on his

way. We'll take her to meet him."

"I have a name," I said, fully aware that any tenuous grip on the situation was slipping away by the second.

"Adamantine," said Janice, smirking. "How cute."

"Yes, and I'm starting to get bored," said Josef. "We've an appointment to keep."

And he and his brother seized me by a shoulder each. A current ran through me, so sudden that I gasped. I twisted around. They'd clamped a metal plate to each shoulder, and they contained some kind of magic source. A powerful one that made my bones rattle.

"Should we up the voltage, so to speak?" asked Josef. "I think when she meets our uncle again, she ought to show him her real eyes."

"Yes, that's true," said Gregor. "Now."

I screamed, my back arching, my eyes flying open. Every cell in my body pulsed with the shock. I was aware that I was falling, that the cousins had caught me, that fingers were pressing into my eyes and I couldn't move, couldn't stop them sliding the lenses out—the slightest sting—and then everything went blinding white.

CHAPTER TWENTY-ONE

KAY

Pull yourself together.

There was nothing to do but head back to Central. I had a fairly good idea where Ada had gone, but I needed to make sure the Alliance had spread the message around and the council members, at least, had left London. I knew they had safe houses for these kinds of situations and the other Alliance branches worldwide and maybe even offworld would be preparing themselves for the worst-case scenario. The Alliance would survive.

Magic was thick in this part of the Passages, and grew more potent as I approached the corridor leading to Central, like a blanket over all the senses, so all I could hear was a dull humming sound, and the world was overlaid with red...

Wait. I could hear something else. Distantly. Shouts. Running. Screaming.

Then I turned the corner, and a wall of sound hit me like I'd walked from a soundproofed room out into a battlefield. People ran everywhere—some people, some dreyverns. Blasts of magic shook the air and sent bodies flying. Someone had put up a barrier so no one offworld would be able to see or hear the fighting.

I swore and went for my dagger in time to intercept a dreyvern's attack. Grinning, it slashed at me with its knife, pit-like eyes glittering. I dodged the blow and went for the weapon hand, broke its wrist almost without thinking, and threw the dagger point first at a second dreyvern who'd spotted me. Right through the throat. The dreyvern went down with a choked yell.

Magic crackled like red lightning, knocking several people flying. I didn't see who'd used it, but it took me off my feet and slammed me into the wall. Who the hell would use second level magic in here? This was the absolute worst place for magic-based combat, all the worse for the number of people here. Alliance members, and others. Not all the opponents were dreyvern. The people fighting the guards wore an odd, scaled-looking uniform not like anything from Earth. Did they work for the Campbell family? Probably.

I'd got back too late. The Alliance was already under attack. Cursing, I pushed away from the wall and ran through the fighting, knocking aside dreyverns and humans alike. Turning into another corridor, I could see the door to London was wide open, though blocked by a mass of bodies. Now I was in the thick of the battle. I wasn't armed nearly enough to deal with so many opponents, with the stunner useless and only one dagger, and magic would do more harm than good here in the Passages.

Someone else had no issue with using it, though, judging by the sparks flying out. As I kicked a dreyvern aside, there was a gap in the mass of bodies, and I saw Ellen—no, Skyla—fighting a group of guards, none of whom seemed inclined to go near her. She'd escaped. Or someone had set her free.

Our eyes locked, and she smiled at me. "Finally, a worthy opponent!" she shouted, the magic seeming to amplify her voice and throw it across the corridor at me. "Get over here, Kay Walker."

And she threw a blast of magic at the writhing crowd, forcing it to part down the middle. Amazingly, the fighting continued, though muted, and behind, I could hear another sound, one that made my blood freeze. A wyvern's cry. *It's not dead?* Not that I could see outside, because Ellen, or Skyla, was in the way of the door.

She grinned. "Pretty good accuracy, right?" She held something in her left hand. Her communicator.

She'd duped us all that day when we'd killed the chalder voxes. To keep us away from her double life's secret Passage.

Dammit. She wanted a fight, I'd give her one. First step was to get her out of the freaking Passages before she blew us all up.

I ran at her, dodging the blasts of magic she fired in the

seconds before I got close enough to hit her with one of my own. One shot—that was all I'd risk. And she didn't even duck, like she'd *wanted* to lure me out onto Earth, I thought, tackling her and sending us both tumbling out of the doorway. She smiled as I pinned her to the ground, her face turning into Ellen's again. Probably an attempt to distract me. It didn't work.

"Last chance to back out," I said, feeling the static build in my hands. Like it had wanted to break out the whole time. It *shouldn't* be this strong on Earth, but at least I could use it.

"Oh, bring it on," she goaded, her eyes teasing me. Would I fire pure magic into a human being, knowing what it would do to them? Perhaps she expected me to back down. Perhaps if I hadn't killed already, I would have done.

She'd killed three innocent people herself, and started a war.

I released the charge.

Boom.

The ground trembled underneath us and Ellen moved suddenly, the bolt of magic striking the tarmac instead. The world flipped over as the backlash struck, sending me flying into a half-crushed car. The impact barely registered as magic slammed into me again, and this time, it was like an electric shock. *Fuck!* I slid down the car's side, the tremor shaking every nerve. I tried to stand, but it pushed me back, relentless. Skyla had got to her feet, still wearing Ellen's face and grinning all over it.

"Knew you had a breaking point somewhere, Kay Walker. I admit, I didn't really think your father would use *you* as one of his experiments. He *hated* magic, from what I heard."

I could still hear the fighting, the screams from the Passage, but it was like I'd been thrown behind that magic soundproofing shield again. Every sound muted, save a roaring in the back of my head. Obliterating everything else.

"He must have really hated you."

The roaring became a crescendo. Forks of reddish-purple lightning burst into life, and I stood, raising a hand, gathered the lighting in my palm and sent it, not at Ellen, but at the road in front of her. She laughed a delighted laugh, but her eyes widened as the magic struck, burning a sizzling hole in the tarmac, then rebounded. The ripple effect sent me staggering back, but it was worse for Ellen. She rose up into the air as if lifted by invisible hands, screaming—and then another lightning bolt descended. She screamed louder and raised her hands, the red lightning reflected in her dark, dark eyes...

And then it dissipated. Like someone had flicked a switch, the magic energy crackling in the air, in me, disappeared. I swayed on my feet, drained of the electric rush, and horrified. Ellen dropped from the sky and hit the tarmac with an audible *thud* I felt even from a distance.

I ran to her, although I already knew she was dead. The roaring in my ears was painful now, more like screaming.

And then I became aware of real voices. Behind me.

"What a shame," someone remarked. "I liked her."

Five strangers had come out of the Passages. All wore magicproof suits like the guys I'd killed on Valeria. One was a teenager with spiked hair. The other three were clearly related. A blond girl followed behind.

And between them was a smaller, redheaded figure with eyes like white orbs, dark pupils in the centre.

Ada.

***

ADA

Delta's father was the spitting image of Josef, except his face was more lined and his hair streaked with grey. Unremarkable, anyway. But then, killers weren't recognisable at a glance, and nor were murdering psychotic businessmen.

"Here we are," he said. "Central. And we're just in time." He laid a hand on my back and pushed me out of the Passages, into the street.

The magic hit me first. It slammed into me with the strength of a boulder, making me sway on the spot. My vision was off-kilter, like I saw the world through distorted glass. Magic pulsed like something living, a cloud covering the houses with their shattered windowpanes, the wrecked cars, the person standing stock-still in the middle of the road—no, now they were running towards a prone body a few feet away.

Oh, God, Kay. And the body was Skyla's. I wasn't sorry. I couldn't afford to be. I needed to get the hell away from Delta and his lunatic family before they used me to blow up Central.

Janice skipped out of the Passages behind me. "What did I miss?" she asked.

"Looks like a magical battle," Delta said. "Who is that?"

Kay. Get out of here. Please.

"No idea," said Janice. "That's the girl who used to visit, though, isn't it?"

"Skyla," said Delta. "Hell, I know who that guy is. Walker. He killed her."

"What a shame," said Josef. "I liked her."

Like in slow motion, Kay turned. Looked into my real eyes.

His own widened in shock.

Get out. Please, Kay.

I couldn't say a word. Not even as Delta's father shoved me forward, his cousins pinning me on either side. Delta in front. He glanced back at his father. "Are we gonna mow him down, or what?"

"I'd stop there," said Kay. My heart sank. Of course he'd challenge them. *Dammit, Kay.*

"Walker, is it?" said Delta's father.

"Kay, actually," he answered. *Oh, for God's sake, get out of here!*

"I suppose he is a magic-wielder," said Delta's father. "And with Skyla dead, we could use the power."

Where was everyone else? What had happened at Central? Delta's father had walked through the battle in the Passages like a god through mortals, and no one had dared follow to challenge him. Not when they'd seen my eyes. Not when they'd seen the magic that surrounded me like a deadly cloak of white lightning. Kay could see it, too. But he'd sacrifice his own life before he let them get at Central.

They were going to use me to kill him.

Delta's father leaned in behind me. He'd strapped a metal-plated contraption to my back. Didn't take a genius to figure out it was a bomb. No—*I* was the bomb. And Kay was...

"Get out of here!" I screamed, cracking. "Save yourself! Please..."

Delta's father backhanded me, knocking me sideways into one of the cousins. Kay swore and took a step forward. Not back. Not away. Oh, God.

"It's pointless," he said. "Central's been evacuated, so's this whole area. You really want to kill me that badly?"

Was he telling the truth? It was impossible to tell.

"Actually," Delta's father said, "We could use some leverage over Walker in case he comes back. Janice? Take him."

"With pleasure," said Janice, skipping forward. Kay watched her, and although he was dead still, I knew he was thinking hard.

"She's a magic-wielder!" I shouted, earning another slap. I barely felt it. The static charge building inside my veins was unbearable, like it *had* to escape somehow, otherwise I'd burn to a crisp from the inside out. But that seemed a preferable fate to wiping out half London in a magical assault.

Janice attacked, but Kay was faster. He avoided the bolt of magic *and* the backlash and sent an equal force back—hell, he was using magic? But I was shaking hard, and my vision blurred more by the second.

"Stop this," I said, through chattering teeth. "If this magic gets out, it'll obliterate us along with everything else."

"On the contrary," said Delta's father. "You will absorb

the backlash yourself. Surely you knew the clue was in your name? Adamantine absorbs magic."

Crap. It does. But... *I* was antimagic? I gaped at him, heart beating fast. No. Adamantine was the most unbreakable substance in the Multiverse. It couldn't be inside my blood. The only place I'd seen it was—

Central.

The building could absorb magic. And no one was in Central anymore.

"Ingenious, wasn't it?" said Delta's father. "To force the Alliance to leave the one safe place in the city. I doubt they got far enough not to be caught in the blast. We have time enough to watch the outcome of this, anyway."

Kay had managed to pin Janice down, but by the tremors rocking the magic in the atmosphere, I could tell both were firing magic at one another. In seconds, one or other of them would be dead.

I ran forward, the movement disturbing the magic. I couldn't intervene without blowing everything sky-high. But the slight disturbance had sent both of them head over heels—Kay slammed into the pavement, and my heart pitched as I saw his hands had taken the backlash and were burned raw red. Janice was in similar condition. Teeth bared in a feral snarl, she leaped at him.

On his feet in a second, Kay raised a hand. His dark eyes

gleamed, the pupils disappearing, almost inhuman. And a fork of lightning shot at Janice. She couldn't avoid it.

She fell.

"More's the pity," said Delta's father, coldly. "Right. Come, now." He pushed me forwards. The others moved, too.

"What about him?" Delta jerked his head at Kay, who still stood beside Janice's body, unmoving. As he did, Kay seemed to come to life again. He turned back and strode towards us. Eyes no longer gleaming, but blank.

Delta's father let out an impatient noise. "Subdue him," he told Delta's cousins. "She's not going anywhere. Not if you threaten *him*."

Dammit.

Josef and Gregor advanced on Kay. They actually looked a little frightened. But they had the advantage of the magicproof suits, and Kay was injured besides. A sharp pain pierced my chest as I saw his ruined hands. He didn't seem to acknowledge it, but I knew it had to really hurt. My heart dipped further. Both cousins carried those magic-charged metal plates they'd used on me.

I couldn't watch. But I did. It was over so fast—one second Kay had pulled a knife, though it must hurt like a bitch to hold it. Next he was disarmed, and Josef struck him over the head with the metal plate. Then he was on the ground, the antimagic shock vibrating through him. I *felt* it, the agony ripping open my own bones. The magic. I could feel the magic…

No. That was *anti*magic I could feel, like magic but its stark opposite. And I'd pulled on it, the same way I did with magic.

That's what's in my blood. Antimagic. Adamantine. To block magic required a substance which had magic origins itself. The equivalent of the reverse reaction. I had more antimagic in my blood than they did in those ridiculous suits. My hands were free. They couldn't have cuffed me, because that would have blocked me from unleashing the source. But that meant I could take in the magic myself. Absorb it. Stop the source strapped to my back from exploding… at the cost of taking the magic into myself instead.

Delta's cousins whirled on me, staring. They'd felt it, too. And from the look on his father's face, he'd also figured something was up. I couldn't hear what he said. The charge had built up to unbearable levels. I could hear swearing—the world had broken into fragments—I blinked, but couldn't clear the film from my vision. It pulsed black, then white, then black again. There was a cracking sound, like breaking metal. The bomb strapped to my back. It fragmented, the plates encasing the bomb breaking away…

I pulled all the magic, all the antimagic, towards me. Took

it all in. They couldn't use it anymore.

My knees struck concrete. Through the haze, I made out Delta and his father, and cousins, and they were shouting at each other. A meaningless jumble of words I couldn't make sense of. Delta's father barked something, and the two cousins turned and strode towards me. They looked scared, but had clearly been given an order.

I lifted my head, held up a hand and the magic gathered in my palm, pure white. Sparks shot out and the charged plates in their hands crumbled. Both cousins yelled as the charge went through them. Building higher. Level three.

They fell.

The charge rippled outwards. I could do nothing about the backlash, not when it rippled through the air and Delta dropped to the ground, when his father took one step towards me and fell, too, screaming…

Everything blurred. *Kay.* Where was he? I couldn't see if he'd been hit. *No…*

The backlash struck me. I cried out, every cell in my body screaming. The world blacked out. Lights burst behind my eyes.

Then… nothing.

CHAPTER TWENTY-TWO

THREE WEEKS LATER

KAY

"Dammit, Markos, I can open the bloody door."

"I beg to differ," said the centaur, and kicked the door to Ms Weston's office in with one hoof. Rolling my eyes, I closed the door behind me and faced the boss.

Three weeks on, and I was still surprised I hadn't been fired yet. It had taken a week for them to clean up Central— I'd actually been right when I'd told the Campbell boss the place had been evacuated. Not that it would have made a difference if he'd really been able to use Ada as a bomb.

London had had a lucky escape. So had the world.

"Kay," said Ms Weston. "I see the bandages are off."

I held up my barely scarred hands. "See? Back to normal. Nothing to stop me running patrols." I was going stir-crazy, and Ms Weston knew it.

I already knew that magic burn didn't leave marks. Not on the outside.

"I'll let Carl be the judge of that," she said, narrowing her eyes. "I hear you want to bring that girl back in. The girl who caused all the trouble."

That figured. I only had to casually mention it and it was around half Central. Inevitable consequence of being the one witness at Central to the standoff with the Campbell family. Like I needed any more attention.

"Yes," I said. "I think she'd be an excellent employee."

Not that I'd told her—or the council—*how,* exactly, she'd killed the Campbells. That she could absorb any magic, including antimagic, unlike anyone else on Earth. All anyone else knew was that she was a powerful magic-wielder—and the Alliance had no way of knowing what that really meant. I'd been the only witness, and the last thing I wanted to do was spread word of Ada's capabilities. Even Earth's council might take advantage.

Ms Weston apparently thought the same applied to me. She hadn't said a word about the experiments, and as far as everyone else was concerned, I was just a normal magic-wielder who'd taken advantage of the unusually high levels of magic on Earth to use it as a weapon. Not that it came from me, that it was part of me.

"She's a liability," said Ms Weston. "We came *this* close to losing control of the Balance—this close to total annihilation."

Yeah. I reckoned half Central was still in a state of shock. To say nothing of all the ordinary people who'd had be evacuated from central London. The Alliance had spent the best part of the past three weeks clearing up the aftermath. The remainder of the Campbell family had been imprisoned back on Valeria. Pity they didn't go in for the death penalty there. Those bastards had almost destroyed the Multiverse.

"That may be," I said, "but if anything like this happens again—like it or not, with magic, it's always a possibility—then we might need her. Besides, I doubt all the Alliance's guards could stop her from helping the Enzarian refugees."

"Yes… about that. You're very lucky the council was amenable."

Lucky. As they were the only people to know exactly what had happened in the standoff with the Campbells—even if I hadn't been able to give Ada's side of the story—they listened. No one could deny the situation in the Empire needed looking into, especially after the information about the hidden shelters in London got out. The Alliance had got hold of the contact details of several other shelters like Ada's family's. The offworld-aid part of the negotiations department had taken care of that, thankfully, and without anyone getting arrested—hopefully, they might even be able to reopen as legal shelters once they'd got through the application process. I had the suspicion that had to do with the team who'd come back utterly terrified from a "meeting" with Ada's guardian. Sounded like she'd scared them into dropping the charges against her family and agreeing that saving the Earth from a magical apocalypse probably merited exemption from the usual consequences of breaking out of jail and attacking the Alliance guard team. Not to mention the trespassing.

As for the offworld transition points, that was a matter for the Law Division, seeing as they involved doorways that were listed in the Alliance's records as defunct. Plainly, someone had tampered with the records to enable the refugees to use doorways the Alliance didn't know about, breaking about twenty laws in the process. But there was no denying they saved too many lives to count, and the New York Alliance's team were negotiating whether to open their new Passage to level two, allowing refugees to get through to the shelter from the transition points—thanks to Simon. Arranging that was pretty much the only thing that had stopped me from going batshit insane stuck in the office all the time. And it was about the only thing I'd managed not to fuck up since arriving at Central.

I hadn't seen Ada once. Not since she'd been in the hospital. Her guardian had told me in no uncertain terms to leave them the hell alone, and only family were allowed in to visit her. I knew she was alive, and that had to be enough. After she'd fallen, knocked out by her own backlash, I'd honestly thought she was dead.

I'd got off easy. Especially considering I'd been inches

away from being caught in Ada's final attack. The one that had killed all four of the Campbells. And almost killed her.

The memory of that was hazy. I'd been half-concussed at the time, but I could recall it in flashes. Waking from the magic shock to see Ada, eyes glowing blinding white, surrounded by crackling white lightning. Then black lightning. Then she'd screamed, and the light had pulsed outwards, knocking two of the guys out. The backlash had taken care of the other two. And when it had hit *her*...

I'd run. Not fast enough. She'd fallen to the ground, and the light had gone out entirely. Next thing I remember, guards had surrounded us, had pulled her out of my arms—when had I picked her up?—and taken her away. I'd tried to stand up but gravity didn't seem to want to cooperate... tried to reach her but my hands fucking *hurt*, like fire flared along every nerve. And then I was being hauled off to the hospital while she was God only knew where and I had no idea if she was even alive.

No one was supposed to absorb so much magic energy. What the Campbells had done had nearly destroyed her. But she'd survived. And once I found out she *was* alive, the first thing that struck me was deep, horrible guilt that I'd been at least partially responsible for her landing in this situation. Because it had been through the Alliance that the enemy had learned about her ability—if we'd just let her go...

Even Ms Weston's keeping my secret didn't seem to matter. Ada had reason to hold me in contempt. Logic told me I should stay away from her, not screw her life up further. But I at least had to tell her that the new Passage was ready to open, that she'd finally be able to help everyone from her homeworld. Once I had Simon's confirmation.

Someone knocked on the office door. "The council want to speak to you," said Aric. *Great*.

"Again? For bloody hell's sake." Ms Weston shook her head. "Fine, I suppose I'll have to… you can go now, Kay. Don't think I'm finished with you yet."

I almost laughed. In the past few weeks, it had relaxed to the point that being called into her office no longer felt like my career was on the line.

"I'm scared to death."

Aric glared at me as I came out of the office. "You're still being an arrogant prick? That's our boss you're talking to."

"Congratulations. I knew you'd learn everyone's faces eventually."

Aric muttered a curse, stifled as Ms Weston marched past, out of the office. "Very funny, Walker."

"Glad you appreciate it," I said, turning to leave. "Is there a reason you're still hanging around out here?"

"I heard what you said." He took a step towards me, in yet another failed attempt to look menacing. "You're really going to bring a dangerous magic-wielder here? That girl should be locked up. I can't believe the Alliance have just let her walk free. She almost killed the fucking *planet*. And then some."

"*She* didn't," I corrected. "She was being manipulated."

"She's a magic-wielder. She ought to have stopped it, not let it get out of hand like that."

"When are you going to get it into your head that magic can't be controlled?" I held up my own hands in demonstration, though the marks had all but healed. "It does whatever the hell it wants. She could only absorb it, not control it. No one can do that."

"That's not what you said two years ago."

"That's *exactly* what I said two years ago," I said, shaking my head. "Magic is a force. It responds to wielders, yeah, but it doesn't give a crap if there's someone else standing in the way. We're like human lightning rods."

Aric glared. "Then you better stay away from *me*, Walker."

"With pleasure."

I slammed the office door so hard, it actually did hurt, a sharp jolt going through my hands. Goddamned magic afterburn never let up. At first, it had been like I'd put my hands on an electric fence and then set them on fire. Now it only shocked me every couple of hours instead of every minute. I could deal with pain.

My communicator started beeping. Simon.

"Is that Central's wyvern-slaying lunatic?"

"Wrong number. This is pest control. Did I hear about gigantic swamp rats?"

"Dammit. And I had some awesome news too. The council have given the plan the go-ahead. We're opening tomorrow."

"You are?" I said, gripping the phone harder. *Ada.*

"Hell, yes. Also, there might be a few people at US Central who want to meet you."

I sighed. "Don't tell me you've been spreading stories."

"Only the truth."

Yeah. Or Simon's version, which involved heroes fighting monsters and saving the Multiverse. Real life didn't quite work like that. No one ever wrote about the aftermath.

I closed my eyes. "Guess I have to visit Ada."

"You don't have her number?"

"She has mine." That spoke for itself.

"Ah. Well, she'll be happy this whole thing's set up now, right?"

"Yeah. 'Course she will." Feeling I owed Simon something of an explanation, I said, "You know who stopped the Alliance from helping Enzar in the first place, right?"

I gave him five seconds. It took three. "Oh, shit."

"Yeah." Yet another reason I hadn't spoken to Ada. Her family hated me, yes, but knowing *she* knew what my father had done...

"Well, good luck. I'll be there tomorrow."

He hung up. I stared at the communicator for a moment. And then double-checked Ada's address.

***

ADA

Nell was pissed off. Nothing new there.

"*Who* are you meeting?" she said, after I'd hung up the phone. The call from Simon, whoever he was, had come completely out of nowhere. Lucky I was in the house. Not that I really had anywhere else to go these days, but still. No job, and Nell being overprotective. Not to mention Jeth, who'd appointed himself my bodyguard after quitting *his* job to help Nell run the business while she recovered.

Now, Nell came out into the hallway, her usual sharp expression back in full force. I was kind of tempted to retreat back into my room. But Alber and Jeth had both poked their heads out of their rooms, wanting to hear the action.

"Kay Walker." Might as well get it over with.

"Walker."

"Yes, I know. Not *the* Walker. His son. He's setting up this arrangement with US Central so the Enzarian refugees—*all* the refugees—can get through the Passages to a shelter there. Look, it isn't as bad as it seems. We can still help people. Just on the legal side. The Alliance... they might be offering me a job." If that still stood after I'd almost destroyed London. I didn't dare consider the alternative.

"And if they don't? We're running out of money, Ada."

"We'll make do. Could always find another supermarket job."

"This isn't a joke, Ada!"

"Nell, come on," said Jeth. "This was bound to go wrong in the end. We stepped on too many toes. Delta's family were dicks, anyway."

Everyone winced at the name. No one had dared bring it up for a week after I'd woken up in hospital—not that I was conscious most of the time. It was too painful to think about, so my nightmares did it for me, with feeling. I'd killed five people, including someone who'd once been a friend. Would the Alliance turn me into a hired killer, too? Like Kay... no, that wasn't fair. He'd killed Skyla, killed Janice, but he hadn't had a choice in the matter. Magic didn't give you one.

I wished I could talk to him. Just once. But Nell always

seemed to be there, reminding me of what the Walker family had cost us. What the Alliance had cost us. It was a mess. Not least because some Alliance officials had showed up on the doorstep while I was still in a coma and recited a ten-minute-long diatribe about all the laws we'd collectively broken, slapped a formal warning onto us, and then charged Nell for damages on behalf of the guards she and Skyla had knocked out. If not for my being unconscious, I'd have had to give a statement. As it was, Nell had screamed bloody murder about how her daughter had saved the Multiverse and if not for me, everyone in the city would be dead. I kind of wished I'd been awake to watch. At any rate, Nell had managed to convince the guards Skyla had been responsible for the damage, so we'd only been charged for the bloodrock we'd stolen. Too bad "only" had sent us halfway to bankruptcy.

Sometimes being a responsible adult sucked. I'd cleaned out my own bank account and it still wasn't enough to help. I didn't *think* Kay was behind the charges—and from what Nell had told me the Alliance officials said, I was pretty sure it was down to him that the times we'd trespassed in the Passages had been overlooked—but I guessed I didn't blame Nell for storming about the house breathing fire in the direction of anyone who mentioned the Alliance.

I shook my head. "Let's worry about that later. I've got to

go find Kay in the Passages. We're meeting Simon halfway, so he can show me where the new Passage open to the public is. Want to come?"

"Into the Passages?" said Alber. "Hell, yes."

"I suppose," said Jeth. "You need someone to supervise you. You're *not* going off to Valeria."

"But. Hover boots," said Alber. "Come on."

"Tell you what, if I get a job at the Alliance, I'll sneak you with me to Valeria," I said. "They let you bring one "extra.""

"Seriously?" said Alber. "Oh my God, Ada. You have to get this job!"

I laughed. Nell narrowed her eyes. "Do I need to remind you to be careful, Ada?"

"Absolutely not," I said. "Are you sure you don't want to come and see?"

"If I had my way, none of you would have anything to do with those people," she said. "I know can't stop you from going. I only wish…"

"Huh?"

"I'm sorry I lied to you, Ada," she said, softly, her face creased with remorse.

I sucked in a sharp breath. This was the conversation we'd never had, the one we'd danced around for three weeks, each wondering whether the other would be the one to break the silence. But I couldn't face another bombshell. Not after what I'd been through already.

"I understand," I said. "I get why you wouldn't want that information getting out."

"It was selfish," said Nell. "I was younger than you are now when they assigned me as your watcher. I saw them do it to you—saw them…" She shook her head. "You don't want to know the details."

"I do," I said quietly. "But later. We're meeting Kay in half an hour. We should go."

"Later, then." She nodded.

The truth weighed heavy on me, heavy as the burden of what I'd done. The deaths I'd caused. And the worlds I'd almost obliterated. I couldn't sleep without reliving that moment in the warehouse when I realised that the magic I'd coveted all my life was never under my control. It was a lie. I was a walking weapon, and I'd almost destroyed the Earth.

In the long hours awake, I couldn't help but wonder if Kay was haunted by the same thoughts.

I never called. I couldn't do it. He'd seen my real eyes. Seen what I was.

Alber and Jeth stood either side of me as we approached the alleyway to the Passages. The road was so torn up, it was a pain to climb over, but at least the Passage entrance still stood. Even if none of us had used it since. I knew that the Cethraxian creatures had been the Campbell family's doing and the Passages were relatively quiet now, but I kept one eye out for danger all the same. All three of us were armed. I had magic, too, of course. But I hadn't dared use it since.

My heart climbed into my throat as we got closer to the halfway point. I hadn't needed to check the map Simon had messaged me, because I knew this part of the Passages backwards.

And I knew the person standing at the other end of the corridor. Lean and dark-haired, dressed in black faux-leather uniform—could he patrol, then? Using third level magic had almost taken his hands off. But I couldn't picture Kay consenting to sit out on the action for long. *Dammit, say something. Stop staring!*

"Hey," I said.

"Hey. These two your new bodyguards?"

"My *brothers*," I corrected. "You've met Jeth and Alber already."

"Unfortunately," Jeth muttered.

"Well, that's nice," said Kay, turning to him. "Seeing as I was about to offer you a job."

Jeth's mouth dropped open, comically. "You what?"

"The Alliance techs were impressed with your invisible communication device."

"You bastard. You gave it to them?"

"I thought they'd be impressed." He shrugged. "Enough

to offer you a pretty good starting salary." And then he named a sum that made my jaw drop as comically as Jeth's.

"Oh. My God. Okay, let me think on that one."

Amusement flashing in his eyes, Kay turned to me. "You're welcome to take the entrance exam for a novice, Ada. Basic probationary period. Ms Weston will tell you the rest, if you come to Central."

"Let me think about it, too," I said, a little too quickly. I think he knew I meant I'd discuss it with Nell. "Is Simon here?"

"We're meeting him. This way." And he strode off without giving us the chance to keep up.

"Holy freaking hell," said Alber, as we followed. "You'd be *mental* not to pass that up."

"I know," said Jeth.

"You'd get all the cool gadgets, too."

"Tell that to Nell," said Jeth. "What about you, Ada?"

"I think..." I cut myself off before I said something melodramatic, like that joining the Alliance seemed the only option I had left, if I still wanted to explore the Multiverse.

Of course I did. The old dream hadn't died, even if I'd felt like it had when I'd woken from that coma. The nightmares would stop, eventually. I had to believe that. Somehow.

Magic was the more addictive for the long absence. I

could feel it pulling at me, tempting me, and I wondered for the first time if Kay could feel it, too. He was the same as I was, after all.

I recognised the route we took as the one we'd been chased down by the wyvern, through the maze of underground corridors and up the hidden stair to the first level. I guessed the Alliance would map out this part of the Passages now. Kay seemed to know where he was going, anyway. But he didn't stop, didn't even look back. Despite everything, a twisting sensation caught at my chest. After everything… did he not even want to talk to me? Hadn't he been the slightest bit concerned about my being in hospital, in a coma? Nell and my brothers hadn't mentioned him asking after me, but I supposed they'd made their opinions quite clear. Kay was a Walker, and even if I worked for the Alliance, Nell would never forgive him.

The twisting sense deepened. It wasn't fair to judge him on that. Even for arresting me. Not now he'd done something we'd never managed to achieve in a lifetime of trying to help people from Enzar. This was actually happening. For real.

I didn't know whether to skip down the Passages or burst into tears. After this hellish month, I finally dared to hope that things might start to look up.

When we caught up to Kay, we found him at a junction

in the maze of endless corridors, talking to a tall blond guy I assumed must be Simon.

"Hey there," said Simon. "You must be Ada."

"Hey. These are my brothers, Jeth and Alber," I said.

Jeth nodded, while Alber muttered, "Hi." That was about as friendly as I expected, considering.

"Right," said Simon. "Well, this is the centre junction where you'll need to direct anyone passing through. That way leads to the upper level—but you know that, don't you? Kay said you know the Passages pretty well."

I nodded, but couldn't help wondering what else he'd told Simon about me. Not that it was any of my business.

"Anyway, we have guards down this path here. They'll direct them the right way."

"Maybe they should signpost it?" Alber suggested.

"They tried," said Simon, grinning at Kay. "But jokers kept rearranging the signs to point the other way. Sounds like something we'd have done, to be honest."

"Yeah," said Kay. "Direct people to Monsterville. I'm hearing there's a disappointing lack of Cethraxian vermin in here these days."

"You've not been back?" I asked. I couldn't help it. "Wait—your hands."

Kay looked at me, hands held palm up. Barely marked, aside from a handful of crescent-shaped scars, fading already.

"No harm done."

Simon snorted. "You'd say that, you lunatic. Hell, you'll probably say it on your deathbed."

Kay smirked. "If you outlive me, ask that they write it on my grave."

"Can we not talk about death in this place?" Alber said, glancing behind us.

"I second that," said Jeth. "Are we done here?"

Kay was still looking at me. "Why don't you show Ada the shelter, Simon?"

"Sure," he said, sounding a little surprised. "Ada? I can bring one non-Alliance person. Sorry, guys," he added to the others.

"I—sure! I've always wanted to go to New York." I turned to Alber and Jeth. "You two can find your way back?"

Jeth nodded. "Sure can. See you later, Ada, okay?"

"Yeah, I won't be long. Bye."

"You owe us for this!" Alber called over his shoulder, as he and Jeth departed. Kay had already headed down another pathway, Simon on his heels.

"Hey—wait!" I hurried to catch up. "For God's sake, stop charging off like that."

"Terrible, isn't he?" said Simon. "He's always running off when you're trying to talk to him. It's the most bloody annoying—"

"I can hear you, you know," said Kay, over his shoulder. But he slowed enough to let us catch up.

"I meant you to," said Simon. "Seriously. I'd be impressed to hear if you'd found a way to get him to stop chasing after monsters for five minutes."

"Not likely," I said, with a sideways glance at Kay. His half smile didn't reach his eyes, which now I saw up close, were shadowed. *Haunted*, I thought, and suddenly wished Simon would leave us to talk alone. The idea made my pulse drum nervously.

"Did you find out what happened to Cethrax, by the way?" Kay asked Simon. "I've been asking around, no one seems to know."

"They've been fined a hundred million credits for aiding the Campbell family," said Simon. "Their Vox leaders aren't too thrilled about it."

"Good," said Kay.

"Yeah. They deserved it." And worse. Twenty Alliance guards had been killed in the fighting, apparently, not to mention the people Skyla had murdered at Central. I still couldn't get my head around that. And Delta, too. The two people I'd trusted outside my family. I didn't think I'd ever get used to it. My life before the Alliance had caught me felt like it belonged to a different person. Someone I didn't know.

I'd spent years helping people who'd been through hell. But none of that had in any way prepared me for dealing with this crushing, overwhelming guilt. The screaming nightmares. The panic attacks. Even my brothers didn't know the half of it. And Nell fluctuated between paranoid and distant, depending on her mood. I was used to keeping quiet, the refugees' problems taking precedence over my own. But now...

I glanced at Kay again. I swore he'd looked in my direction then turned away just as quickly.

Was he avoiding my eyes? Why? Because I hadn't called? I didn't think so, somehow. Things like that seemed to bounce right off him.

"Here we are," said Simon, breaking the silence. "Welcome to the NYC Alliance." He pushed open the door.

"Do all Passages lead to alleyways?" I asked. It was still daytime here, the midday sun blinding over the glittering skyscrapers piercing the skyline. I could see a street at the end of the alley, and Simon headed that way.

"The Alliance often uses the ones which are easily concealed," said Simon. "There are five here in the Big Apple. I'd show you the sights, only we've got maybe an hour before the next patrol goes into the Passages. And I'm supposed to be on that patrol, so..."

"Dammit," I said. "I always wanted to come here."

"Come on, you got to go to *Valeria*," said Simon. "And Kay said something about stolen hover boots?"

"One hover boot," I said. Admittedly, that had been the one fun part of that whole fiasco. I didn't mind discussing that. "I'd have preferred two. It was a bit lopsided."

"I wanted to try out one of those hover bikes," said Kay. "Next time, I'm hiring one."

"You think the Alliance will let you go back there after you violated half their traffic laws?"

"Considering I just got promoted to Ambassador? I hope so."

"Shit, Kay. You kept *that* quiet!" said Simon.

"Only happened today," he said, with a shrug. "They lost a couple of Ambassadors in the fighting so there was an opening."

"Wow," I said. "Guess you get to see the Multiverse?"

"I could kill you right now," said Simon.

"Well, you already know what to put on my grave." Now his smile definitely didn't reach his eyes.

"Damn," Simon muttered. "That is *not* fair. Tell me you rubbed it in Aric's face? Just a little?"

"I'll send him a postcard."

"I could send Nell a postcard from here," I said, making a sweeping gesture at the towering skyscrapers. "It'd probably get there in a week."

"Ha. You should do that," said Simon. "Nell's your foster mother, right?"

"Uh-huh." I glanced at Kay again, but he didn't seem to notice. "He told you everything about me?"

"Don't worry. Your secrets are safe with me," said Simon. "We're here," he added, leading us down a side road.

The apartment building was unremarkable, the same as its neighbours. I could see people inside. Offworlders—even some from Enzar. Children running around. I smiled. Dammit. I would not start crying in the middle of the street.

"Pretty cool, right?" said Simon. "Kay—oh, for God's sake, he's off again."

Kay hadn't come up to the house with us. He'd wandered down the road instead, looking up at the skyline.

"What's up with him?" I asked, safe in the knowledge that he couldn't hear us. "He's acting... I don't know."

"You're not what I expected," said Simon, disregarding the question. "Kay said you were... look, I promise I won't tell anyone this." He drew in a breath, while I blinked, slightly confused. "I know you're from Enzar. I know the Walker family gave your world a shitty deal. But Kay had nothing to do with that."

Huh? Was that the problem? "I know. His father did, right? Did you ever meet him?" I checked again that Kay wasn't within hearing distance. He wasn't.

"No." Simon shook his head. "Got the impression he cleared offworld before Kay came to the Academy. He never said, and I didn't like to ask. Well, Walker's reputation precedes him. But Kay, well, he might have been a total overachiever at the Academy, but he never used the Walker name if he could help it. I mean, his family owns properties across three universes, they were amongst the original founders of Earth's Alliance. They're billionaires several times over. Everyone at the Academy knew that. But in five years, he never brought it up once. Not a word."

I stared. "He told me he'd never been offworld," I said, because I had to say *something*.

"He hadn't, until now, I guess," said Simon. "It's difficult to get answers out of him."

"Tell me about it," I said. "I asked what happened to his parents. He said they were *dead or otherwise absent.*"

"I thought his mother died. He never talked about that, either," said Simon. "Nor his life before the Academy. He only ever talked about the future. The Multiverse, and the Alliance."

Given that his father had volunteered him as a human experiment, I could put two and two together and get a hell of a painful answer. Maybe I didn't *want* to know.

"Has he ever mentioned the wyvern incident?" asked

Simon.

"Mentioned it," I said. "What happened there?"

"He saved my life."

"He did?" I asked, startled.

Simon nodded. "We were kind of idiots. Third year at the Academy, we got bored and decided to explore the Passages. Started out as a competition with Aric and his friends. Sneaking into the Passages, picking fights with offworld creatures. Then, well, it got complicated. Ended up with a wyvern getting loose in there. We never did manage to prove it was Aric who did it, but it must have been. Only Kay would throw himself into the path of a rampaging wyvern. He damn near died, and you know, the first thing the lunatic said when he woke up in the hospital was ask if everyone else was all right. I mean, how many people would do that?"

And now I wanted to cry. I'd been awful to him. The things I'd said—I couldn't take them back.

"I saw the scars," I said, instead.

"Wait, you've seen?" Simon whistled.

"It's—it's not like that."

"Hmm."

"Quit it," I said feebly. "We're probably going to be colleagues at Central. I'm not going to screw things up before I even start."

"How do you know you'll screw it up?"

"I have a terrible track record with relationships." *Why the hell did I tell him that?* I couldn't stop shouting my mouth off lately, apparently. "And an overprotective guardian who hates the Walkers."

"Well, you're the first girl he's paid attention to for longer than a week since the wyvern incident, so that's a start." He paused, and I had the feeling that he'd been about to say something else, but had held back. "If I were you, I'd go after him before he gets lost."

"Is that likely to happen?"

"God, no. Guy has a photographic memory."

"I thought so," I said. "All right."

And I ran after him. I caught up before I reached the street's end, though the crowded path had slowed him down. Kay stood apart from the crowd, gaze still fixed on the sky— until he saw me and turned his head. And, to my own total surprise, I wrapped my arms around him, tight. I felt him stiffen in shock.

"Ada—what?"

Dammit. I blinked back tears. "I'm sorry."

I couldn't seem to let go. The world disappeared around us, reduced to the sound of his fast-beating heart against mine, to the seconds as I tilted my head and our lips met in a surge of electricity infinitely better than magic. And I felt him smile, and I didn't care that we were blocking the path and people were having to step around us, annoyed. Because I wouldn't miss this for anything in the Multiverse.

"I think we should get out the way," Kay said, breaking off the kiss.

"Spoilsport." But I drew back. The question *what now?* hovered between us like a tangible presence. I drew in a deep breath. "Yeah. I'm joining the Alliance." I grinned. "You're not getting rid of me that easily."

Thank you for reading!

If you enjoyed *Adamant* and have a minute to spare, then I'd really appreciate a short review on the retailer site where you purchased the book. Reviews are incredibly important to authors because they help more readers discover our books!

Find all of my books at www.emmaladams.com

About the Author

Emma spent her childhood creating imaginary worlds to compensate for a disappointingly average reality, so it was probably inevitable that she ended up writing speculative fiction. She was born in Birmingham, UK, which she fled at the first opportunity to study English Literature at Lancaster University. In her three years at Lancaster, she hiked up mountains, skydived in Australia, and endured a traumatic episode involving a swarm of bees in the Costa Rican jungle. She also entertained her creative writing group and baffled her tutors by submitting strange fantasy tales featuring dragons and supernatural monsters to workshops. These included her first publication, a rather bleak dystopian piece, and a disturbing story about a homicidal duck (which she hopes will never see the light of day).

Now a reluctant graduate, Emma refuses to settle down and be normal. When not embarking on wild excursions and writing fantasy novels, she edits and proofreads novels for various publishing houses and reads an improbable number of books. Emma is currently working on the Alliance series, a multiple-universe adult fantasy featuring magic, monsters, cool gadgets and sarcasm. Her upper-YA urban fantasy Darkworld series is published by Curiosity Quills Press.

Website: www.emmaladams.com
Blog: http://throughthegateway.blogspot.co.uk/
Twitter: https://twitter.com/ELAdams12

Acknowledgements

I would like to thank my beta readers and critique partners, who first read this book and assured me that it didn't suck, then helped me make it a hundred times better. Thank you so much to Cole, Erin, Jessica and Laura!

Thank you to Amy, for your fantastic work on the cover designs for this series, and for turning my vague ideas into gorgeous covers!

I would also like to thank my family and friends for being so supportive of my crazy job/obsession. :)

Thank you to Jed, for being awesome.

And as always, thank you to my readers. You're the best.

51622157R10228

Made in the USA
Charleston, SC
29 January 2016